THE PAUSE

JOHN LARKIN

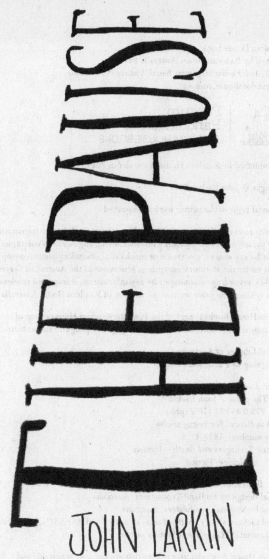

THE PAUSE

JOHN LARKIN

RANDOM HOUSE AUSTRALIA

A Random House book
Published by Random House Australia Pty Ltd
Level 3, 100 Pacific Highway, North Sydney NSW 2060
www.randomhouse.com.au

Penguin
Random House
RANDOM HOUSE BOOKS

First published by Random House Australia in 2015

Random House Books is part of the Penguin Random House group of
companies whose addresses can be found at global.penguinrandomhouse.com.

National Library of Australia
Cataloguing-in-Publication Entry

Author: Larkin, John, 1963–
Title: The pause / John Larkin
ISBN: 978 0 85798 170 7 (pbk)
Target audience: For young adults
Dewey number: A823.3
Subjects: Teenagers and death – Fiction
          Suicide – Fiction

Cover illustration and design by Astred Hicks, designcherry.com
Internal design by Midland Typesetters, Australia
Typeset by Midland Typesetters, Australia
Printed in Australia by Griffin Press, an accredited ISO AS/NZS 14001:2004
Environmental Management System printer

Random House Australia uses papers that are natural, renewable and
recyclable products and made from wood grown in sustainable forests.
The logging and manufacturing processes are expected to conform to the
environmental regulations of the country of origin.

For my wonderful children Chantelle, Damian and Gabby, the brightest stars in the darkest night. And for Louisa, for helping me find my way back into the light.

For in that sleep of death what dreams may come,
When we have shuffled off this mortal coil,
Must give us pause

William Shakespeare, *Hamlet*,
act 3, scene 1, lines 66–68

FIVE HOURS BEFORE

My name is Declan O'Malley. I'm seventeen years old. I come from a loving and supportive family. I go to a top-notch selective high school. I have the sweetest, most gorgeous and intelligent girlfriend in the world. And in five hours' time, I will kill myself.

I'd like to report that my death actually meant something. That I'd stepped in front of a bus to save a little girl who'd chased a much-loved pet onto a busy road. Or that I'd saved an old lady from thugs on a train, despatching them with a potentially lethal combination of kung-fu, karate and UFC — only the gang regrouped and stabbed me in retaliation. Or that I'd dived into the pounding surf to rescue two naive but breathtakingly cute tourists, who'd quickly found themselves out of their depth — only to find myself quickly out of mine, my premature demise ever so slightly compensated for by my being posthumously awarded the legion of something-or-other for bravery, and both women eventually naming their firstborn and a small maple tree after me.

If only I'd lived as creatively as I died then my brief flicker of existence might have meant something.

As it was, my passing was neither glamorous nor meaningful. It was brutal. It was violent. And for the few unfortunate souls who had the misfortune of witnessing it, it was horrifying.

So soon I will be gone and quickly forgotten. Another tragic statistic. Oh, sure, my former school friends might raise a glass to me on the occasion of our twentieth school reunion, shaking their heads at the futility of my life, before spending the rest of the evening getting slowly wasted and bemoaning the futility of their own. This will be the final time that I will be remembered publicly. I may just as well never have existed.

But let's not focus on my death. There'll be time enough for that. Let's instead focus on my life, which will shortly come to its premature and bone-crunching conclusion.

FOUR HOURS BEFORE

It's late morning when I finally drag myself out of bed. It's Saturday and I've got nothing to get up for except my phone, which I check in a nonchalant manner. Though who am I kidding? When it flatly refused to beep throughout the night, I switched it to silent mode hoping to be pleasantly surprised by its winking when I woke up. Nothing.

I checked in at 6.00, 6.10, 6.23, 6.47, 7.00, 7.30, 8.05, 8.23, 8.56, 9.11 (not that I'm obsessed or anything) and at ten- to fifteen-minute intervals since. Nothing. Even factoring in delays, Lisa's plane would have touched down on Lantau Island about eleven hours ago. You could, I suppose, stretch out a trip back to Hong Kong Island to a couple of hours max, but that's only if you're being picked up and the roads are gridlocked. But Lisa was taking the Airport Express, which — according to the omniscient Google — is quick and efficient and puts our own beleaguered rail network to shame.

So even allowing for Sydney-like delays and an out-of-season category five typhoon, Lisa would have been at her aunt's home for at least eight hours now.

She said she'd phone or Skype as soon as she could. Not only did she promise to text me from the airbridge or the baggage carousel in Hong Kong, but also from the departure lounge at Sydney. Yet my stupid phone steadfastly refuses to ring. I even try resetting it by taking out the battery in the hope that there's some sort of kink in the connection hosepipe and this will unblock it and I'll be inundated with a stream of messages. But no. Nothing.

I try shaking my phone and hurling it against the stupid wall, but this doesn't work either and I end up tearing my Bombay Bicycle Club poster instead. Crap! We went to that concert together. The last time we were happy together. Our last date. And the whole reason Lisa's been sent to Hong Kong, after her psycho kraken of a mother found out. She thought Lisa and I were going to a Christian rock concert (which, to be honest,

I've always thought of as an oxymoron) with Lisa's crusading buddies.

I sticky-tape the poster back together, hoping that this symbolic action of rejoining it and us will kickstart my phone. I try glancing at it out of the corner of my eye but again it refuses to flash. Useless piece of ancient crap. Maybe my throwing it at Bombay Bicycle Club has damaged it. I try resetting it again. Again, nothing. I hate the guy who composed the Nokia start-up theme. What a douche.

I slump on my bed and try not to think about Lisa and how this isn't her fault and how I won't get angry with her. Though she knows what a text or a call from her would mean to me. She obviously doesn't give a stuff about me anymore. Couldn't care less how I feel. She has a new life now and I no longer figure in it. Despite her tears, she's accepted The Kraken's decision and moved on just like that.

If only I'd known that The Kraken had confiscated Lisa's phone before she went through customs at the airport.

If only I'd known. Then I might have lived through the day.

SEVEN MONTHS BEFORE

We gather at that great teenage social hub: the train station. It's kind of like the launch pad for all the high schools within a twenty-kay radius. There's an equal mixture of schools and groups, all of us trying to climb the social hierarchy and impress each other on the way up. There are the Reeve Road High students, who don't belong with the rest of us. They're okay when they're together, but put them alongside those of us who have some-how obtained social skills and they look about as comfortable as a bogan at the ballet. They could give you a quantum analysis of their bus's atomic composition or design a rudimentary hydrogen engine, but a lot of them would struggle to hold a conversation with the driver. And then there's us: Redcliffe Boys' and Grosvenor Girls'. Technically we may not be as smart as the Reeve Road students, but we get invited to parties, generally wear our pants at a socially acceptable height, and are coordinated enough to swing a baseball bat at PE without decapitating the teacher, catcher or the guys in the outfield. We even have emos at our schools. Straight-A emos. I'm kind of going that way myself, allowing my hair to fall insouciantly over one eye, proving to the world that I'm almost too cool to be allowed out in public, at least without my stylist.

I'm standing on the platform with the early-morning sun on my face. I'm an hour early but I'm waiting for this girl I like and, as the year has progressed, I've learnt to give her a bigger and bigger window of time to arrive. I've already let two trains come and go without me. It's Monday morning and I'm not going to start the week without seeing her.

'Hey, Toke, 'sup?'

Chris and Maaaate approach. Chris is South Korean and Maaaate is ABC (Australian-born Chinese). They call themselves bananas: yellow on the outside, white in the middle, and reckon I'm an egg: white on the outside, yellow in the middle. We've been tight since year seven.

Chris lives with his mum just up from the station, while Maaaate's a full-on westie. He has to get up at six to make all his buses and trains, but he reckons it's worth it. Or at least his old man does. Maaaate's dad puts all his hopes and dreams into Maaaate and Maaaate's older sister who's doing medicine at uni. Maaaate, though, is struggling. He's smart enough but he's never going to be a neurosurgeon or a physicist. He might study economics or science which is okay, but that's not what his old man has in mind. But even economics or science will be a struggle for Maaaate. The disappointment from home is starting to weigh on him. He's piling on the weight and kind of withdrawing. He's not really into anything apart from FIFA and Call of Duty. I'm going to have to keep an eye on him or he'll wind up shutting himself off in his room, gaming, eating pizza and calling it a life.

Chris has got it all together. He's topping our year in everything including sport, which is kind of unfair. He's also so good looking that he makes the rest of us look like the result of an industrial accident. All the girls think he's hot. Not that he seems to notice. The bastard has the audacity to be humble, too. A-hole.

We give each other a complicated handshake as if we're from the hood. Seriously, though, no matter how much we try to act like lads — or how provocatively we wear our hair — we wouldn't last ten seconds in the LA projects. Then again, I doubt that the Crips or Bloods would cope too well in an exam situation with us.

The girls from Smith Street High and Grosvenor hug each other but we're guys and that's not allowed so we start with the baiting instead. Remembering a news article I'd read in the paper on the weekend, and ignoring the North–South divide, I open the batting.

'Hey, Chris. Shouldn't you be locked away in a Pyongyang lab with some weapons-grade plutonium and a centrifuge, trying to build a massive weapon for His Shortarseness?'

'Supreme Leader has a *huge* weapon,' replies Chris. 'Or at least he thinks he has.'

We laugh and talk about short man syndrome, about overcompensating, about how the North Korean people are eating bark soup and grass but can look up with pride when they see a home-grown ballistic missile passing overhead. We solve the world's problems with ridicule and humour like the intellectual radicals we consider ourselves to be.

And then there she is strolling along the platform. My IQ is immediately halved — all I can think about is her. She's walking a little awkwardly this morning and I wonder why. Does she play weekend sport? Is she into equestrian and had a fall? Is she a gymnast and strained her back? I don't know. I won't know. I'll never know. I've had this huge crush on her for almost a year now and all I know about her is that her name is Lisa Leong. And although we've glanced at each other a few times, for the whole year I've spoken a grand total of zero words to her. I'm normally confident around people – even girls – but when it comes to speaking to Lisa, I have about as much backbone as a jellyfish.

'Give it up, Toke,' says Maaaate. 'Even if by some miracle you somehow manage to develop the power of speech around her, her parents wouldn't let her date a *gweilo*.'

'Don't be so racist,' I reply without once taking my eyes off her.

'It's not racist if *I* say it,' says Maaaate. 'I tell you, her parents wouldn't let you within a kilometre of her.'

Chris looks over at Maaaate. 'How do *you* know? Do *you* know her parents?'

'Not really,' replies Maaaate. 'But we used to go to the same church and last year her mum went psycho when she found out she was dating this guy called Justin –'

I don't know who Justin is but I hate him.

'— and he was Chinese *and* Christian,' continues Maaaate.

'I'm kind of a Christian,' I say, defending my Italian-Irish-Catholic heritage.

'You're kind of a douche,' suggests Chris.

I look at Lisa standing there all alone, in her Smith Street Girls' High uniform. If she's got any friends I haven't seen them. She's usually by herself. She's all glasses and bookish but I see her. I see beyond her sadness — and she seems to have too much of that hanging over her.

I want to race over to her and wrap her in my arms and ask her if she's okay. But that is never going to happen because right now our relationship is perfect. She's the perfect girlfriend and I'm the perfect boyfriend. And I'm certainly not going to ruin that by actually talking to her.

But I did and destroyed both our lives.

TWO HOURS BEFORE

I sit at the breakfast bar hunched over my second coffee. Mum has made scrambled eggs with smoked salmon but if I have so much as a mouthful I'll hurl across the room. I've never felt anything like this before. It's unbearable. It's as if all my nerve endings are being twisted and contorted. There's no relief. There's nothing I can do. There's nothing I want to do. I just want the pain to stop. I want my nerve endings to stop crying out as if they're about to rupture. But that's not about to happen. Ever. I'll be stuck with this agony for the rest of my pathetic existence.

My sister, Kate, comes bounding into the kitchen like a puppy that's just slurped up an entire jar of Nutella. She's in year eight at Grosvenor Girls'. Her enthusiasm alone makes me want to puke. We usually get on quite well, but these are not normal times.

She looks at me then over at Mum. 'What's up with douche?'

I don't look up. I don't even acknowledge her existence.

Mum's silence tells me that she has just signalled Kate a reminder that my girlfriend has been carted off to Hong Kong.

'Forget Lisa,' says Kate, whose closest relationship is with her Build-A-Bear. 'You should go out with Ashleigh Singh. She likes you.'

I can feel the wind from Mum's arms twirling in circles, basically telling Kate to shove a sock in it.

But Kate's on a roll. 'You should think about it. Ashleigh Singh's cute. She has a really attractive left eye. Well, it must be, because her right eye keeps looking at it.'

Even if Kate didn't mean it to be funny, Mum can't control herself and lets out a snort which she tries to turn into a sort of cough.

Kate just doesn't get social cues. She's a walking encyclopedia, particularly when it comes to science. But send her up to the shops for some milk and she'll totally forget the milk and return home with a dozen doughnuts and a form to sponsor a child in Sierra Leone. Seriously, she's like Jack from that beanstalk story. Luckily we don't own a cow or we'd wake up one morning with a gargantuan weed in the middle of the lounge room and an enormous goose crapping golden eggs all over our heads.

Thankfully, though, having Kate burst in like a honey badger into a candy store has taken my mind off Lisa for the moment. Or at least it did until I started thinking about how she'd taken my mind off Lisa and so now my nerves are screaming at me again.

But that's what I need to do. Think about other stuff. Not about how Lisa is probably locked in a dungeon in Hong Kong somewhere. And of course, the minute you start to stop thinking about it, you start thinking about how you've stopped thinking about it and that starts you thinking about it and then the agony washes over you again. There's just no escape. No way out.

'Do you want a game of Uno?' says Kate, which is kind of nice of her. Even she can see that I'm in a mess, and we always challenge each other at Uno when we're not doing too well. It certainly beats talking about stuff.

But Kate's kindness makes me feel even worse. 'No thanks,' I reply. 'Not right now.'

As if things aren't bad enough, Dad decides

to come in from whatever the hell it is he thinks he's doing out there in the garden. What began as a retaining wall is now starting to resemble a sort of half-arsed pyramid of Giza. Widely regarded as the worst handyman on the face of the planet, he once blew up a toilet – a *toilet* – in the process of changing a washer. Seriously, how do you blow up a toilet? And because it's October, he's started growing his annual mo ready for Movember, which is death by embarrassment, because he couldn't be like a normal human and grow a regular mous-tache. Oh no. He's has to go for one of those British Brigadier numbers, the type that only an elderly male walrus could carry off. And even then, only just.

Dad's a total sports nut and he's been miffed at me since I quit both soccer and cricket. He used to coach us in the under eights. I know I let him down and I kind of hate myself for it but the passion had gone. My passion for most things went south the day Great-Aunt Mary . . . well, the day Dad's aunt did what she did. I don't blame him for what happened. I don't. *I don't*. And I'm not trying to punish him. Or at least I don't think I am. I love my dad. I really do. But he kind of hurt me when he didn't believe me when I told him that Aunt Mary was nuts. And since then I've been kind of guarded with him, even though I don't mean to be. We're trying to find some sort of common ground but unless I take up accountancy, begin losing my hair, start wearing battery-operated Hawaiian shirts, or electrocute myself while hammering a hook into the wall, it's hard to imagine just where that common ground might be. Dad thinks I've turned into the clichéd embodiment of a sullen teenager and he winds me up about it. He just doesn't get what I'm going through right now. How could he? How could anyone?

Dad takes a swig from a bottle of mineral water and, showing scant regard for those of us whose lives are falling apart, hits his first joke of the day. 'What do you get if you cross a French dog with a rooster?' I can sense Mum's eyes roll back in her head. I stare at my coffee. KMN.

'I don't know,' says Kate, always eager to please. What happened that day with Aunt Mary united me and Mum, and Kate was left to be Dad's favourite by default.

'A cockadoodlepoodle,' says Dad.

Kate dissolves into paroxysms of laughter, though she probably doesn't even get the joke. She's pretending she does just so Dad's ultimate dad-joke doesn't fall flat.

Dad went to Trinity College in Dublin and became, if you can believe it, an accountant. It doesn't seem right, does it? You just don't hear of Irish accountants. Writers: yes. Comedians, musicians, political activists, actors: certainly. But accountants? It's wrong somehow. Kind of like Angelina Jolie and Brad Pitt being insurance claims assessors or Stephen Hawking working as a cinema usher.

'What's up, Dec?' he says. 'Girl trouble?'

I can sense Mum slip into semaphore mode again, her arms waving about like a baton twirler.

'Not to worry, pal,' he says, ruffling my hair. 'Plenty of other fish in the sea.'

I push his hand away. 'Well then, why don't you go and fuck a tuna?'

Mum gives me a look as if I've gone too far, but cuts me some slack and doesn't say anything.

'Looks like someone needs a happy pill,' says Dad.

'Give him a little space, Shaun,' says Mum in diplomat mode. 'He'll be all right.'

'He shouldn't speak to Daddy like that,' interjects Kate as if her opinion actually counts. I hate it when she calls Dad 'Daddy'. She just does it for effect. To be all cutesy and cuddly, to the point where I want to beat her over the head with her My Little Pony. I hate myself for behaving this way to Dad and Kate, but I can't help it. My nerves are screaming and they just don't get it.

'Could you go and check the pool temperature, darling?' says Mum, to Kate. 'Summer's well on the way and I fancy having a dip when I get home from work.'

Kate races out the back like a demented chicken and Dad follows when Mum gives him a nod. Mum comes over and gently puts her arm around me. It's a half-hug. She knows the rules. But unfortunately I can't hug her back, not even half. Life doesn't work like that. I haven't been able to hug her since I turned thirteen. And yet I really need to. I need her to draw me into her and let me cry like a baby. But that's not about to happen.

'Hang in there, Dec,' she says. 'The sun will smile on you again soon. I promise.'

As she makes the promise, I feel it building in my chest, welling in my eyes, but I choke it down and blink it away. And apart from my screaming nerves, I'm okay. For now. At least Mum, Dad and Kate didn't see me cry, and that's the main thing.

'I'm here if you want to talk about it.'

I wish she hadn't used that pronoun at the end. That tells us all that there's a specific 'it' that's bothering me, and we all know what 'it' is.

I don't even manage a grunt.

SIX MONTHS BEFORE

True story: a little nuggety guy walks up to an extremely tall woman in a nightclub and says, 'Hey, baby, what's the weather like up there?' The woman looks down at the guy in disgust, hoicks up a throatful of phlegm, spits on him and says, 'It's raining.'

That would have to be, without a shadow of a doubt, the worst pickup line in history. Though I think mine runs it a pretty close second.

It's the last train we can catch to school without getting a late notice. Chris and Maaaate tell me to give up. She's not coming this morning. She's either sick or her parents have driven her. Besides, Smith Street Girls' High is only two stops up the line: she can afford to catch a later train. With five stops to Redcliffe Boys', *we* can't.

We scramble onboard, climb the stairs and grab a three-seater. Chris and Maaaate talk about an upcoming English exam. I zone out and stare out the window as the rain streaks down it. Each day I don't see her is a day lost.

'Mate,' says Chris, elbowing me in the ribs. Maaaate looks over at us but then realises that Chris has omitted the extra 'a's.

'What!' I snap. They know to leave me alone to let me wallow in my pathetic, poetic misery on the days I don't see her.

Chris nods over to the far stairs, which Lisa has just wafted up. She sits down in a vacant two-seater but because we're in the last seat we will be going backwards, so I can discreetly—or not so discreetly—gaze at her for the entire length of the journey, which is probably about one kilometre. Oh, lucky, lucky me.

She takes a book out of her bag and finds her page.

'Snap,' says Chris.

'What?' I say, listening to but not looking at him.

'*To Kill a Mockingbird*?' says Chris. 'Man, if that's not destiny sending you a message, then my nephew is a simian.'

'What the hell are you talking about?' says Maaaate.

'A monkey's uncle,' I reply. Our gags often lose a little impact when we have to explain their meaning to Maaaate.

'Get in there,' encourages Chris. 'You'll never have a better chance.'

Although she's at the far end of the carriage, we can see Lisa's book cover and I know Chris is right. I don't believe in that whole destiny crap any more than I believe that God has a tailored plan just for me – I mean, who the hell am *I*? – but I'm prepared to suspend my principles when it suits me.

'Go on,' says Chris. 'Your fate awaits.'

'Shut up,' I hiss at Chris but he's enjoying himself too much.

'Don't be a pussy all your life,' chimes in Maaaate.

'Pussy? Me?' That's it. I have no choice. Maaaate's at the bottom of our friendship pyramid and Chris is at the top. If I chicken out now, Maaaate and I will have to swap places and that would just suck.

My heart starts pounding in my chest like a set of bongos as I get up. By the time I'm halfway down the aisle the train lurches out of the station and I have to do that weird walk where it looks like you're attempting to make your way forward in the face of a force ten gale. Very cool, Declan.

There's a Grosvenor Girls' year eighter or something sitting diagonally opposite Lisa but the seat in front of her is vacant. They are both clearly aware of my presence, and as I've left my backpack with Chris and Maaaate, whose muffled catcalls and whistles are still reaching me from their seat (remind me to kill them later), it's quite obvious why I'm here. I flop down opposite Lisa like it's the sort of thing I do all the time.

'I hope that's not an instruction manual.' And there it is. The second worst pickup line in history. It's so bad I'm half-expecting Lisa to put down her book, rear up and spit in my face, and the Grosvenor year eighter to join in. The fact that neither starts spitting at me like a pair of puff adders is testament to the social graces taught at both Smith Street Girls' High and Grosvenor Girls'.

'Excuse me?' says Lisa.

'Your book. To Kill a Mockingbird.' And then rather than attempt to climb out of the hole I've just dug myself, I opt to dig even deeper. 'It's not some sort of weird ornithological genocide kit, is it? I mean, you're not going to spend the afternoon wandering around the park poisoning the pigeons, are you?'

And there it is at the corner of her mouth. It's just a suggestion but there's no mistaking it. It's the beginning of a smile. The beginning of a relationship.

'It's about racial prejudice in the Deep South of America.'

I want to play with this a bit more but with only two stops to Lisa's station, I have to make it count.

'So what was it with Harper Lee and birds?'

Lisa gives me a quizzical look. 'It's not about birds . . .'

'To Kill a Mocking*bird*? Atticus *Finch*?'

She turns the book over and examines the back to see how I could possibly know this.

'You've read it?'

'It not only made me ashamed to be white, it made me ashamed to be human. Do you know there are some people who believe it was actually written by Truman Capote?'

'Really?'

'Well, he and Harper Lee grew up next door to each other. Can you imagine that? Two of the greatest figures in American literature playing together in the sandpit?'

We're pulling into Lisa's station and this is a good bailout point as we're sort of mid-conversation and this positively demands continuing tomorrow. But then Maaaate has to go and stick his big, fat, bulbous nose into it.

'Tell her you won a prize for your essay!' he yells from the back.

Lisa looks at me. 'You won a prize?'

'A book voucher,' I say. 'No big deal.'

'I have to do an essay on it next week,' says Lisa. 'Maybe you could . . .' And if it wasn't for the fact that Maaaate's aftershave smells like essence of dead cat, I could kiss him.

'Sure,' I say. 'We could meet up at Ciao Latte after school.'

'I have to go straight home,' she says, deflating my balloon slightly. 'My mother . . .' But she doesn't have to say any more.

'Okay,' I say. 'Give me your number, and I'll –'

'I can't,' she says, and this time *she* looks deflated, which gives me hope. 'It's kind of difficult. My mobile's only for emergencies.' She thinks for a moment as the train comes to a stop. 'Give me yours,' she says. 'Your home, not your mobile. My mother –' sounds like a pain in the arse '– goes over the bill.'

The doors are opening so Lisa quickly pulls a pen out of her bag while I rattle off my home number. She writes it on her hand. She writes my phone number on her *hand*.

I try playing it cool by not waving at her through the window but I can't help myself. At least, I try to wave to her but by the time we pass her on the platform, Maaaate has me in a headlock and Chris is ruffling my hair. The Grosvenor year eighter calls us losers and plugs herself into her iPod.

And with that I'm officially in love.

FIVE MONTHS AND THREE WEEKS BEFORE

I follow Lisa's directions to her leafy address in the burbs. The house is imposing, with huge skeletal gum trees looming up behind it like something out of a Maurice Sendak book. Actually, the house itself is quite ordinary; it's what I've heard goes on beyond the front door that is imposing. And I'm not about to be disappointed.

I take a deep breath and ring the doorbell. When I hear no *ding*ing or *dong*ing coming from inside, I knock on the glass panel. Nothing. I try again, harder this time. It would be just my luck to temporarily turn into my dad at this point and put my fist through the glass and sever an artery. Fortunately both glass and arteries hold.

I hear clomping down the hallway and if it's Lisa, she's not exactly light of foot. But I know it's not. Seeing how tense and nervous Lisa becomes when she talks about her mother, she probably doesn't have door-answering privileges. I think my being here might be the biggest risk she's taken in a long time. Our daily phone calls over the last week were big enough, our Ciao Latte get-togethers huge, but this . . . this is taking things to a whole other level.

The front door swings open and I have no option other than to immediately nickname Lisa's mother The Kraken. It's the look she's directing at me. It's not exactly hatred, more a glare of total contempt, the sort of look she might reserve for her husband if she found him in a compromising situation with a chicken. It reminds me of the way my mother once glared at a cockroach that was doing the backstroke in her bowl of cornflakes.

She's a lot older than I thought she would be. She must be at least sixty. I do the maths in my head and it doesn't make a lot of sense.

'Lei ho ma,' I say, having googled a Cantonese greeting before I left home.

Lisa's mother looks at me as if I've just informed her that her pet goat is on fire and that I've sold her tennis racquet into slavery, and, I suppose, given that Cantonese is a tonal language, there is a very real chance I have.

'I'm Lisa's friend,' I offer. 'From school.' And as soon as I say it I realise it's a mistake.

'Lisa goes to a girls' school. You're a boy.'

There's no fooling The Kraken.

'We catch the train together. We're friends . . .' Oh, Lisa. Where the hell are you? Save me from this . . . this thing. Lisa certainly wasn't exaggerating when she told me about her mother. In fact, now I can see that far from exaggerating, she was actually holding back. 'We talk about English.'

'Of course you talk in English. Do you speak Cantonese?'

Evidently not. At least as far as goats and tennis racquets are concerned. 'I mean the subject, not the language.' For eff's sake, Lisa, get out here and rescue me.

And then I hear her padding down the hallway. A gentle hypnotic glide across the earth like a cat, not the steady, heavy, pre-lunch stomp of a Komodo dragon.

'Oh, hi, Declan,' she says, all sweetness, but we both know she's going to be in big trouble for this. 'I see you've met Mummy.'

'Mummy'? Seriously? Hearing Lisa call this woman 'Mummy' just brings out the difference between them even more. This thing gave birth to a child? A human child? And an angelic one at that. Jeez! Evolution works fast around here. From Morlock to Eloi in one generation.

'Mummy, this is Declan. Declan — Mum.'

Lacking any high-calibre firearms with which to shoot me — and with an almost breathtaking show of magnanimity — The Kraken proffers a talon, which I tentatively take hold of. It has all the warmth and texture of a three-day-old dead fish. I don't know whether to shake it or batter it and serve it with chips.

'Come in, Declan,' says Lisa. Well, of course it was Lisa. These were not words that were about to spring forth from The Kraken's spittle-flecked lips anytime soon.

Now that Lisa has invited me in, The Kraken has to step aside or put on a scene. And if she puts on a scene she will lose face. And from what I've heard from Lisa, face is paramount to The Kraken.

The three of us stand there in the entrance. You could cut the tension with a chainsaw.

'I'll just grab my books,' says Lisa. She heads off towards her bedroom.

Oh no. Left alone in the vestibule with The Kraken, my heart rate begins to quicken. This is what it must feel like when you're alone at sea, being circled by a shark. I smile at her. A sort of well-isn't-this-nice smile, but she just glares at and through me, as if I'm the spawn of the devil. For a moment I'm sure I can see flames dancing in her eyes. She continues to look me up and down.

'Have you been here long?' I ask, breaking the silence. Lisa told me that her family had bought this house a few years ago, so I latch on to the fact to make conversation.

'About twenty years.' She thinks I mean how long since she moved here from Hong Kong. 'You?'

'I was born here, like Lisa.'

'Lisa was born in Hong Kong.'

Again I do the maths. Lisa was born in Hong Kong but they've been here twenty years. It's not quite adding up. 'Oh, but I thought you said that you'd been here . . .'

'Doesn't matter,' snaps The Kraken, and I wonder if I've inadvertently stumbled onto something.

'My parents are from overseas,' I add in some sort of bizarre hope that being the child of a fellow immigrant will make me appear slightly more acceptable.

'Where from?'

'My dad's from Ireland and Mum's Italian. Well, her parents are.'

'You speak Italian?'

'I understand some, but when they all get together for Christmas and stuff they speak too quickly.' Arms flailing around like those bendy-balloon guys outside car yards.

'What do you want to do, after the HSC?'

I'm going to go out with my mates and get completely shit-faced. 'Go to uni and study English.'

'Why English? You already speak English.'

'To teach. I want to be a high school English teacher, or else work overseas teaching English, in Shanghai or Beijing perhaps.' I throw in this last bit hoping that my altruism towards her country-men (women, persons . . .) might change her initial opinion of me.

'Teachers don't make much money,' says The Kraken.

Oh, please hurry up, Lisa.

'But Lisa wants to be a teacher, too.'

'Lisa is a girl. It doesn't matter too much what she does. It matters what her husband does.'

'My mum's a barrister,' I say, brimming with pride.

The Kraken glares at me as if having a barrister for a mother is all types of wrong.

Did the last forty years not happen? But luckily, just as I'm wishing I had a bra and some kindling for a fire, Lisa returns with her books. She gives me a look. We both know what she was doing: she wanted to leave me alone with The Kraken to see how well I would cope. Had she left it any longer she might have returned to find me nothing more than a pile of spat-out bones and a couple of blinking eyeballs on the floor.

The Kraken gives me one last look and then stalks off towards the kitchen. When she gets there she calls back, '*Lisa! Fai-di yup lei choo fong!*'

Lisa gives me a smile, rolls her eyes and beckons me to stay where I am.

Of course, I've no idea what The Kraken just said, but judging by what happens next, it was probably something like, 'Lisa! Get your butt in the kitchen pronto!'

The kitchen is obviously the hub of the house. The aroma is intoxicating. Over the years the culinary odours have seeped into the walls, giving the house a strange yet delicious essence. Cooking clearly plays a significant role in the Leong home.

Adopting what seems to be the custom, I kick off my shoes and place them with the thirty or so pairs already in the vestibule. From where I am I can see into the lounge room. I notice there's a jade Chinese dragon on top of the piano. There's also the ubiquitous bare-bellied Buddha smiling at me like someone's just told him the one about the priest, the rabbi and the lawyer who walk into a bar and the barman looks at them and says, 'Is this some sort of joke?' Man, that is one rotund enlightened being. For a guy who started the movement in abject poverty, he certainly stacked on the kilos once it got going.

Chris and Maaaate's homes look nothing like this, their parents having embraced Freedom and Ikea. My dad emigrated to Sydney from Dublin when he was in his early twenties and yet the only Irish thing in the house, apart from him, is a shillelagh, which is kind of like an Irish nunchucka. It's a heavily polished, short wooden stick which Mum lets him keep on display for no other reason than it could possibly be used to beat a spider into compliance.

There's a bamboo cane leaning against the wall near the piano and a single chopstick next to the Buddha, which seems a bit out of place. There's also a family portrait on top of the piano which, judging from Lisa's age and the stupid hat that her father is wearing, was taken last Christmas. Lisa's brother and sister look to be well into their thirties. Lisa must have been some sort of accident. A happy accident. Though looking at her beautiful face in the photo, she doesn't appear too happy. But the weird thing is, as I look at all the other photos on the walls and cupboards and so on, I notice that the Christmas photo is the only one that contains Lisa, and even in that one it looks like her sister is holding onto her, trying to keep her in the shot. Maybe she's kind of like the Harry Potter of the Leong family.

The whispered debate wafts in from the kitchen along with the smells. They speak in English: it's The Kraken's way of telling me that she knows what I'm up to. Lisa *had* told Mummy that her friend was coming over to study. The same friend who has been helping her with her English studies on the phone. Mummy acknowledges that this was indeed the case, however Lisa neglected to mention that this particular friend was in possession of a penis. All Lisa's friends have boyfriends! But Lisa shouldn't have boyfriends. When Lisa's mother was a girl, *she* never had any boyfriends. Lisa counters with the slightly heartbreaking chestnut that I'm not a boyfriend but a boy-space-friend. Mummy replies that Lisa shouldn't have either a boyfriend or a boy-space-friend. Lisa tries to shush Mummy and this escalates an already tense argument. Mummy argues that she is in her own home and will not be shushed by anyone, particularly her selfish, ungrateful, horrible, shameful, good-for-nothing daughter who doesn't give a damn about her own mother. The same shameful, disgusting, ungrateful, good-for-nothing daughter who has no respect at all. At this point I'm forced to lose interest in the debate when it switches to Cantonese. I keep an ear out for *gweilo* (white devil) which, apart from *yum cha* and my goat-tennis-racquet greeting, is the only other Cantonese word I know. I don't hear it. But I guess I don't need to.

Eventually some sort of compromise is reached and Lisa and I are allowed to study at the kitchen table, which is where I expected us to be located anyway. Hell, if I'd been The Kraken (and it's the sort of thought that could wake me up screaming at night) I wouldn't let me study in Lisa's bedroom either.

The Kraken makes herself scarce (though unfortunately not extinct) for a while and Lisa and I get down to deconstructing *To Kill a Mockingbird*. We decide that Atticus Finch was a precursor to Clark Kent/Superman, choosing to ignore the fact that Superman actually appeared first. We discuss the Deep South, we discuss slavery, we discuss what's happening now – the demonising of boat people for political gain – and we arrive at insights into racial issues that no one in the world has ever thought of before. We are so clever we can hardly contain ourselves. We determine that as the races continue to interbreed (though we hate the term 'interbreeding'), eventually there will be no such thing as racial purity (another term we loathe) but one big, happy race, so humanity will have to find other things to go to war over – borders, religion, oil, wealth. It's at this point we look at each other and go 'Duh', though mine comes out more like Homer's 'Doh'.

Occasionally I attempt a couple of sneak attacks to brush the back of Lisa's hand, but she's too quick. She pulls away and stares at the doorway in case The Kraken has suddenly materialised. I notice the faint red welt marks on the back of Lisa's hand and now I think I know why there's a single chopstick on the piano, lying next to the gag-cracking Buddha.

The Kraken keeps suddenly materialising but she's not using the irregularity of Chinese water torture. You could set your watch by her: two minutes between security sweeps. Maybe she's working off some sort of ancient astrological chart that's informed her that it is impossible for a man, even a red-blooded, depraved *gweilo*, to get her daughter pregnant in the space of two minutes.

On The Kraken's third passing, I finally hit paydirt and manage to stroke the back of Lisa's hand. Clearly Lisa has also calculated the timing of The Kraken's orbits and doesn't pull away this time. Her skin is all soft and silky smooth. She gives me the sort of coy look that only Michelangelo or that guy who was really into painting angels (Botticelli?) could come close to capturing. And on The Kraken's eighth passing I lean across and kiss Lisa on her cheek. She turns to me and gives me a stunned expression but then, risking life, limb and possible dismemberment, she — *she* — reaches over and kisses *me* on the mouth. I have never experienced anything like it, in heaven or on earth. Our lips melt into one and the tingling sensation throughout my entire body makes me feel as though I'm simply going to float away. And when, with The Kraken inbound, we finally pull apart and look at each other, I know, I just know with every ounce of my being, that I am going to love this angel forever.

I was right. I *did* love her forever. What I didn't expect was that forever was going to be over in less than six months.

ONE HOUR BEFORE

I toss a couple of things (wallet, novel, keys) into my backpack and tell Mum that I'm going to catch up with Chris. Mum thinks this is an excellent idea as it will take my mind off . . . things. I wish she hadn't said anything about '. . . things' (especially with the gap), because now I'm thinking about '. . . things' again and my screaming nerve endings are just about ready to rupture and bleed permanent insanity into my system.

Had I known that this would be the last time I would ever see my family, I might have made a bit more of an effort. Dad and Kate are still out the back, raking leaves, cleaning the pool, being inseparable, so I don't even say goodbye to them. The last thing I said to Dad was that he should go and fuck a tuna. I said next to nothing to Kate, apart from knocking back her offer to play Uno. These are the last memories of me they will carry around for the rest of their lives. They deserve better. They all do. I wish I'd known what was coming. About the destruction and devastation I was about to leave in my wake. But how could anyone in my condition know what lay ahead? And that's the thing I realise now that I'm here in nowhere or whatever this place is. It *was* a condition. A condition that slowly crept up on me and took over my sanity, my logic. A condition that with time, help and medication, I would have gotten through. After some time I would have started cutting back the meds, the trips to the psychiatrist, the outpatient group therapy, and moved on with my life as Lisa would have started moving on with hers. I would have truly begun healing. Lisa and I would have eventually emailed or Skyped and she would have come back in a few years' time, even if just for a holiday, and we would have seen each other again. We might have even dated. We probably would have more than dated. Because no matter how psychotic and controlling you are, you can't go around beating a nineteen/twenty-year-old, not unless you want them to start fighting back.

But I didn't give it a chance because the agony was too much, my nerve endings had ruptured, my sense of logic and scale had vanished. It was too much because I had no reference point. I called it quits on an impulse when all I had to do was ride it out until it had passed. And pass it would. Mum said the sun would eventually shine on me again. But I didn't believe her. It didn't seem possible. I just assumed she was speaking in platitudes. Telling me what I wanted to hear. I was seventeen. I didn't have the experience. I thought I would be stuck with this agony forever. But I just had the wrong mixture of chemicals whirring around in my brain. But how was I to know? How was I to know? *How was I to know?* My mind was broken. And when your mind breaks you need help. External help. Because the thing you rely on most to get you through the screaming darkness is the very thing that's broken. And that's where and why it all falls apart.

*

When your mind cracks and your nerve endings are rupturing, it's weird how grey everything looks, even on the most perfect days. There isn't a cloud in the sky as I step outside and make my way down to the village, but as I'm walking through the park, the day simply couldn't be any darker. Even though it did nothing to me, I punch a tree in retaliation as I walk past. Unless the tree has feelings, it hurt me more than it did the tree.

Despite a gentle breeze, the temperature is already nudging thirty when I slide into a booth at Ciao Latte across the road from the train station. I look down at my painful, rapidly swelling hand. That's the only way I know that any of this is real. The pain. Bad as it is, my damaged hand is nothing compared to my ruptured nerve endings and broken mind. God knows why I've come here. It certainly isn't to meet Chris or Maaaate. I don't want to see them. I don't want to see anyone. I don't want to do anything. I don't want to be anywhere. I just want this to stop. I want it to end. I think I'm doing it to torture myself. That's the only way I could explain it. I was proud of my mind before it broke. Now I wouldn't wish it on anyone.

Although after that night when I met The Kraken I was banned from helping Lisa with her homework again, Lisa started informing (not asking) The Kraken that she would be catching up with friends after school because that's what every other year-ten girl in Australia did (even good *tang wah* girls), and what's more, these catch-ups just wouldn't be to study but to hang out. And further-more, if The Kraken didn't like it then she could get down on her knees and kiss Lisa's butt. Though

I'm pretty sure Lisa omitted this last bit from her side of the debate. Lisa of course was a shameful, good-for-nothing disgrace to the family. Lisa was beaten regularly, whenever she arrived home late from 'catching up with friends', but she didn't care. Her new-found freedom was worth it and she assured me that the day was rapidly approaching when she would fight back.

I order a coffee, my third of the morning – not exactly good for my already screaming nerve endings – and think about the first time we met up here. It was the day after our *To Kill a Mockingbird* moment on the train and about a week before Lisa tested the water by inviting me over to study.

I buy Lisa a Tim Tam chiller and the first thing she wants to know is why we call Maaaate 'Mate'. Nothing about Harper Lee, Truman Capote, Atticus Finch or racial prejudice in America's Deep South (or Australia's public transport network), and I'd smashed out some study on all of them the night before. Instead she wants to know about Maaaate. *Maaaate?*

'It's not "Mate",' I reply. 'It's "Maaaate".' I hit the extra 'a's, making it sound deep and guttural.

'Maaaate,' says Lisa, mimicking me as best she can.

'That's better,' I concede, 'but try to make it sound more like a dog growling.'

'*Maaaaaaaaaate*,' says Lisa, slightly overdoing it and possibly damaging her vocal chords.

'Now you're getting it.'

'Which brings us back to my original question.'

'It's from those beer ads. The ones where the father and son-in-law get locked in the sauna. All they can say when they get out is, "Maaaate". It's kind of a westie thing and Maaaate's from there, so it kind of stuck. Or we stuck it to him.'

'Do *you* have a nickname?'

'I'd tell you but I'd have to kill you.'

She takes a sip of her chiller. 'Sounds like it might be worth it.'

'It's "Toke",' I say. 'And if you can guess why, I'll give you my firstborn, Rumpelstiltskin-style.'

She thinks for a moment and then admits defeat.

'At the end of year seven I went to a maths camp with Chris and Maaaate.'

Lisa bursts out laughing. 'You went to a maths camp? Why?'

'I thought it might be fun.'

'And was it?'

'No. It was about as interesting as it sounds. Anyway, I was the only . . .' I trail off. I'm not going to call myself a non-Asian, Anglo, whitey or skip. I've entered a political-correctness mine-field and I don't know where to tread. 'I was the only . . . European.'

'European?' she says. 'You're European?'

'Yeah. Italian, Irish.'

But she's just playing with me. 'Ah,' she says. 'Token whitey.'

I smile at her. Cute, bookish and smart. I don't want to give her my firstborn; I want her to bear it, and my second, third . . .

'So what about you,' I say. 'Do you have a nickname?'

'I do,' she replies. 'But it sounds better in Cantonese.'

'What's it in English?'

'Well, loosely translated, it means: shameful, ungrateful, nasty, worthless, useless, good-for-nothing little bitch.'

'I think I'll stick with "Lisa", if that's okay with you.'

'Whatever's easier.'

I laugh at this point. I seriously laugh out loud. And I see that beneath the bookish exterior, Lisa has a subtle, dry sense of humour and if it turns out she likes art-house movies and indie music as well, I just might have to ask her to marry me this afternoon.

*

After that we kind of become inseparable. Well, we do for about fifteen minutes on a school morning and half an hour in the afternoons. And when she kisses me (*she* kisses *me*) in her parents' house for the first time, I become a walking cliché. We hold hands every morning walking along the station platform as I float along beside her. She has one hand in mine, fingers interlocked, while in the other she's generally holding the latest poem I'd written the night before. If Chris or Maaaate get hold of my poetry – and it gets back to school – I'll be forced to commit ritual seppuku out of sheer embarrassment. I even try my hand at haikus, if you can believe it, creating, in seventeen syllables, a pictorial symbiosis of a cherry-tree leaf in autumn and Lisa's stunning good looks. Some of my haikus even make sense. Well, they do to me. And all of a sudden pop songs of the type peddled by the sort of boy bands that shouldn't be allowed out in public, at least without adult supervision, start to reveal their greater hidden depth and I get them. I understand them. I truly do. Naturally I baulk at logging onto iTunes during this period for fear of what I might inadvertently buy. I have enough of my former self lurking within the confines of my mind to know that any potential crimes involving music downloads will be pounced on by Chris and Maaaate and the sordid details will be plastered about school the following Monday. That I find subtext in the music of vacuous boy bands should tell you all you need to know about my state of mind at that point. Which, when all is said and done, was a damn sight better than the state of mind I ended up with.

Lisa is a member of a Christian Crusaders group, which she dutifully attends weekly. It doesn't take much convincing for me to put aside my existential leanings and join her brethren for Friday evening worship and games.

It takes us a while but we work out that although Lisa has to *go* to the Crusaders meetings and be collected afterwards, the bit in between – the actual attending bit, the crusading – is optional. Around pick-up time, her father would park his car down the road and, with a couple of beers under his belt, generally doze off. All Lisa needed to do was to climb in the car around crusading knock-off time and no one would be any the wiser. So we use this time to jump onto a train to the megamall to go to the movies, ice-skate or hang out at Max Brenner.

But as is the way when you're crazy in love, you don't always think things through. Eventually, questions regarding Lisa's ongoing absence from Friday-night Crusaders were bound to be asked. The answers to which The Kraken wasn't particularly going to like. Eventually there was going to be hell to pay – in this life and possibly the next.

I can only imagine the horrible sound of the *swish* of bamboo through the air and the *thwack* of it on raw skin, when Lisa arrived home from 'Crusaders' six months into our relationship to find The Kraken lying in wait, arms folded and foot tapping like a dog with a serious flea problem. Apparently The Kraken had been tipped off by Reverend Tong, the youth minister, when Lisa hadn't turned up yet again.

When The Kraken went out shopping the next day, Lisa phoned and told me what had happened. It was pointless lying to her mum because the facts were all there. And what's more, there were at least thirty witnesses and a much-respected youth minister to testify against her: that she had been ditching Christian Crusaders for dates with me. The caning she took was a significant one. She described each blow: how hard it was, where it fell, the look on her mother's face . . . All the time she was telling me this, I just lay on my bed with my jaw practically down to my knees. Amazingly she managed to make me laugh when she told me how she hadn't realised her mother was left-footed until she'd started stomping on the floor in her rage, and then how her father had to run for cover when The Kraken turned on him. Apparently it wasn't sufficient enough for him to drop off their shameful, good-for-nothing, useless, disgrace of a daughter at Crusaders and pick her up afterwards. No. Part of his brief, which he hadn't realised, was to make sure she went inside so she couldn't be molested and corrupted by youthful, demonic, penis-possessing *gweilos*. Lisa's father had fled outside before the *swish* of bamboo turned into a *thwack*. I was in stitches at how she described the way her father had torn off up the street and probably hadn't stopped until he arrived at the pub.

And when she told me this I fell even deeper in love with her. She'd deliberately brought up both her mother's left-footedness and her father's fleeing to the pub and probably embellished both in order to lighten the moment, to make me — to make *me* — feel better.

My stomach lurched when she informed me that The Kraken was threatening to send her to live with her equally psychotic aunt in Hong Kong, but that I needn't worry as rarely a week went by without The Kraken threatening to send Lisa to live with this equally psychotic aunt in Hong Kong. It would pass, Lisa assured me. It always did. We would just have to give it time. Not see each other for a while. She'd been through this before apparently when she'd been seeing that Justin kid in similar circumstances — I didn't know him but I still hated him. And not only was Justin

Chinese, he was a member — an *actual* member, not an existential/agnostic blow-in — of Crusaders. I would have thought he had ticked all the boxes and yet The Kraken still told him where the door was and what to do with himself once he was on the other side of it.

Lisa's immediate fate would involve her father or some other relative driving her to and from school and she would be Rapunzelled up in her room for the foreseeable future.

But what we didn't realise was that as we were chatting on the phone and trying to reassure each other that everything was going to be just fine, The Kraken was at the travel agent making final preparations. Preparations that had begun the previous evening with a phone call to Hong Kong as Lisa cried herself to sleep. But there had been nothing unusual about this. The Kraken regularly phoned Hong Kong. Just as Lisa regularly cried herself to sleep.

MINUTES BEFORE

I'm re-reading Sartre to try to make sense of the bleakness of the world, my place in it and the agony I'm feeling. Okay, if I'm going to be honest I'll admit that I started reading Sartre so that chicks on the train would be impressed by my bookish intellect and not just my smouldering blond (Italian, Irish) emo looks. However, the more I read, the less I care what anyone thinks about me and if I ever find myself in a serious relationship then my girlfriend will also have to read Sartre or it just won't work. Lisa read Sartre. The Bible and Sartre. She liked to keep her options open. Life everlasting or the bottomless chasm of nothingness. Either way, she was covered.

But now, with my third coffee downed and my ruptured nerve endings bleeding permanent and poisoned insanity into me, not even Sartre can help. Apart from the bleakness of existence — I'm all over that. Not that I need a short, bespectacled, nihilistic Frenchman to point it out. The evidence is all around.

I pack away my book and make a decision. It's not a great decision but at least it will keep me moving, give me something to do rather than just dwell. I decide to go to the airport and look up the departure board for flights to Hong Kong. I won't be catching any of them, of course. My part-time job at the supermarket is enough to keep me in movie, ice-skating and Tim-Tam-chiller money, with the occasional blowout such as tickets to see Bombay Bicycle Club. My budget certainly doesn't stretch to international flights.

After I've checked out the airport, I'll try to find that beach that Dad used to take us to when we were kids and Mum was jetting off somewhere for work or just needed some space while she was finishing her master's thesis. It's the one near the old air traffic control tower. You can walk along the beach and watch the planes take off and climb up the rocks and practically onto the runway. Although he'd left years ago, I think there were times Dad yearned for Ireland and this was his way of connecting with it. He's never been back. Not once. Perhaps he idealised the place through the movies of Neil Jordan, the novels of Roddy Doyle and the music of The Pogues. Occasionally he would visit Irish-themed bars and, over a pint or three of Guinness, gaze nostalgically at milk churns, rusty bicycles, hurley sticks and other kitschy symbols of the old land that are nailed to the walls of thousands of Irish pubs around the world except, curiously enough, the ones in Ireland.

I check Google and find that it's 4583 miles/ 7375.63 kilometres/3982.52 nautical miles to Hong Kong, which means it would probably be quicker and more efficient — not to mention cheaper — for me to swim there. However, given that I can only manage about two hundred metres before I have to come up for a rest and a Red Bull, that probably rules that out.

I slouch across the footbridge and buy a ticket to the airport. It's more than I expected. Much more, and I can only just cover it, mostly with coins. Had I known what was coming, I would have only bought a one-way ticket. As the guy behind the glass partition scoops my coins out of the stainless steel tray, he grunts at me like he's evolved from warthogs, and even then only recently. I don't bother with any of the obligatory pleasantries such as 'please' or 'thank you'. When you fall through the cracks and your nerves rupture, social graces are the first thing to go. Apart from your mind.

I take the escalator down to the city-bound platform but, step by step, the closer I get to Lisa, the further away I feel. The airport isn't going to bring us closer. Nothing is. Instead, it's going to accentuate the distance.

My phone still refuses to ring.

I can feel the wind from the approaching train as it makes its way through the tunnel, pushing out the warm air ahead of it. I can't stand the pain anymore. I feel physically sick. I crouch down because the agony is such that I can no longer stand. I feel as though I'm about to vomit.

I watch the train emerge from the tunnel. The train can take me away from all this. It can stop the pain. It can heal my ruptured nerves, silence my screaming mind. And it will be quick. It will be efficient. It will be final. Everyone will be better off without me. I'm practically a stranger to Dad and Kate anyway and without me being a weight around her neck, Mum will be able to get on with her career and might even make it to judge. And Lisa. My darling Lisa. Before I'd *To Kill a Mockingbird*-ed my way into her life, she was doing just fine. Well, she was doing okay. She would have made it into uni, come of age, started dating whether The Kraken liked it or not. She would have had her own life. But now, thanks to me, she's probably stuffed in a shoebox bedroom in a foreign country. No wonder I haven't heard from her. She's obviously taken one look at her new life and begun to despise the pain — both physical and emotional — that I've brought down on her. She hates me. I'd hate me, too, if I were her. Hell, I hate myself for ruining her life. Lisa will definitely be better off without me. And my phone is a silent testimony to the fact. But I don't want to live in a world without her. I don't want to live in a world with me. I don't want to live.

The train is almost here now. I have to make it quick. I can't hesitate. I stand up and run but for a moment I do hesitate. Just for a moment and it's enough. Because it's here I feel my life split in two.

But despite the hesitation I follow it through. I have to stop this pain.

I thought it would be instantaneous. Boy was I wrong. Very wrong. I drop my backpack and jump. I have a moment's peace as I'm flying through the air and then my path and the path of the train intersect and there was only ever going to be one winner. My face slams into the driver's windscreen and I can feel my nose and my teeth being driven back through my skull and into my brain. My teeth and mouth are immediately destroyed and I feel so guilty because Mum and Dad paid a lot for my braces and I've only had them off for a couple of weeks. All that money; they work so hard. All that money wasted. What have I done? The look of horror on the driver's face will stay with me forever as no doubt will the memory of my shattered face on his windscreen. He will wake up in a cold sweat every night for the rest of his life. Yet another life I'm destroying. But I didn't think. I just wanted the pain to stop. What have I done? But the pain doesn't stop. My knees practically liquefy on impact and while my ears remain functional I can hear screaming. My mouth no longer works and probably can no longer even be recognised as a mouth, as my jaw is being driven through my neck. So the screaming isn't coming from me; it's from a combination of the train's brakes and the people on the platform. Little kids off for a day shopping or a day at the movies will also wake up screaming at night. I have become the bogeyman and I hate myself for it. What have I done? The train begins to slow and I slide down the front and fall beneath the wheels. My arms splay to the side so that both my hands are immediately severed. What have I done? I look at my hands as they fly away from me. What have I done? What have I done? I love my hands. Or rather, I loved my hands. I can still feel Lisa's fingers interlocked in mine, the way an amputee can feel a phantom itch in an absent body part. But it's not even over yet. What have I done? Something catches me beneath the train and I am tumbled along and mangled beneath it, my bones and tendons snapping, breaking, shattering and tearing with each revolution. By the time the train finally comes to a stop, I don't so much need a body bag as a bucket. What have I done?

As I lie there I can feel the last electrical surges transmitting through my dying mind. But there is only one thought. Only one word repeated over and over and over: Why?

And then it's over.

Only it isn't. There's worse to come.

Much worse.

NON-SPACE

I don't know where I am, but it's not where I wanted to be, and I wanted to be nowhere, to not exist. Instead, I'm here, wherever or whenever here is. It's not heaven. It's not hell. It's not even purgatory. It certainly isn't nirvana. I could only call it non-space. An abyss of infinite nothingness. I'm not a thing, just an essence. A shadow of that which I once was and that which I might have been.

I'm dead but instead of not existing, I'm wracked with guilt. Instead of destroying myself, I've destroyed the lives of the four people I love. I only realise now, as I watch the police and paramedics peering beneath the train and a couple of the newbies vomiting at what they find there.

It's now that I start to contemplate the damage I've left behind. My parents will have to identify the body. *My* body. How could I do this to them? Who's going to tell Kate? Who's going to tell her that her brother, her Uno buddy, is gone forever? Who's going to break it to Lisa? Who's going to tell her that the future we'd planned on our train ride to see Bombay Bicycle Club is over? Our future of motorcycling through Europe, of living together and teaching English in Hong Kong or Shanghai, of digging wells and teaching in Africa, will never happen?

If I'd gone to Chris's place rather than the station we would probably be having a laugh now, or else we might have taken the footy to the park and had a kick or played a game of chess. He's good at taking people's minds off their problems. He's good at taking his own mind off his own problems. I should have gone to see him; I would have been okay for the moment. Instead, I'm currently splattered across one hundred square metres of train track, severely disrupting the mid-morning rail timetable and the rest of my family's lives.

*

It's said that when you're dying, your life passes before your eyes. What you never hear is that when you commit suicide, the life you lost passes before your eyes. And that is a whole other type of hell. It seems that before I can move on or fizzle out, I'm forced to narrate the road not travelled, the life unlived.

The whole of time — past, present and future — is with me at once.

So now I get to see, in vivid detail, the life that I gave up. And I deserve it.

SECONDS BEFORE

The train is almost here now. I have to make it quick. I can't hesitate. I stand up and run, but for a moment I do hesitate. Just for a moment. And it's enough. Because it's here I feel my life split in two. Part of me carried it through, but the part of me that wanted to live, the part that knew that at some point the agony would stop, was stronger. Just. And although I have to stop the pain, this is not the way. So I pause.

I slump to the ground and curl up in a ball. I feel that if I can make myself as small as possible, the pain won't be as intense. It won't find me. I'm wrong, of course, because my nerve endings are still rupturing, but at least now they're not being splattered beneath the train's wheels, though a strange sense of deja vu will not leave me.

Various arms scoop me up and half-drag, half-carry me over to a bench. Someone wants to give me water; someone else wants to give me air. No one seems to know what's wrong with me. They think I've had a seizure, that I've fainted, that I've OD'd, that I'm drunk. An ambulance has been called as have the police. A blanket appears from somewhere as if my problem is temperature related. A young woman in a business suit gently squeezes my shoulder while someone else strokes the back of my hand. A tradie in a bright orange shirt is kneeling down beside me as if asking for my hand in marriage. He might as well be because I can't hear or understand a word he's saying. He pats me gently on the head with a hand the size and texture of a baseball mitt. I look at the elderly lady who is stroking my hand. She smiles at me in that grandmotherly way that transcends generational, cultural and racial divides. Her tenderness, and that of the young businesswoman and tradie, tips me over the edge and I slump forward so that no one can see my tears. Crying over what I almost did. Crying over the agony that I must endure so as not to destroy the lives of those I love. Crying over the kindness of strangers. Crying because I don't think I'm worth anything.

The police arrive first — two young constables. One sits down next to me while the other talks to the witnesses. The one next to me asks me if I've been drinking or taken drugs. Slouched forward, I shake my head because I seem to have lost the power of speech. She asks me to look at her and although my eyes are bloodshot, they are not bloodshot in a way that concerns her.

Another train enters the station and my fairy grandmother squeezes my hand tighter, her grip vice-like. She's not letting go. Not until the train passes. She gets what no one else seems able to grasp.

The paramedics arrive and with no crime seemingly committed, the police are happy to hand me over.

The paramedics check my heart rate and my blood pressure and even give me some oxygen which, compared to the fetid air of the platform, is as sweet and crisp as strolling through a Tuscan meadow in spring. Not that I've ever strolled through a Tuscan meadow in spring, but still.

The paramedics ask me a series of rehearsed questions but I don't really hear them. I look about me but the tradie, the young businesswoman and the old lady have gone. Spirited away by a train.

Despite my grunts that I am fine, the paramedics insist on putting me on the stretcher and keeping me covered with the blanket. The older of the two, Sandra, orders me about in a bluster-ing matronly way. Despite her outward veneer of functionality, as they're wheeling me towards the ambulance she never lets go of my hand.

The looks I'm drawing as I'm wheeled across the concourse give me a brief taste of what fame must feel like. People staring at you in that not-staring-at-you kind of way, whether you want them to or not.

They roll me into the back of the ambulance and Sandra hauls herself in after me. Her partner, a young guy not much older than me, I'd say, seems happy to drive. He doesn't put on the siren. He doesn't need to. There's no rush for this. All of us know that my problem, and its solution, is long term.

'So why did you do it?' asks Sandra after she's given me another taste of oxygen.

'I didn't.'

'Look, Declan. We spoke to the police, who spoke to the people on the platform. You bailed. Only you know how close you came to actually going through with it. Maybe you should think about your family. Can you imagine what this would have done to them?'

'I didn't do it.' Or did I?

'There's something I tell kids like you. Reckon you should get it tattooed on your forehead backwards, so you can read it in the mirror each morning. Wanna hear it?'

My ruptured nerve endings are screaming at me so I don't say anything.

'What you think is insurmountable today will probably be irrelevant in a month.'

I look over at her. 'Who said *that*?' I manage to slur.

'I did.'

I try to smile at her but my face can't quite manage to pull it off and it comes out more like a grimace.

'Hang in there, kid. Someone loves you. And if they don't now, someone will one day. You don't want to miss that, do you?'

Sandra sounds just like someone's mum. She sounds just like *my* mum.

'Okay,' I say, but I don't sound too convincing. Not even to myself.

Sandra gently squeezes my hand all the way to the hospital. I have neither the strength nor the will to squeeze back.

ONE HOUR AFTER

Even though the waiting room is quite crowded, Sandra has a word to the receptionist and I'm wheeled through to a small consultation room. Sandra helps me down from the stretcher and into a seat. She then slips into boss-mode and orders her offsider to go and make her a cup of tea. As an afterthought she asks if I want anything but I shake my head as words are beyond me. I feel as though I'm holding her up, that she has more important things to be getting on with, sicker people to attend to, but as if reading my mind, she tells me that she will stay with me until the nurse appears. No sooner has she had her first sip of tea than that's exactly what happens. Sandra wishes me luck and tells me that she is going to dance at my wedding. Although I keep my eyes glued to the floor, I think of me and Lisa getting married and Sandra doing some sort of spectacularly uncoordinated mum-dance at the reception and I manage a sort of half-smile, just to be polite.

When Sandra goes, the nurse asks me what happened and I try to explain as best I can (I reckon I'm going to be doing a lot of that over the next few weeks). I don't mention Lisa or The Kraken, Hong Kong, Great-Aunt Mary who's long dead, or anything like that. Instead I tell her about my nerves. About them being twisted and contorted until all I can do is scream my silent scream and curl up in a tight ball. She tells me that she can give me something for the pain but that I'll have to see the doctor first. Before she goes she wants my home number as well as my parents' mobiles.

'Can't I just go home?' I mumble to the floor. 'Do they have to know?'

'You've had a close call,' she says. 'And now we're here to help.'

I tilt my head to look up at her. 'What sort of help?'

'Sometimes when we're young,' she says in almost a whisper as if we're in on a great conspiracy, 'we have to be protected from ourselves.'

'You mean a padded cell?'

She shakes her head. 'That doesn't happen any-more. Well, not here.'

She asks me if I want anything — tea, book, magazine. When I decline, she wants to know if I'll be okay alone while she phones my parents and tracks down the doctor. Although I don't want to be left alone with my thoughts, I nod that I'll be okay. For a little while. She nods her understand-ing, tells me that there are nurses just outside and a camera on the ceiling so I just have to wave if I need anything, and closes the door behind her — though it doesn't appear to be locked. I don't know what my rights are but I guess I'm free to go if I choose. Surely I can't be held against my will. I do want to escape, though not out the door. I want to escape — from me, from the world, from my shattered mind and my screaming nerves, from what I almost did — so I curl up as small as I can in the chair and close my eyes. I drift in and out of consciousness but sleep, real, escapist sleep, eludes me.

*

Outside the consulting room I can hear my parents talking to who I assume is the doctor. I don't know how they got here so quickly, or even if they did get here quickly. Time has no meaning. I look down at my hand where I punched the tree. It's a little swollen and it's stiffened up a bit, but I don't think it's broken and I feel a sense of relief that it's still connected to me and not lying on a railway sleeper somewhere, reaching out to me. I stretch out my fingers. They're sore but they'll be okay. People will think I'm mad anyway. Probably best if I don't mention anything about beating up the local flora. They might just throw away the key. Hello padded cell.

The door swings open. 'Hey, Dec,' says Mum gently. 'What's going on?' Her soft touch tells me that she knows exactly what's going on but is at a loss as to how to handle it (that dreaded pronoun again). It's not every day your eldest child almost kills himself. She's not trained to deal with it. Or to know what to say. Parenting manuals don't really cover this.

Mum, Dad and the doctor crowd into my little consulting room, stepping carefully on eggshells as they do.

'Declan. This is Dr Hitchiner. He's the psychiatrist at the hospital.'

I look up and feel guilty about Mum's smeared mascara.

'I'm so sorry,' I manage to choke out.

She immediately drops down and hugs me, her body wracking with sobs. She tells me that everything is going to be okay. That she'll protect me. That she'll wrap herself around me. That she'll quit her job if she has to.

I tell her again that I'm sorry, but it sounds half-hearted, even though it's not. I really am genuinely sorry for the hurt I've caused her. She doesn't deserve this. What was I thinking?

'You should bloody well be sorry.' Dad joins the discussion in his own subtle way.

Mum gets up and glares at Dad. 'Shaun. There are times when we have to shut up and just listen.'

'Mr and Mrs O'Malley. This isn't really helping anyone.'

Dad glares at the psychiatrist. 'So we're all supposed to pussyfoot around him now, are we?'

'Piss off, Dad!'

'That's it!' snaps Mum in what turns out to be the beginning of the end of their marriage. More guilt to shovel my way. 'Get out!'

Dad folds his arms. 'I'm not going anywhere.'

'Some things are just too important to leave to chance,' continues Mum, 'and I'm not risking this. So either get out, or I'll throw you out.'

Dad stalks out and Mum follows him. She closes the door behind them and basically tears him a new one.

While Mum and Dad go at it, Dr Hitchiner attempts to ask me a few questions, perhaps hoping to draw my attention away from the divorce proceedings that have begun outside the door. I don't really hear him as I'm too busy listening to Mum slicing and dicing Dad. When it comes to a verbal joust, an accountant isn't going to be much of a match for a barrister at the best of times, but listening to their one-sided debate is kind of like watching Ironman taking on Mr Bean. It isn't pretty. She tells him in no uncertain terms that he is to be either part of the solution, or else seek his accommodation needs elsewhere. Either way he isn't allowed back in and *no*, she will not be taking a taxi home. *He* has to.

He tells her that he doesn't have any money, that he left his wallet at home. On hearing of Dad's impoverished state, her sigh is so deep and long that for a moment I mistake it for the breeze. She must have had a fifty on her because when she comes back in it's just her, or else Dad is hitch-hiking home.

I kind of feel sorry for Dad, in a way. He can't tell me that he loves me. He's never been able to. The only way he can deal with what's happened is by getting angry. Getting angry with me. I realise that this *is* his way of telling me he loves me. That he's angry at me for almost leaving him. How messed up is that?

Mum and Dr Hitchiner take charge of my life. I drift into the background, content to let them.

Dr Hitchiner will give me something that will take the edge off the anxiety. He recommends that I be admitted to the hospital's emergency psych unit to get me through the next couple of days. After that he suggests a private hospital that will be better suited to my needs. Listening to them discussing my future, discussing various medications and facilities, I finally accept what should have been patently obvious from the beginning. I am sick. Desperately sick. And I need help.

When you get a viral infection you can literally feel it entering your system. You start to feel off, get the shivers or the sweats, your temperature rises, you lose your appetite. Mental illness is different. It leaches into your mind like a thief in the night. You mightn't realise you have it, even as you lay splattered beneath the wheels of a train, as you dangle from a rope in your bedroom, or as your severed arteries bleed what's left of your existence into the bathtub. It is an insidious and silent killer. For the unlucky ones, it's only when your body is being loaded into a drawer at the morgue that your family and friends backtrack and come to the agonising realisation that you were infected by the black dog. I'm one of the lucky ones. Now that it's out of my blind spot, I see it for what it is. And it's huge. It's so big, in fact, that I can't believe I didn't see it creeping up on me. It took up residence the moment Aunt Mary disappeared into the mist and was let loose on the day I lost Lisa.

The ward nurse shows me to my room while Mum and Dr Hitchiner talk about hospital options. There are four rooms on the ward, each containing only one bed. Clearly we crazies don't like sharing. The other rooms are vacant at the moment, but the nurse assures me that it's early and they are usually full come Sunday night – depression, and its close cousin anxiety, are obviously more active on weekends. This part of the hospital is all safety glass and stainless steel, its gleaming surfaces a stark reminder of the functionality of the place. The psych unit's role is to keep us alive, get us through the first couple of nights, and move us on to a more long-term facility.

I don't know how Mum found the time, but somehow, following the phone call, she packed a little bag for me, which brings such a weight to my chest that I can barely breathe. The bag contains my PJs (boxers and T-shirt), toiletries, a few clothes and some books. My life cut down to the bare essentials. I think of an old man going into hospital for the final time, his life pared back to almost nothing, everything he's earned and accumulated over the years counting for squat. He's left with a toothbrush, a shaver, and an old robe as his life begins to ebb away. The only things he'll need for the next plane of existence or oblivion are his memories.

The nurse now goes through the bag that Mum lovingly packed while her mascara made a break for freedom and her world was crashing around her. She sorts through it with a fine-tooth comb as if somehow my mother might be complicit in my self-annihilation. I loathe myself for the pain I've injected into her heart, infected her soul with. The pain that came within a whisker of permanence. How could I have even contemplated it?

The nurse sits me on the bed and removes my shoelaces. She does it as subtly and gently as possible but there's an elephant in the room the entire time. When they're under lock and key she shows me the bathroom, my Nikes flapping on my feet like flippers. The bathroom is more soulless stainless steel. The toilet doesn't even have a seat. You're obviously supposed to perch yourself on the thin metallic rim, or do what Lisa calls 'hovering', which isn't as easy as it sounds. The opaque mirror is built into the wall and is either plastic or perspex. I guess they don't want us either slashing our wrists or gazing too long at the shadows we've become.

Back in the room I notice that the blind is sandwiched between two thick glass panes. You can adjust the daylight or the dark by turning a dial built into the frame but otherwise there's no escape through either the window or the cord.

Even though it's still morning, the nurse helps me into bed and returns minutes later with the promised pills. I attempt to display an interest in my recovery by asking her what they are, but I couldn't care less. Anything's got to be better than this. She tells me that it'll calm some of my anxiety and help me sleep.

'It will take a little while,' she says, 'but you need to reboot. We all need to reboot sometimes.' She smiles at me. 'Not everyone gets a second chance. You're one of the lucky ones. From this point on, each day is a bonus.' She pats me on the leg. 'Make the most of it.'

I think she's probably going beyond her job description by saying this but I know she's right. I came so close to throwing my life away and so now I owe it to myself, my friends, my family, Lisa or the girls I'm yet to meet, and the children I'm yet to have, not just to survive but to prosper. But first I must heal. First I must reboot.

I swallow my meds, already familiar with the language of the psych unit, and the effect that washes over me is almost immediate. It's like gentle waves lapping at your feet on a blistering summer's day. I want to plunge into the ocean and be carried away but Mum comes into the room to hug me goodbye and tell me that she'll be back later and ask if there's anything I need. I try to tell her that I don't need anything, not even Lisa, but my speech is slurred, because of the drugs, because of the day.

The pills gently unravel my twisted nerves so that I can breathe again. I try desperately to fight off the sleep it brings so that I can enjoy the effects a little longer. I reach for my phone to send Chris a text to tell him that I won't be able to hang at the mall with him tonight. I see that it's flashing. I pick it up and try to adjust my vision to the screen but the drugs aren't helping my focus. I adjust my eyes enough to see that someone has sent me a text. I open it but I don't recognise the number.

Hey D. Hope you're surviving.
Mum took my phone.
Email when I can. Love L XXX

Through the haze of drug-induced semi-consciousness, I hardly even have time to process the idea that the text was from Lisa before sleep cradles me and carries me away.

NON-SPACE

Here's an interesting fact. You don't exist. You can't possibly. The author/mathematician Ali Binazir sat down and calculated the chances of your existence, sparing you the tedious necessity of having to do it yourself. At a mathematical level, your existence comes in at one in $10^{2,685,000}$. Which is so close to zero it *is* zero.

First of all there are the chances of your parents actually meeting. If your father was particularly sociable — and not too keen on sleep or actually doing any work once he got to the office — he could have met about two hundred million women before he turned forty, not including those who volunteer to appear as the studio audience in infomercials and should be automatically excluded from procreating. A slightly shy male, providing he doesn't attend Star Trek conventions (which would disqualify *him* from procreating or at least meeting someone to procreate with) would meet around ten thousand women. Even allowing for these conservative odds, the chances of your mother being one of these women is about one in twenty thousand. Having then met, the chances of them getting along, hanging out, being attracted to each other, dating, marrying and staying together despite various incompatibilities and disputes is now one in two thousand. Overall, having come this far, the chances of your existing is one in forty million.

Now let's duck down to the biological level (your father's happysack if you will) because it's here that things start to blow out, so to speak. Your mother makes about one hundred thousand eggs in her lifetime. Mercifully she isn't a chicken or she wouldn't get a moment's peace. Your father is even busier, producing around four trillion sperm during the years you could conceivably be conceived. So the chances of the one egg and the one sperm that made you actually bumping into each other in the darkened confines of your mother's fallopian tubes are – wait for it – one in 400,000,000,000,000,000. That's one in four hundred quadrillion, which is rather a lot. But that's just your parents. You now need to track your unbroken lineage back four hundred million years, starting with your grandparents and ending up with some single-celled organisms floating around the primordial sludge. The chances of all that happening (your two parents, your four grandparents, eight great-grandparents, sixteen great-great-grandparents — keep going back four hundred million years . . .) come in at one in $10^{45,000}$. That's a ten with forty-five thousand zeros after it, which is somewhere beyond mind-blowing. But then you have to remember at each step along the way, from grandparents down to the single-celled organisms — which are really not a lot of fun to be around though significantly more interesting than the studio audience of an infomercial — the same rule of the single egg and the single sperm meeting applies, which comes in at a jaw-dropping one in $10^{2,640,000}$. That's a ten with two million, six hundred and forty thousand zeros after it. So now we have to consider all that together. $10^{2,640,000} \times 10^{45,000} \times 2000 \times 20,000$ puts your chances of existence at one in $10^{2,685,000}$.

All of which points to two patently obvious facts. Firstly, Ali Binazir has way too much time on his hands. Secondly, your existence is a miracle.

And I abandoned the miracle of my own existence because I didn't know how to ask for help.

ONE DAY AFTER

Time stopped the moment I entered the psych ward and so now I live in a sort of bubble. Disconnected from the outside world. From reality. It's as if none of this is real. It could be the drugs but I feel like I'm living a dream. Someone else's dream.

On my nurse's advice, I'm sitting in the common courtyard outside my room giving my eyelids a suntan. I've never done this before and it feels okay. The warmth flowing through my eyes, through my body. This is what we depressives need, apparently: vitamin D. Vitamin D and not killing ourselves. It's amazing how when you almost die it's the simple things that matter.

I don't want to hoon through Surfers Paradise in a Bugatti Veyron, climb Mount Everest, or go to my year-twelve formal with a supermodel. I'll take the sun on my face, a hazelnut latte (don't tell Chris or Maaaate), a good book, a walk along the beach at sunset with Lisa's fingers interlocked in mine. I had all of that and yet I still gave it up. Almost. Maybe because at that moment on the train platform, at my crossroads, I felt for sure that none of these would give me any pleasure ever again, and no amount of Bugatti Veyrons, Everest expeditions, or trysts with supermodels could come close to compensating for what I'd lost. Hope.

I stare at Lisa's message again:

Hey D. Hope you're surviving.
Mum took my phone.
Email when I can. Love L XXX

She must have used her aunt's phone. I can't risk texting her back in case her aunt is anything like The Kraken.

Lisa's message positively drips with subtext. She hopes I'm surviving? Clearly she realised just how much her leaving was going to mess me up. Obviously more than I did. And of course The Kraken took Lisa's phone. I should have known.

Even though Lisa and I had bought her a new sim card just for us. That evil old scrote thinks there's nothing wrong with beating seventeen shades of shit out of her own daughter, sending her to live overseas, and just generally hovering over her like a demented buzzard.

Lisa's banishment was ordered by The Kraken, and for the moment it's easiest to blame my close call on the station and hospitalisation on her. If she'd stepped aside and let us be normal teenagers rather than the controlling, manipulative, racist old bag that she is, then none of this would have happened. Lisa and I would probably be sitting in Ciao Latte right now solving the world's sociopolitical, ethno-religious problems over a chiller and giant cookie, instead of me being stuck in a psycho ward and her in a shoebox bedroom 4583 miles/7375.63 kilo-metres/3982.52 nautical miles away.

As I'm sitting here basking lizard-like in the sun with time stopped, my mind wanders and I start fantasising about all the punishments I could dish out to The Kraken. It's clear what I have to do. I have to slay her. Only then will things return to normal and Lisa and I can be together again.

I couldn't kill her outright, of course. I just don't have murder in me. The guilt demons would haunt me for the rest of my life. I have to be cleverer than that. Do something that will lead to

The Kraken's demise but leave me only indirectly responsible at worst. Maybe as she's walking up the street with her groceries I could leap out from behind a tree dressed as Death, a ninja warrior or Ronald McDonald. Something that will startle the old bat enough to leap out of her shoes and hopefully give her a chest-bursting heart attack. Or maybe I could somehow tie a steak around her neck or baste her in mutton sauce and set a bunch of pit bulls on her. Or maybe I could get some killer bees and somehow dress her as a bear and –

'Hello, Declan.' My meds-induced homicidal fantasies are interrupted by the sudden arrival of Kate.

'Declan'? She hasn't called me that in years. I'm either 'douche', 'douchebag' or 'loser', depending on her mood or whether or not I've kidnapped her Build-A-Bear or My Little Pony and hidden them for ransom. 'Declan'? Obviously she's been prepped to tread on eggshells around me. It'll be fun seeing how long it lasts. I give her five minutes tops.

'Where are Mum and Dad?' I ask, as Kate begins surveying my new environment.

'It's nice here,' she says. 'I like the fish.' She's referring to the oceanarium wall on the far side of the courtyard which has been painted by either an artist or a patient or perhaps someone who was both.

'Mum and Dad?' I remind Kate.

'What about them?' says Kate, who has the same sort of attention span as the very fish she's staring at.

'Where are they?' I sigh. 'Or did you drive here by yourself?'

'Are you nuts?' Kate kind of cringes when she remembers where I am. 'Er, Mum's talking to the doctor and Dad's getting coffee.'

In a minute she'll either start counting the fish, or else complain about their anatomical inaccuracies. The fun part will be to keep interrupting her so that she'll have to begin counting all over again.

'Do you reckon this was painted from memory, or did someone take a photo and bring it in? And this one's fin looks weird.' Some poor artist has barely managed to keep death at bay by painting this picture and all Kate can do is complain about a lopsided fin.

'Kate. You do realise that this is a psycho ward?'

'Yeah, I know that. So?'

'It's just that you'd better be careful or they mightn't let you out. There's a padded cell at the end of the corridor with your name on it.'

'Shut up, douche!'

I check my watch. Two minutes forty.

Mum comes in all smiles and carrying a green recycling bag stuffed full of books and clothes.

She's obviously heard or decided that I'm going to be in here for a while.

'Hello, darling. Sleep well?'

'Like a log.'

'That's good.'

'A log?' says Kate.

'Yeah. Woke up in the middle of a forest covered in wombat poo.'

Kate turns away from the seascape. 'Really?'

Sometimes Kate is about as much use as an ashtray on a hang-glider.

'Oh, Kate,' sighs Mum. 'Go and see where your father's got to.'

'Okay,' she says brightly. She loves being given things to do. Probably keeps her mind from eating itself. Kate will probably end up curing cancer or coming up with a unified theory of the universe, but when Dad told her the joke about how Irish astronauts had landed safely on the sun because they went at night, she believed him. She even told her teacher and the rest of her year-two class the names of the two astronauts: Pat MaGroin and Phil Macavity. Dad felt so bad he went up to school and apologised personally to the teacher.

'You'd better drop breadcrumbs behind you,' I suggest to Kate as she starts to leave. 'Or you'll never find your way back.'

'Dec,' chastises Mum gently.

'I don't have any breadcrumbs,' says Kate.

I look at her and shake my head. 'Yeah. That's the only thing wrong with *that* plan.'

'Douchebag!' snaps Kate as she heads off to look for Dad.

'And don't step on any cracks in the tiles,' I call after her. 'Or you'll have to come back and start again.'

'Why do you have to wind her up so much, Dec?'

'Because it's fun.'

Mum raises her eyebrows. 'She could say one or two things about you right now, you know.'

'Yeah. But you've drilled her not to. And it's killing her.'

Mum comes around behind me and kisses the top of my sun-drenched hair. 'Oh, you're nice and warm. You did sleep well?'

'Yeah. Had a little help.'

'We all need help at times.' Mum comes around and sits next to me. She holds my hand. There's no one else around so it's okay. 'Do you want to talk about it? Before they get here.'

'Not really.'

'It might help.'

'I'm not sure I understand it.'

'How are you feeling?'

'Better than yesterday. Well, a bit anyway. The pain's not as bad.'

'Do you understand what it would have done to us had you . . .' She trails off. It's just too big. 'You have to know when to ask for help. I couldn't have survived if you'd . . .'

I shrug. 'I didn't know I needed help.'

Mum wipes her eyes. How could I have not realised that this is what it would have done to her, to Kate, to Dad? But that's the thing when your mind cracks. You don't know that it's cracked, because the very thing that lets you know that you *have* a cracked mind is the very thing that's cracked.

'Your dad's sorry about yesterday.'

'Yeah, right.'

'No, Dec, he really is. He wants to take you fishing.'

We've never gone fishing in our lives. 'Fishing?'

'I know, but let him. It's his way of dealing with it.'

I look at the seascape opposite. I have a psycho moment and so now marine life has to die. Hardly seems fair. I don't know why we just don't wander off into the wilderness *Lord-of-the-Flies* style and slaughter a goat or kill a pig.

'Was it just Lisa or was it . . . the other stuff with —'

'I don't know,' I interrupt, because I don't want to hear her name. 'Can we leave it?'

86

I knew that Mum would eventually want to open that particular can of worms when I'd prefer to let sleeping dogs (or worms) lie. She still carries the guilt with what happened with Aunt Mary, but she has to let it go. I have. Or I thought I had.

'I need to know, Dec.'

'She's dead, Mum. She can't get any deader. Just let it go!'

'If I could have taken your place . . .'

'Enough, Mum. Jeez. You're supposed to be cheering me up, not workshopping crap about that psycho.'

'Don't call her that, Declan. She was sick. That's why she did what she did.'

'Okay. I'll call her "the fucking nut job", then. That better?'

'I'm sorry, Dec. I'm so sorry. I should have known. She always had a vile temper. You told us that she used to hit you.'

'Mum! I don't want to talk about it.'

'But you have to. The doctor said you've bottled it up.'

'How does he know?'

'You blame me, don't you?'

'No, I don't. You couldn't have known that she —'

'You do. And you're right. I'm the one who left you alone with her that day. I could have taken the day off —'

'Stop it, Mum!'

Never have I been more pleased to see Dad and Kate. Mum was seriously about to go off on one. And I don't need that. Whatever skeletons remain in that particular closet have long since turned to dust and are best left undisturbed.

'Hey, Declan, what's happening?' says Dad, trying to act casual.

'We're going paragliding this afternoon.'

'Oh, really?' says Kate. 'Can I come?'

'He's not serious, Kate,' says Dad. He looks over at me to check. 'You're not serious, are you, Dec?'

I give him a look.

Dad gets to work on his tray of coffees. 'So that's a skim cap decaf for the love of my life.' He hands Mum her coffee and plants a kiss on her cheek. I can't imagine what they got up to last night after they made up. Actually, I *really* don't want to.

'A hazelnut latte for the big fella.' Dad's voice bellows around the courtyard like the grunt of a mating bull.

'Keep it down a bit, Dad.'

'Why?' he says. 'Is a hazelnut latte too girly for the hospital?'

'No, but *you* are.' It's the worst comeback in the history of comebacks but, hey, I'm drugged up to the back teeth. 'Seriously, the loonies need their sleep.'

'Declan,' chides Mum. 'Don't call them that.'

'"Us", Mum,' I say. '"Us". I'm one of them, remember?'

'Double espresso for moi,' continues Dad, 'because if I was any more manly I'd grow hair on my teeth.' And everyone within earshot rolls their eyes.

'And a soy-milk hot chocolate for Katie Bear.'

'Because allowing Kate access to caffeine would be like giving the Duracell rabbit rocket fuel.'

'Shut up, douchebag.'

'Do you even know what a douchebag is?'

'Yeah, it's you.'

'Stop it, you two,' pleads Mum. 'For God's sake, give it a rest.'

Dad looks around the courtyard and nods. 'This is okay, isn't it, Dec?'

I shrug. 'Best nuthouse I've ever been in.'

'I mean, it's nicer than the hospital your Aunt Mary was in, God rest her soul.' He appears thoughtful for a moment. Mum looks at me and I shake my head.

'Mum tell you we're going fishing?'

'Yep,' I say. 'I can hardly wait.'

'Dec,' whispers Mum. 'Come on.' Dad is still surveying the courtyard so he didn't detect the sarcasm.

I take a sip of coffee. 'Can I bring a book?'

Mum sighs but smiles. She squeezes my knee, happy I've made a concession.

'Bring as many as you like,' he says. 'But it's deep-sea fishing. We're going to be heading out from the Central Coast. Out into the deep. The wild blue yonder.' I don't know if he's taking the piss or if he's serious.

'Maybe if you spot a white whale,' I say, 'you could turn into Captain A-hole.'

'Captain A-hole?' says Kate while Mum snorts with laughter.

'Don't be a Moby Dickhead,' says Dad, and he immediately bursts out laughing at his own cleverness.

Kate didn't get the whole A-hole/Ahab thing, but she thinks Dad warning me about being a dickhead is the funniest thing she's ever heard. Meanwhile Mum and I, on team Dec, are still laughing at my A-hole joke. Pretty soon we're all at it. We haven't laughed this much in years. At least not at the same time and at the same joke. It's usually me and Mum laughing at something Kate's said or something Dad's done involving a structural wall and some sort of power tool. But now we're all in on it. We're practically rolling around on the floor. And if it wasn't for my being in a psycho hospital having come within a whisker of splattering myself beneath a train, then it would have been a real Instagram moment.

ONE WEEK BEFORE

I approach the house stealthily, like a ninja. I even reach for the imaginary sword that isn't sheathed on my back. One wrong move. One error of judgement. One twig crack and the game will be up and I'll be one hundred and forty dollars out of pocket. Why couldn't I have fallen in love with a girl who doesn't have The Kraken as a mother? But we don't choose who we fall in love with any more than we can choose our sexuality, our parents, our Gods, how long we'll live, and, I suppose, our friends. Stuff like that's beyond our control. You just have to go with it.

Maybe the fear of getting caught is part of the thrill. Maybe Lisa and I are star-crossed lovers, without the ability to speak Italian. Well, I do. A bit.

If Juliet or Lisa had a mobile phone (or rather, had a mobile phone that she was actually allowed to use) then things might have turned out differently for both of them. But Juliet was prevented from owning a mobile phone because she lived in the Elizabethan age when technology basically sucked (well, that plus the added fact that she didn't actually exist). And Lisa? Well, Lisa lives in Forest Place where her mother basically sucks. So I travel back to the troglodyte days of Romeo and throw a small rock at Lisa's bedroom window. When nothing happens I try again. And again. When nothing continues to happen, I scoop up a handful of gravel and hurl it at the window. In times of yore, Juliet would have appeared backlit on the balcony and Romeo would have started banging on about the light being soft and it breaking from the window and Juliet being the sun and everything. The story would have undoubtedly lost some of its appeal had the Capulets' front porch light gone on and Juliet's mother appeared on the doorstep, her hair Medusa-ed up in rollers while she yelled, 'Who's out there?'

The ruse up, I have no choice other than to step out from behind my tree.

'Oh, hi, Mrs Leong,' I say so sheepishly that you could hack off one of my hind legs and serve it with mint sauce. 'Is . . . er . . . is Lisa in?'

'Why are you throwing rocks at the window?' she says, not unreasonably.

'Because I, er . . .' There is absolutely no justifiable reason I can think of for throwing rocks at Lisa's window. In the end I opt for honesty. 'Because Lisa isn't allowed to use her phone.' It's at this point I decide that we are going to buy her a new sim card.

'I know Lisa is going out with you tonight,' says The Kraken, hands on hips. 'She told me.'

'Oh, right. Er . . .' Lisa had told me that she'd informed The Kraken that she was going to a Christian concert tonight, but I couldn't remember if she told her that she was going with me, or with her crusading friends, or both. That's the trouble with living a lie. You need a good memory.

I approach the front porch half-expecting The Kraken to pull a crucifix from her pocket and for me to burst into flames. 'Sorry about that.' I gesture towards the window.

'Lisa,' yells The Kraken. 'Declan's here.'

Lisa emerges from the house as gorgeous as ever. She's wearing *my* look – jeans, black T-shirt and second-hand Vinnies jacket. Luckily I've opted for a white T-shirt tonight or we'd look a bit cheesy.

'Ready?' I say.

'Yep,' replies Lisa. She gives The Kraken a peck on the cheek and walks down the steps.

'Goodnight, Mrs Leong,' I say.

We turn and head off down the path.

'Declan,' calls The Kraken.

We both turn around.

'I expect her home by eleven. Not one second later. You understand?'

'Yes, Mrs Leong,' I say. No, Mrs Leong. Three bags full, Mrs Leong. What a total suck I've turned into.

'One more thing,' says The Kraken. 'The next time you throw rocks at Lisa's bedroom window so that she can sneak out to be with you, it's probably best if you throw them at *her* window, not mine.'

I acknowledge The Kraken's wisdom with a nod.

'You were throwing rocks at the window?' says Lisa quietly. 'May I ask why?'

'I'll tell you on the train,' I say.

Following the twenty-minute walk to the station, we get ourselves comfortable on the train and disappear into the couple bubble, my first experience of this phenomenon, where no one else exists apart from the two of us.

Lisa snuggles into me. 'You got the tickets?'

'Yep.' I pull them out of my pocket and look at them. 'Slight problem. The concert doesn't finish until eleven. Then we have to get a bus back to the station and a train home. Then there's the walk to your place. We'll have to leave early, I guess.'

Lisa looks up at me and smiles. 'Screw her,' she says.

'But she said you have to be back by eleven.'

'She's a whack job,' says Lisa.

'Your mum?'

'Who else? I hadn't realised just how nuts she was until I met your mum.'

'Yeah,' I agree, 'but my mum's different. She gets it.'

'She's what a mother should be, Declan. She loves you but she doesn't control you. She loves you unconditionally. Everything you do she doesn't take as a reflection on her. What you do isn't *about* her, it's about you and she's there to support you.'

No matter what Lisa says, I know that my mum *is* pretty special.

'But your mum seemed quite nice just now. She even had a bit of a joke with me about the window. She was okay. Better than last time anyway.'

'Depends which way the wind's blowing. Yes, she knows I'm going out with you tonight, but she also thinks we're going out with a big Crusaders group. Everything I do with you is hidden by lies and deceit, and I'm sick of it. I'm sick of her. You know what she said to me when I told her that you were coming to the concert, too?'

I shake my head.

'She said, "The Devil has you now." What sort of a fruitcake of a mother would condemn her daughter to hell because she's going out with someone she disapproves of?'

'She disapproves of me?'

She shrugs her shoulders, but not very convincingly.

I feel slightly deflated. 'She doesn't even know me.'

'Hey,' she says when she realises that I've been stung. 'It's not a reflection on you, it's a reflection on her. She thinks she's so pious but she's just self-righteous. I wish she'd just drop dead.'

'Lisa, you shouldn't say that about your mother. Even *your* mother.'

Lisa reaches over and kisses me on the cheek. 'I've just told you that she talks smack about you and yet you protect her. You're wonderful, Declan. You're worth two hundred of her. You're more of a Christian than she is and you're an atheist.'

'Agnostic,' I remind her. 'I'm worried, though, Lisa.'

'What about, babe?' I just *love* it when she calls me 'babe'.

'You haven't been to Crusaders for about two months. We're going to be late home tonight. If she hates me already, what about after tonight?'

'She hates everyone.'

'Still. I'm worried what she might do.'

'Declan. She can't hurt me anymore.'

'What do you mean?'

'I've built a shield around myself.' She taps her head. 'She can't get in here.' Lisa nuzzles into me again, even closer this time. 'Now stop worrying.'

Bombay Bicycle Club's music doesn't necessarily lend itself to moshing but boy does it go off. Free from her Rapunzel tower, Lisa really parties. She leads me round the mosh pit like a writhing wild thing. Despite the fact that my dad has all the rhythm of a plank, as far as movement is concerned, I appear to have absorbed my mother's Mediterranean blood so I am able to match Lisa's moves.

I'm still only seventeen, but I bump into a couple of year-twelve guys from school and they sort out drinks for me (imported Italian beer) and Lisa (pina colada) and I am soon intoxicated though not so much on the beer as on Lisa. If nuzzling into your girlfriend's neck during a slow song isn't the best feeling in the world then I don't know what is.

For one night we are truly allowed to be ourselves and it's perfect.

By the time we begin our walk back to the station it's already eleven o'clock. On the station I stare down the line and check my watch knowing that I've well and truly stuffed up.

'Relax,' says Lisa when she sees that I'm worried. 'I told you. She can't hurt me now.'

But it turned out that The Kraken could hurt Lisa. She could hurt both of us. And although on the train journey home we talk about going to uni together and then teaching English in China, or building wells and teaching in Africa, or motorcycling through Europe, in the back of my mind comes the horrible realisation that this isn't for keeps. That this is just one of our stolen moments.

THREE DAYS
AFTER MORNING

My stuff's packed so while I wait for Mum to pick me up I head back out to the courtyard for some more sun. It's peaceful out here. A safe haven from the world. A world that is about to come and get me.

As I walk out I see a girl sitting in my spot. She looks about my age, maybe younger. She's wearing long red flannelette Mickey Mouse PJs and reading *The Diving Bell and the Butterfly*. I open Sartre's *The Age of Reason* to show her that I'm intellectual and stuff, too.

She looks over at me and nods.

'Hey,' she says. 'I'm not in your spot, am I?'

Yes. 'No.'

'I'm new,' she says. 'Got in last night. Not sure of the rules, other than you're not supposed to kill yourself.'

'Yeah,' I agree. 'They frown on that. It looks bad on their résumés if you do.'

She smiles at this and it's a stunning smile.

'Everything okay?' I say, then realise that this is a seriously dumb question.

The girl laughs.

'Sorry.'

'It's fine,' she says. 'And yeah, I'm doing okay. Better than yesterday, anyway.'

I want to know what happened yesterday but as I don't want to be pushed myself, I have to show her the same consideration. We return to our books but there's a bit of, I don't know, tension in the air. Things unsaid.

'Are you allowed to smoke out here?' she says.

I shrug. 'I haven't seen anyone. They don't really supervise us much. Not out here anyway. I suppose you could.'

'It's just that there're butts on the ground and you can smell it. Makes me want to puke. God, smokers are pigs.'

'Oh, I thought you wanted . . .'

She closes her book. 'My uncle used to smoke. Could smell it on him. That and his cheap bourbon.' She drifts off, deep in thought.

I sense that her uncle did more than smoke and drink bourbon around her but I don't know if she wants to talk about it. I don't. About Aunt Mary, that is.

'Why are you here?' she says. 'You look normal.'

'Don't we all?'

'I suppose.'

'My girlfriend . . .' I don't know how much I want to tell her. I don't really have the energy. 'It's a long story.'

'Did you get her pregnant?'

'No,' I say. 'Nothing like that. She got . . . she got taken overseas. Against her will.'

'So you tried to suicide?'

'Sort of.'

'You'll get over her.'

'Not sure I want to.'

'That's what it seems like now. You just have to get through this bit.'

'And you?'

She looks thoughtful for a moment. 'My uncle, he . . .'

'It's okay if you don't want to talk about it.' Actually, *I* don't want her to talk about it. I don't want to hear what her uncle did.

'He killed my mum and then tried to, you know . . .'

I feel myself turning white at the thought of Aunt Mary.

'What about your dad? Couldn't he . . .?'

'Mum stuck a carving knife through Dad's neck, which is why my uncle killed her.'

She says this so matter-of-factly that I feel my blood turn to ice. It makes my own issues seem kind of lame.

'Used to bash her. Couple of times a month. She's been in here before. Not this hospital but one like it. They should have kept her here, where she was safe.'

'Did your uncle . . .?' I trail off. It's too big.

'No. I got out. Lived on the streets for a while – or the trains. Slept in the rail yards mostly. Just stayed out of sight, in the shadows. Eventually I got sloppy and he found me.'

I look at her and gulp.

'It's okay. He blew his brains out. Not that he had much to begin with.'

'When was this?'

'Yesterday. My teacher – actually she's more than my teacher, really – reckons I've seen too much. So here I am. Need to work it out, I guess, rather than bottle it up – or they reckon I might go postal in a few years.'

I stare at this girl, this beautiful girl, and shake my head. Sometimes the world is just so messed up you have to wonder if everyone's insane.

She looks over at me as I stare back at her.

'Don't worry,' she says. 'This is the happiest I've been in my whole life. He'll never hurt me again.'

Mum comes into the courtyard carrying my stuff.

'Hey, Dec,' she says brightly. 'Ready?'

'Are they letting you out?' asks the girl.

'Going to a different hospital,' I say.

'Good luck,' she says. 'You'll be fine.'

'Yeah,' I reply, getting up. 'You too. See you around.'

'She's very pretty,' says Mum as we walk out of the hospital to the car.

'She was homeless.'

'Why?'

I realise that if I mention her uncle then Mum will probably start up about Aunt Mary again so I let it go.

'Drugs,' I say, because it's easier.

We go via home so that I can pack some more of my stuff. It's weird but it doesn't feel like home anymore. It's as if they've all moved on without me. It kind of feels as though I don't belong here. There's a space. A hole in the air where I once was. The normal me, that is. I've only been gone for a few days but I'm homesick for the hospital.

Mum's made soup because apparently that's the law when someone's sick. Cold coming on – pea and ham. Viral pneumonia – vegetable.

Thwarted suicide bid — chicken and sweet corn. So Mum's made soup.

I sit at the breakfast bar and try to work up some enthusiasm for my liquid lunch but it's a struggle. Dad's at work and Kate's at school so it's just me and Mum.

I think about the girl. I think about how strong she's had to be. How she lived in the shadows. Maybe that's what I could do. Maybe I could live like that. Slink through life in the shadows so nothing can get to me again. But it won't work. Life will always come and get you in the end. And if it doesn't then you'll probably find yourself lying on a park bench in a disgusting overcoat, mainlining a goon cask every night, looking after a dog that no one wants, while the dog looks after a human no one wants. That's a life. Though it's not a life I want. So I have to live again. Slowly. I have to find my way back.

NON-SPACE

Two groups of early primates climbed down from the trees and stared out into the savannah. One group said (actually, they didn't say because they couldn't speak yet), 'Why don't we go see what's out there?' – And off they went. The other group said, 'Stuff that for a joke, it's not safe,' and scampered back into the trees. The second group's ancestors we now gaze at adoringly at the zoo and think, 'Oh, they're so cute.' The first group are doing the gazing. They're us.

Group two didn't need to evolve much. They were already well suited to their environment. But group one had to change drastically. They had to adapt. They had to walk upright in order to peer over the tall grass, to make sure there weren't any sabre-toothed tigers or other bitey things lurking about. They also had to communicate to warn each other about the bitey things, and they had to work collaboratively in order to hunt as they changed from herbivores to omnivores.

And the extra protein in this new diet started to do amazing things to their brains. One day a loner, let's call him Ugg, was wandering around the plain on his own when he was attacked by a bitey thing. In a wild panic, Ugg picked up a heavy stick and thwacked the bitey thing on the head, killing it instantly, which put a bit of a crimp in its day. Ugg gazed down his stick and thought, 'You know what? If I were to attach a sharpened rock to the end of this stick, I would have something that I would call, oh, I don't know, a spear.' Ugg returned to his tribe and showed them what he'd made, and a couple of the blonder ones said, 'Dude, that's totally gnarly,' before they migrated to California.

And so technology and surfing were born. Communal living led to collaboration and cooperation. This in turn led to contemplation as the advent of technology gave our early ancestors free time to sit around the campfire shooting the breeze and telling stories. And the trouble with free time is that eventually you'll get around to contemplating the nature of existence. Which will invariably lead to some troublesome questions. Why are we here? What's the point? What's our purpose? This can lead to a thirst for knowledge, or else to the depths of despair as we come to the realisation that there is no why, there is no purpose. There just *is*. We are alone in the universe. The lucky ones skim across the surface of life content with shopping, watching home renovation shows or sport on TV, and accumulating stuff they don't need to fill the void of their inevitable non-existence. The luckiest ones take comfort in an afterlife. They don't accept the randomness of the universe but instead attribute it to a benign creator. The unlucky ones plump for self-annihilation when the void becomes too much, too empty, too painful. And that is a uniquely human trait. No other species on the planet commits suicide. Animals will fight to the death to defend their young, but that's sacrifice not suicide.

Being human, it seems, is the greatest gift there is. It is also, for some of us, the greatest curse.

THREE DAYS AFTER AFTERNOON

Mum wants to do a bit of shopping before we go so I sit and read in the hammock by the pool until she gets back. By the time we get to the hospital it's around four-thirty. I think she wanted to give me some time alone. Time to see what I would have missed had I . . . to see how lovely our home is and she's right, it *is* lovely. But I don't want or need stuff. I want and need Lisa and to not feel this sense of desperation, of nothingness. I sense that Mum has her sad moments, but I don't think she knows what it's like to feel emptiness, this bottomless chasm of emptiness. At least I hope she doesn't. She doesn't deserve to feel like this, no matter how guilty she feels about what happened to me.

We get to the next hospital and I meet my nurse. His name's Andre and he's from Nigeria. He's a large friendly guy with a beaming, welcoming smile. No sooner am I settled in my room than he's filling out my dinner order for me. Dinner, he says as he checks his watch, is in about an hour. He tells me the directions to the dining room, which is basically down a kilometre-long corridor and to the left. I should have brought my skateboard.

Mum gives me a hug and a goodbye kiss. 'You'll be okay?' she says.

'That's the plan.'

'Do you want anything before I go?'

I think for a moment. Lisa is obviously out of the question. She hasn't called or texted again and we're not allowed to use the net so I don't have access to email. Besides, if Lisa's aunt is anything like Lisa's mum then she probably beat Lisa senseless over the text message.

I shake my head. 'I'm fine.'

'You sure?'

'Maybe get Chris and Maaaate to drop over sometime.'

Mum likes this idea. 'I'm here for you, Declan. Please be here for me.'

I nod. 'I'm not going anywhere, Mum. I promise.'

She hugs me again, cries into my hair.

'Your mum's nice,' says Andre, after she's gone.

'She's amazing.' I can say that to Andre 'cause she's not here.

'Is she married?' asks Andre before bursting into laughter. 'Only joking.' He then goes through my bag looking for alcohol or anything sharp. But he's a little more discreet than the nurse at the other hospital. He doesn't ask about my laces, which I didn't bother rethreading, figuring they'd only be taken from me again once I got here. It seems this place is a little more laid back. I suppose the first hospital was emergency care. It was their job to keep me alive. Nothing more. I'm here to get better. To reboot.

I wonder about life on the outside. The real world. My friends, school, ordinary stuff. Lisa. I don't really want to be here – another nuthouse – but then again, I don't really want to be anywhere. It's difficult but I have to trust Mum and the doctors. Left alone, I almost ended it because I didn't even know that I was sick so, to use Mum's expression, I have to outsource my recovery to others. I'll take my medicine and my therapy. I'll take whatever they dish up because the alternative is too horrifying to contemplate.

Andre has finished going through my bag and now goes over the notes at the foot of my bed. 'My friend,' he says, 'just take your time. There's no rush. Ed will be along later. Ed Chiu. You'll like him. Everyone likes Ed. He's the psychologist. Good man, Ed. Anyway, Declan, get yourself down to the dining room by six before the sharks start circling your dinner tray.' He laughs again. It's a loud, infectious laugh and I can't help but smile.

By the time I shuffle along the corridor to the dining room it's already quite full. The trays are laid out on the tables and have everyone's names on them. I find mine and luckily it's on a table by itself so I don't have to sit with anyone. The other patients are mostly middle-aged women. They're seated together and in on some joke that apparently happened at one of the group sessions this morning. One of them has a laugh like a hyena on nitrous oxide. It's actually more like a screech and it occasionally goes above the threshold of the human audio range: her mouth's open but there's no obvious sound coming out; dogs within a twenty-kay radius are probably looking around and thinking, 'What the hell was that?' Maybe that's the big joke. Maybe everyone else is laughing at her laugh. God knows why they're in a psychiatric hospital if they're laughing so much. Perhaps if they stop laughing, they'll start crying.

A couple of them look over and say hello. I nod back. It's the best I can do. I'm not comfortable around strangers. Not large groups anyway. I was okay with the girl at the other hospital but that's because it was just the two of us.

Suddenly I feel really anxious and don't want to be here anymore.

'Excuse me,' I say to the group of cacklers.

'Yes?' says the hyena, turning around.

'Do we have to eat in here or can we . . .'

'Oh no,' she says. 'You're allowed to eat in your room if you want.' She then gives me a wonderful warm smile and I feel awful for thinking so poorly of them.

I try to smile back at her but it's a total fail.

I pick up my tray and shuffle out of the room. And that's the thing. I've noticed that since it happened – or almost happened – I've started shuffling like an old man. I'm even wearing this ancient pair of Dad's slippers that Mum made me bring in because I refuse to own slippers on general principle. It takes me about five minutes to shuffle back down the corridor to my room. I close the door behind me and turn on the TV. I don't want to think too much. I find the cartoon channel, content just to be. To live in the moment. That's all I can handle for now. That and the luke-warm chicken pasta and jelly and ice-cream. But things will get better. They will. They *will*.

After dinner I go and ask the ward nurse if I can have my meds early. She checks my notes and agrees that it should be okay. I then shuffle back into my room and curl up in a ball in bed. According to the list of activities there's a group session on after dinner, but I've had enough for today.

Although it's only seven o'clock, I've made it through another day without Lisa. I met an inspirational girl, I had a bowl of chicken and sweet corn soup, moved hospitals, had dinner, watched *The Simpsons*, and took my meds. That was my day. And I'm happy with my achievements. Considering the fact that had I not had that moment's hesitation on the station, today would probably have been my funeral. Because of that pause, that fork in the road, Dad's probably out in his shed attempting to cobble together the sort of birdcage that no bird in its right mind would ever think about living in, and Kate will probably be in her bedroom doing whatever it is that Kate does in her bedroom (extracting nuclear fusionable material from a Lego brick or something). And Mum will be enjoying a glass of wine on the sofa rather than crying into her pillow with her heart torn out knowing that life will never be the same again. I'm glad I'm able to give that to them. Spare them that agony. On Saturday on the station I thought they would be better off without me . . . That everyone would be better off without me. I now see such thoughts for what they are. The ravings of a madman. Which is why I'm here. This is where I belong. For now, at least.

I'm just drifting off to sleep when there's a knock on my door.

The man enters my room like he's done this a thousand times. 'G'day. You must be Declan. I'm Ed Chiu, the psychologist here.'

I sit up in bed and shake Ed's hand. His voice has a gentle quality like a warm and relaxing hot chocolate. I immediately feel at ease.

'You've settled in okay?'

'Fine.'

'You've probably seen the list of activities for tomorrow.'

I nod. Words are not my strong point at the moment.

'Just do what you want – though we do kind of make group compulsory. You can give this evening's session a miss if you want, though, seeing how you just got here. Tomorrow's starts at ten and I'd like you to attend. After that just take your time. There's cooking, art, tai chi. I think they're going for a walk up to the shops tomorrow, too, if retail therapy's your thing, which, if you're anything like me, it's not.'

I smile and think of us loonies doing the baby-elephant walk up to the nearby mall in our dressing gowns, tracksuits and slippers, and parents gathering their children closer to them as we pass. Ed's right. I think I'll give that little outing a very wide berth.

'What's happened to me, Ed? I don't really understand it. Everyone's been great but no one's saying what went wrong.'

'I've been going over your notes from the emergency psych unit,' says Ed. 'And although it's a term that's fallen into disuse, I believe you've had a mental breakdown. It's hard to say without talking to you in more detail but there was probably a trigger.'

I think of losing Lisa, of the injustice of her life. Our lives. The violence, the physical and emotional abuse that she's had to endure. Her gentleness.

'But the chances are that something was always there – or has been there for a long time – and the trigger just released it.'

'Will I be all right?'

'It'll take a little time but we'll teach you various methods of how to cope, plus how to spot the negative thoughts piling on top of each other. Basically, given what's happened, your brain has to rewire itself. I have every confidence that in a couple of weeks' time, you'll be running down the corridor, eager to get back to your life.'

When Ed goes I switch on the TV again. *The Big Bang Theory* is on, but I don't feel like laughing so I turn it off. Right now I'm just in the moment.

I have no past and no future, no drive, no ambition. I just am. I'm just a collection of fractured nerve endings and although deep down I want to carry on, if I were to be wiped out by a meteor or tsunami right now it wouldn't bother me. And if that *did* happen, if I did get smacked in the face by a meteor or a tsunami, then I don't want to be reborn. I don't want there to be a heaven or a hell. I'd rather be dispersed. To no longer exist.

My whirring mind starts to slow as I feel the meds washing over me, carrying me away. I check my watch. It's just after eight o'clock but for me the day is long over. Before I can reboot, I need to shut down. I switch off the light and drift off to sleep so that my brain can begin the process of rewiring itself.

*

After breakfast we do a tai chi session. If Chris, Maaaate and Lisa could see me they would totally lose it. The instructor has this permanently demented smile attached to her face and I wonder if she's also a patient. It's so hard to tell. We work on breathing more than movement and it's okay. I never really thought about breathing, what with it being involuntary and everything, but now that I stop and think about it, and I mean really think about it, it's kind of nice. If you just focus on breathing – I mean really focus and try to stop your mind chattering by thinking about your body, about breathing, about being in the moment – everything else kind of goes away and time stops.

After tai chi the clock kicks off again but there's a half-hour break before group so I shuffle back to bed and read for a while.

I get to group early so I don't have to walk into a room full of strangers. The women from last night arrive shortly after me. They're still laughing at some side-splitting in-joke but they all smile at me and are so welcoming it's impossible to think badly of them. There are a couple of guys sitting by themselves, lost in some sort of mental maze, but a complete absence of anyone my age, which is interesting. Maybe adults, with their experience, learn to ask for help, but I haven't learnt how to do this. It was easier to call it quits.

The leader of the women appears to be a mop of frizzed-up hair called Sharon. Sharon's group talk quietly amongst themselves without excluding me, which is nice of them. They seem to sense that I don't want to talk but although they're sitting across the room from me, their body language is open should I want to join them.

Ed Chiu bustles in and is greeted by a cheery 'Good morning' from the women – he is clearly a hit with all of them. He looks over at me and nods, trying not to draw too much attention to my status as the newbie. His understanding eases my nerves a little. There's a bit of banter before Ed gets the session under way. Given the sparse attendance compared to the full dining room of last night, it's obvious to me that group is not as compulsory as Ed likes to think it is.

As I'm the only newb, Ed takes it on himself to introduce me.

'Everyone, this is Declan. He arrived yesterday. You might have seen him around.'

'Hi, Declan,' say the women in singsong voices.

I look at the carpet rather than say anything. I'm not being rude — well, not deliberately — it's just that their greeting took me back to kindergarten and I'm trying not to laugh.

'Could you tell us why you're here, Declan?' says Ed.

'Depression,' I reply to the carpet. 'And anxiety.'

This elicits a series of sympathetic noises from the women.

After my introduction, the spotlight is removed from me while we make our way around the group and everyone workshops their issues, so that everything is out in the open and we can all try to help. And that's the interesting thing about group. Ed keeps us on track and retains the focus but the group sort of runs things. A clear case of the lunatics taking over the asylum.

I hear stories of rape and drug, alcohol and physical abuse. There are tales of neglect, child-hood trauma, children forcibly removed, poverty and utter helplessness. Things that make me wonder what on earth they were all laughing at during dinner last night. And maybe my initial thought was right. If they stop laughing, they'll start crying – or worse. One woman, who is sitting alone, is so dosed-up on meds that she may as well not be here. Her eyes are so glazed and glassy they look like marbles. Her mind, or what's left of it, is elsewhere. She doesn't, nor is she asked to, contribute to group. Remembering her own name would probably be beyond her.

Eventually, after everybody else has had their say, the focus returns to me.

'So, Declan,' says Ed, trying to ease me into things, 'tell us a little bit about yourself if you could.'

I don't really want to tell them anything but after hearing from everyone else, it seems that to hold back would be unfair.

'Well, I'm seventeen years old. My dad's an accountant who thinks he's a comedian. Trust me; he's not.'

Everyone laughs at this.

'I have a younger sister who should probably be in here more than me.'

More laughter.

'I mean, she's totally nuts.' I look at my fellow loonies and want to slap myself for being so insensitive. 'Sorry. I didn't mean . . .'

'It's okay,' says Sharon, smiling at me. 'Everyone's a bit nuts. We're just the ones who admit it.'

'Please continue, Declan,' says Ed.

'My mum's a barrister and my hero.'

A large round of 'ah's.

'I'm in year eleven at Redcliffe Boys'.' I suddenly realise that there's not much to my life. Not yet, anyway. I'm really just getting started, I suppose. 'I like reading, movies, playing chess, and hanging out with my friends. Probably sounds pretty boring.'

Everyone happily agrees that it's not.

'How long have you had depression, Declan?' asks Ed, gently reminding us that this is a mental hospital and not the first night of an evening cooking class.

'Since I was young.'

'Because you're so old now,' says Sharon and everyone laughs again. Though the way Sharon says it, they're laughing with me not at me.

Ed prods me as gently as he can. 'How old were you, Declan?'

'Young,' I repeat. 'Really young.'

'Did something happen that led to it?' asks Ed. Obviously this question is too big for Sharon's group and so they lapse into a rare silence, waiting for me to respond.

I look up at Ed. What has Mum told him?

'You obviously know something did,' I say.

'Do you want to talk about it?'

'Not really.'

Ed and I lock eyes. I quickly look down at the floor. Ed's trying to open the door to my recovery, but it's up to me to take the first steps and I'm not ready. Not yet.

'Maybe you and I can talk privately,' says Ed.

'Whatever,' I reply, because I can get away with it.

'Has anything else happened recently that got too much?'

I look up at Ed again. I know that he knows. And he knows I know that he knows. But I guess the healing, the rewiring, can't start until it's out there.

'I broke up with my girlfriend.' It seems so lame compared to everyone else's problems I can hardly stand myself.

'But it wasn't just a breakup, was it, Declan?'

I can feel Sharon's group staring at me, eager to have their minds taken off their own stuff.

'She was sent to live in Hong Kong.'

This elicits a huge round of 'oh's, head shakes and 'that's terrible's from the group. They are so wonderful and supportive that I choke up. I try to hide it but the game is up. Compared to what they've been through I feel so pathetic, but they sympathise with me as if I've lost my whole family in a car crash. Huge chest-heaving sobs wrack my body. My muscles tense as I try to mask what's happening to me but the game is up.

Sharon comes across the room and puts her arm around me. 'Let it out, Declan. You deserve it.' She hugs me. I mean, really hugs me, drawing me into her, wrapping herself around me. Her kindness consumes me with grief. My head is resting against her chest as my tears cascade down my cheeks and onto her flannelette PJs. I hardly even know Sharon but for the moment I feel as though I've come home. That I'm safe. That nothing can get to me. And right at this moment, cradled in the arms of an almost perfect stranger who had been molested by her father since she was a little girl and then abused and neglected by her own husband, I feel myself begin to heal.

ONE WEEK AFTER

People come and go in the psycho ward. Most arrive in a drug-induced state of serenity, transferred from another hospital or medical centre, or else they're back for their second, third or twentieth stint. Some, however, arrive kicking and screaming, but those people don't tend to stay long, spirited away in the night never to be seen again.

On my second night, an elderly lady went berserk, wailing up and down the corridors like a banshee until she was dragged away by the police in handcuffs. Where do you take someone who goes insane in a mental hospital? Wherever it is, I don't want to go there.

There are a few men but they don't last long either. Loners, every one of them, they spend their time out in the courtyard smoking and trying hard not to think too much about what they've lost. Trying not to think about what went wrong in their lives. Trying not to think too much at all. In group they have neither the language nor the desire to unpack what's happened to them, so they zone out, waiting for time, for life, to pass.

There's a high-school history teacher called Neville who's too young to retire but feels he's too old to embrace or understand the iPad generation that's taking over his classroom. He can barely operate the mobile phone his son gave him, let alone prepare an interactive SMART Board lesson for their sister school in Nepal. When he tells me he's always wanted to write a book on World War I, I try teaching him Word when Mum brings in my laptop, but it would be easier to teach a fish how to use a pogo stick. When he can't even grasp the notion of creating a file and saving it, I shake my head and tell him that there are remote tribes in the Amazon jungle that can put together a PowerPoint presentation and regularly Tweet about their isolated status, but he just laughs and tells me that his kids, his wife and his students did the com*poo*ter stuff for him. After several lessons we both admit defeat. The digital age has consigned him to the past. With a master's degree in ancient history, he's thinking of starting a lawn-mowing business or else stacking supermarket shelves at night.

A huge tattooed trucker, Bill, joins us for a while. His muscular forearms and sausage-like fingers make his cigarettes look like toothpicks. I learn from Sharon that his wife died of breast cancer a few months earlier and he's attempted suicide a couple of times since. Three days after Bill was admitted I came out of my room around midnight to make a cup of hot chocolate only to see his bulbous sheet-covered silhouette being wheeled down the corridor. He found his way back to his wife via his dressing-gown cord and the bathroom doorknob.

The day after Bill left, a young girl, Ellie, joins us. She's in year nine but looks more like year five. Her arms are sliced to ribbons, the fresh scars not quite covering the old ones. I chat to her over coffee in the games room but we have little in common apart from our age. I figured anyone *that* determined to die would, like Bill, get there eventually. But Sharon assures me that Ellie doesn't want to die, she wants to live, and the self-harm, the slicing and dicing of her arms, is her way of feeling something. Anything. Her parents are divorced, so Ellie divides her time between her mother's mansion on the North Shore and her father's penthouse in Dubai. Like a lot of depressives, she has everything to live with, but very little to live for, so she cuts herself to feel alive.

The woman who floated into group and sat there in an upright coma with her mind far, far away is escorted down the corridor and returned to her family when two-and-a-half bottles of vodka are discovered in her bag that some 'friends' of hers had obviously smuggled in. The hospital makes it quite clear on arrival that the staff are here to help us get better, but we have to at least meet them halfway by wanting to.

A bipolar patient believes she knows how to communicate with God and attempts to fly down the emergency exit stairwell. She's unsuccessful on both counts. God fails to heed her call or cushion her fall and she winds up with two broken arms, a fractured skull and an adjustment to her medication.

The girl from my first hospital eventually joins us. Her name is Danica and she's trying to forget or get over everything she's seen and heard. The death of her parents, life on the streets, the trains, the abandoned houses.

There are additions and subtractions to Sharon's group, too, but the nucleus remains the same and Sharon's position at the helm is unquestioned.

We haven't really spoken much since that first day in group. At least not about what happened. Somehow it's too big. Beyond words. But she gave something to me that day. I regressed to my own ground zero as Sharon cradled me. No amount of drugs, psycho- or retail therapy, tai chi, cooking and art classes could give me what Sharon gave me in five minutes. And I think Ed, the wily fox, knew what was going on, which is why he didn't intervene. For a few minutes I let Sharon become Aunt Mary, or the Aunt Mary my dad remembers – the one full of kindness and charity before the drink and demons leeched into her mind – and I am finally able to close the door on her. To let her go. And I now know that when Aunt Mary let go of my hand and disappeared over the edge and into the mist, she saved me because when it mattered most, the decency that was buried beneath all her other stuff broke through to the surface. And it was enough. Just.

I learn from one of the group members that Sharon lost a baby boy when he was only three days old. He would have been my age now, apparently. I wish I could help her the way that she helped me. Help her in some small way. But there's nothing I can do.

*

There's no wi-fi in the hospital and up until now, Mum has been reluctant to buy me an internet dongle. But I guess she thinks I'm getting better because after a few days she gives in. When I finally get it working, I check my email as casually as I can but my heart is racing. When I log in to my mail server I have to wade through the morass of crap that has found its way past my spam filter. There's a bunch of messages from a Russian chick called Svetlana, who is wanting to meet a man like me and would like to send me a photo of herself if I give her my address. There are about twenty emails from various companies wanting to sell me discounted Viagra. Seriously? I'm seventeen years old and, when I'm not in mental hospitals, hornier than the sharp end of a stampeding rhinoceros. I don't need Viagra. I need the opposite. An antidote. Down, boy! But there, amongst all the spam (I don't believe in capital punishment but spammers should be shot at dawn without trial) are several messages from Lisa. The first one is kind of chatty. She lets me know that she's okay. That she's settling in. That she's sorry for what happened. That she misses me more than air (boy does that bring a smile to my face). She still considers us to be boyfriend and girlfriend despite the distance and she hopes I do, too. She then confides in me that at night, when she thinks about me, about our kisses, and about that time in my bedroom when we did a little more than kiss, she has to muffle herself with a pillow so that her aunt doesn't come rushing in or call an ambulance. On reading this I immediately need some anti-Viagra and am forced to miss group and take a long cold shower instead. By her fourth email she has heard, from one of her friends, that I'm in hospital but doesn't know why. She also understands if I never want to see, talk to, or email her ever again. That she not only has zero respect for her mother but she hates her. Hates her with such venom that she wants to stay in Hong Kong, at least until she's finished school. And when she has finished school she will come back to Sydney to be with me and live with an elderly aunt on her father's side who also loathes her mother. My heart sinks a little when I read her last email. She hasn't heard from me so she has accepted that I've either moved on or else I don't want anything to do with her, which she understands completely. My fingers are just a blur as I type out a reply. I tell her that I've been sick, that I've been in hospital, that I'm *still* in hospital (though I don't go into details), that I haven't had access to email up until now, that I can't live without her and that we *are* still together. That we are still a couple. That no amount of demented mothers or aunts (hers or mine) will keep us from being together. That I love her. That I have always loved her and *will* always love her.

I hit 'send', and then refresh my inbox every minute on the minute waiting for her reply. She must have been at school because it takes seven hours before she replies. She tells me that she has been crying because my email is so wonderful. She has read it over and over and over again. She wants to know why I'm in hospital, though she suspects it's related to depression. She tells me that we *are* going to be together forever. That we will get through this. We will negotiate the hurdles. And while there is a small, rational part of my brain that knows that this is probably what everyone feels in their first real romance, I don't want rational. I don't want wisdom. I want Lisa. And although we are 4583 miles/7375.63 kilometres/3982.52 nautical miles apart, we are back together.

I think back a week ago to the train platform and what might have been. The wreckage I would have left behind in that moment of pure insanity. Thank God I paused.

ONE WEEK AFTER

I've been prescribed antidepressants for my long-term mental health, as well as something to help me sleep. To help me reboot. I'm on so many meds that if I run, I rattle. The funny thing is that before all this I didn't take anything. Didn't believe in it. Mum's a bit of an earth mother (well, an earth mother in a power suit), and she always encouraged me and Kate to let our natural antibodies fight whatever ailments we had coming on – headache, flu, tummy upset, couldn't-be-arsed-going-to-school-because-it's-cross-country-carnival-day. So it's kind of part of my DNA not to take medication, but now . . . Mum's eager for me to scarf down whatever pills the doctors throw my way.

Because when your mind cracks you need more than positive thinking, incense sticks and a set of bongo drums to stitch it back together again. You need hard-core pharmaceuticals.

I'm in the process of writing an email to Lisa when there's a knock on my door.

Danica enters without being invited in. 'Party in Nathan's room,' she says. 'Under twenties only. His mates smuggled in goon.'

'What if we get busted?' I say rather pathetically. 'Won't we get in trouble, like what's-her-face?'

'You mean we might get expelled from a psychiatric hospital?' says Danica. 'Oh no. Whatever shall we do?'

'Okay,' I say. 'You can turn off the sarcasm now. Be there in ten.'

'You sexting Lisa?'

Sprung. 'No. I'm just sending her an email.'

Danica grins. 'Yeah, right. See you soon.'

There're five teens in the psycho ward now. Me (the almost suicide), Danica (who's seen too much), Nathan (bipolar), Ellie (arm slicer), and Samantha (another almost suicide). Danica's the alpha of the group and she instructs me to smuggle five cups from the tearoom but to be obvious about it and not sneak around like I'm up to something. Nathan opens the cask. Given that it's almost lights out, we're all dosed up to the back teeth on meds.

It heightens the effects of the wine, which tastes like paint thinner.

'Jeez, Nate,' I say, having taken a sip and involuntarily dry-retched. 'Couldn't your mates have smuggled in a couple of bottles rather than this cardboard shit? I mean, how did they get the cat to piss into the cask?'

'I'll tell you what, Captain Connoisseur,' says Nathan. 'You and your mates can cater our next event. Okay?' He talks at a million miles an hour but I think I get the gist of what he said.

'Fine by me.' Chris'll raid his mother's private stash. Nothing under twenty-five dollars a bottle.

It's kind of like a cross between a party and group therapy. Once it's fully underway and Nathan's wine has stripped the tastebuds from our tongues and the backs of our throats and reduced our collective IQ significantly, it's clear that Ellie and Samantha don't talk much but Nathan hardly shuts up. Given the speed of his speech, and how he tends to answer questions that he hasn't even been asked, he's obviously heading towards the manic cycle of his particular flavour of psychosis.

'It's just awesome dude when the highs hit you feel like you can fly and you feel like you kind of like know the mysteries of the universe and how to cure cancer and shit like that and you do that's the thing you really do only when you try and write it down you forget so then you come up with a whole new religion that everyone can embrace because it doesn't have any rules or commandments or Gods or killing people and blowing shit up and stuff like that because religion is supposed to be peaceful but then you start thinking that if you start a religion it kind of makes you God and maybe people will start worshipping you like you're God or Allah or Krishna or or or or that mad asshole in America who thought he was the second coming of Jesus only he and his followers stashed away a bunch of AK-47s and grenades and shit which is not something you could imagine Jesus doing up there on the cross pulling out from behind his back a Kalashnikov semi-automatic assault rifle and saying "Take that you mothers . . . eat lead Pontius Pilate – where's your plane if you're a pilot, ha ha ha" – and so when the FBI turned up and said "What the eff" they had the shit kicked out of them because although what they did was completely and utterly messed up beyond belief what we should never forget is that the governmentcandowhateveritwantsand there'sfuckallyoucandoaboutit . . .'

Danica pours Nathan another large mug of wine before our ears start to bleed.

Unlike the rest of us, Nathan doesn't want to be cured because he lives for the highs of bipolar, even if the lows almost kill him. It's a balancing act, he says, using a thousand words when fifty would have covered it. The important thing is to try to avoid leaping off a building during the manic phase because you truly believe you can fly, and then not throwing yourself off the same building in despair when the black dog shows up.

Danica talks of her life on the streets, the bus shelters, the parks, the trains, the rail yards, the megamalls. Meanwhile, Ellie, whose parents are loaded, informs us that she really doesn't want to live in this world anymore. We tell her that she's wrong. That she's an amazing person. That life can only get better. But seriously. Who are we to offer advice to anyone? We're the broken ones.

Samantha doesn't want to reveal why she did what she did. She never says anything in group. Though she will have to wear the scarf around her neck for the rest of her life to cover the rope burns.

And then it's my turn. Danica knows about Lisa, but life on the streets has made her smart beyond her years and she knows there's something else.

'So what about this aunt of yours,' she says. 'Ed mentioned her in group. She jerk you off or something?'

I shake my head. 'No. Nothing like that.'

Nathan perks up. 'She blow you?'

'He wishes.'

'For God's sake, Danica. She was my aunt.'

'Technically she was your father's aunt, so she was your great-aunt.'

'She was also seventy-five years old.'

'She could have taken out her false teeth first,' says Nathan.

Even Samantha laughs at this. Everyone does. Everyone but me.

'Sorry, Declan. We're just messing with you,' says Danica.

'She committed suicide,' I say. 'While I was . . .'

There's silence for a moment.

'She do it in front of you?' asks Ellie.

I nod.

'That's totally messed up,' says Nathan.

'She tried to take me with her.'

Danica puts her arm around me. 'Sorry, Declan. We didn't mean to . . .'

'It's okay,' I say because it is. 'I've never really talked about it.'

'How old were you?' asks Samantha.

'Six.'

The silence is so overwhelming that you can almost hear the gutrot wine eating through the cardboard cask.

'That's really messed up,' says Nathan, the combined effects of the wine and his meds having finally brought him back to neutral.

'I didn't realise just how much it got to me . . . . Thought I'd buried it.'

Danica gently rubs my back.

'I suppose she put it in my mind that suicide was an option, when really, life is bloody awesome.'

'Were you close to her?' says Danica.

I look around the group. Everyone respectfully waits for my affirmation. 'I hated the bitch,' I say. 'I wished she'd killed herself sooner.'

There's a long silence before Danica snorts with laughter and then, having started us off, we're all at it. And for a moment, just for a moment, I get a brief taste of Nathan's mania and can understand why he's reluctant to give it up.

*

By the time I stagger into group the following morning, it feels as though someone has hacked my brain in half with a machete. I don't know how I got back to my room last night without assistance, or even if I *did* get back to my room without assistance. I kind of vaguely remember a nurse coming into the room at some point and laser-beaming her torch into my eyes.

Danica wanders in and slumps down into the chair next to me. She looks like I feel.

'What happened last night?' she says. 'How did we get back to our rooms? And was that like the worst wine in history? Was it wine or kerosene?'

I nod and immediately regret it. It feels like my brain is bouncing around inside my skull like a pinball.

'What happened to the cask?' asks Danica.

'The nurses took it,' says Samantha.

'They finish it off?' says Nathan, hopefully.

'Evidence.'

Oh, crap!

Ed Chui bounds into the room like he's on a mission. He doesn't run today's session but hands over to a trainee. Straight out of uni, she focuses on negative thoughts, how to spot the signs, and the strategies that we should employ to overcome them. It really is psychology 101 but I just want the session to be over so that I can go back to bed and lapse into a goon-induced coma. One thing's for sure and that is that I'm never drinking again. Ever. Well, not out of cardboard anyway. That stuff is potentially lethal.

When the hour's up, Ed invites Danica, Samantha, Ellie, Nathan and me to stay behind. We are clearly in deep shit.

When everyone has left the room, Ed reaches into a plastic bag and pulls out the offending cask. We all stare at it and silently curse its very existence, for making us feel like something the cat crapped out, like someone has pierced our eyes with a red-hot needle.

'Well,' says Ed, 'do you have anything to say for yourselves?'

'Any left?' says Nathan. 'Hair of the dog?'

Ed smiles at this, though I don't think the rest of us know what it means. Well, I don't.

'Who's responsible?' says Ed.

I put up my hand.

'Declan,' hisses Danica.

'We all are, Ed,' I say. 'We all got stuck in. Well, apart from Sam. Does it matter where it came from?'

'Are we out?' asks Nathan.

'Discharging you would be as irresponsible as the five of you were last night.'

'But what about what's-her-face?' says Danica. 'She got kicked out for having vodka in her bag.'

'Monica? She was thirty-eight years old,' says Ed. 'And she knew the rules.'

'So did we,' argues Danica, who seems in favour of our expulsion, at least on ethical and equality grounds.

'You're teenagers,' says Ed. 'And no matter how much you think you know, no matter how intelligent you think you are, not only has your cerebral cortex not fully developed yet, you don't have the benefit of experience behind you that Monica had.'

'Cerebral cortex?' says Ellie. 'What the hell does that mean?'

'I didn't even know I *had* a cerebral cortex,' says Nathan.

'It means,' says Danica, 'that we don't know shit from a hot rock.'

'In a nutshell,' says Ed. 'But you are on a warning. All of you.'

'Can we go?' says Danica. 'I've got a couple of Nurofen with my name on them.'

'In a moment,' says Ed. 'But first I want to tell you a story. About an uncle of mine.'

We look at each other and realise that we have very little choice but to listen. Ed's given us a reprieve so now we are his captive audience. This is our penance.

'Poor Uncle Jimmy,' continues Ed, 'had the great misfortune of being killed by a thumbtack.'

Danica snorts but attempts to turn it into a cough to spare Ed's feelings.

'That's okay, Danica,' says Ed. 'Uncle Jimmy was . . . How shall I put this in a way that you would easily understand . . . Oh, I know. All right. Uncle Jimmy was an asshole. In fact, if an asshole had an asshole, it would look a lot like Uncle Jimmy.'

We openly laugh at this.

'Despite his being an asshole,' continues Ed, 'his death does serve as a warning. Now, Uncle Jimmy spent his whole life ripping people off.

Family, friends, associates; he didn't care. He'd rip off anyone and call it business. He ran massage parlours. Okay, let's call a spade a spade. He ran brothels and exploited young women. Made him a lot of money. And to further highlight what an asshole he was, when his eight-year-old daughter started crying at her swimming lessons, he took her to the local pool and threw her in the deep end fully clothed. Some might say that he was mean. Some might say he was trying to toughen her up. I would say that he was a prick. He was also a raging drunk. In fact, he drank so much that he actually bought a house because it was close to a bottle shop.'

'So he died from what, liver failure?' asked Nathan. He obviously assumed, like the rest of us, that this was Ed's anti-booze lecture.

'No. I already told you, he died from the effects of a thumbtack.'

We look at each other again. How the hell do you die from a thumbtack?

'So what happened?' asks Nathan.

'Well, of all the idiotic ways there are to die, I think Uncle Jimmy takes the cake. Though I'd prefer to call it karma. One night he shouts us all dinner. Big man. Big show. And he hit the bottle pretty hard that night, let me tell you. He left the restaurant in much the same way the five of you left Nathan's room last night.'

'Four,' says Samantha. 'I didn't drink.'

'You were party to it,' says Ed. 'No passive bystanders here. Anyway, a couple of us manage to pour Uncle Jimmy into a taxi and give the driver his address. And when he arrives back at his McMansion, he somehow staggers to the top of the staircase — barefoot, you understand — and steps on a thumbtack that had been dropped there. But rather than suck it up, old Uncle Jimmy starts leaping up and down like a one-legged kangaroo, yelling the house down about who the hell had dropped the thumbtack at the top of the stairs. Now I know that Uncle Jimmy's grandchildren were staying over that weekend because the same child who had dropped the thumbtack at the top of the stairs had also carelessly left his skateboard just next to the thumbtack, and in his animated leaping about to draw attention to the fact that a thumbtack had been dropped at the top of the stairs, Uncle Jimmy inadvertently leapt onto the skateboard, which was, unluckily for Uncle Jimmy, facing the staircase.'

I can feel Danica shaking next to me desperately trying to hold back a snort. I try to avoid locking eyes with her as I'm busy biting my lip.

Ed looks over at Danica but solemnly continues. 'Now Uncle Jimmy, it must be said, was not a very proficient skateboarder. In fact, the best that could probably be said is that he was a rank amateur, and not a very gifted one at that. And it would take an extremely proficient skateboarder — some might even suggest a *professional* skateboarder — to be able to pilot a skateboard down a marble staircase . . .'

Unable to hold it together any longer, Danica's snort erupts out of her nose, her eyes, her ears. It's like her head is spontaneously combusting. Tears stream down her face.

I look across at Ellie, Samantha and Nathan, who are doing the best they can to hold it together, covering their faces with their hands as if they're deep in contemplation or immensely saddened by the events that Ed is recounting in deadpan.

'Please, Danica,' says Ed. 'A little respect for the departed if you don't mind.'

Danica tries to cry out that she's sorry but she's too far gone and she sounds more like a pig snuffling through a trough.

'As there were no witnesses or security cameras present to capture or recount the events as they unfolded,' continues Ed, 'it is unclear just how far Uncle Jimmy was able to manoeuvre the unfamiliar craft down the spiral staircase. Did I mention that the staircase was spiral?'

I cover my face with my hand and shake my head because I've lost the power of speech.

'What the autopsy report did reveal, however, is that Uncle Jimmy's head connected with most, if not all, of the stairs on his journey down and at some point along the way he acquired massive and fatal brain damage.'

Ed is forced to stop his recount of his Uncle Jimmy's demise at this point when a magma of snot erupts involuntarily out of Nathan's nose, and, in order to continue breathing, Samantha is forced to use her asthma inhaler.

Ed looks to the heavens. 'Rest in peace, Uncle Jimmy.'

The five of us eventually end up rolling around on our chairs like upturned sea turtles and begging Ed to stop.

It takes a good five minutes before we've all recovered the power of speech. No sooner do we regain our composure than someone would snort and we'd all be off again.

'Was that true, Ed?' asks Danica, her eyes still brimming with tears.

'For the most part,' says Ed. 'He was found dead on the staircase and there was a skateboard in the immediate vicinity. The rest I've sort of embellished.'

Ed's polished delivery suggests that this wasn't the first time that he's told the story of Uncle Jimmy's passing.

'What's the moral of the story?' asks Nathan. 'Don't drink? Don't be an asshole? Always be on the lookout for skateboards on stairs?'

'There is no moral,' says Ed. 'The point of the story is the story itself.'

We look around at each other, unsure what to make of it.

'Look,' he continues when he sees us struggling, 'you've all been through a really difficult time. Some of you are still going through it. Three out of the five of you have attempted suicide. What did Uncle Jimmy's story make you feel?'

'Like pissing ourselves,' says Danica. 'I haven't laughed that much in years.'

'Raise your hand if you feel like dying right now?' says Ed.

No hands go up.

'Life is about enjoying the little moments. You've all just had a moment. I dare say you had another one last night during your little get-together. And isn't that life? Little moments stitched together. We're all going to fall on bad times and go through sadness, through breakups, through death, bereavement and depression. It happens. It's a part of life. But those moments will pass and you'll have good moments again. You'll have great moments. You'll have beautiful moments.' He hesitates as if considering what to

say next. 'When I was at uni my then girlfriend –
technically she was my fiancée – told me that she
was seeing someone else and that our relationship
was over. Well, it almost destroyed me.'

Ed and I share a look at this point.

'I pretty much abandoned my life, wallowed
in self-pity for months and hit the booze. I was
studying economics at the time but I dropped out
of uni and had suicidal thoughts. Although I didn't
actually stand on the edge of the cliff, the thought
was constantly on my mind but there was no
way I was going to act on it because a small part
of me knew that just beyond the horizon there
were other possibilities. There were moments
and adventures and travel that I was yet to have,
women that I was yet to meet, a child or children
whose very existence and guidance would be my
responsibility. It wasn't much but it was something
to hang on to. A little glimmer of hope. I knew
that I had to stay alive. Not for the life that I was
having at the time, because frankly it sucked, but
for the life that was just beyond the horizon. And
so I was admitted to a place not unlike this one
and spent five weeks putting myself back together
again. Eventually with psychotherapy and some
medication I was able to move on. I went back
to uni but dropped economics and switched to
psychology where, one week into the course,

I met the most wonderful woman who has ever existed.'

Ed takes a breath before landing the knockout blow. 'Our daughter will be nineteen next month.'

We look at each other and nod, but then someone mentions Uncle Jimmy and the skateboard once more and we're off again.

Ed looks at us and smiles. 'Now get out of here, you booze hounds – and you'd better not let me catch you drinking again.'

I have a quick shower and then lie on my bed to process everything Ed told us. Life *is* about moments. Beautiful moments. The rest you just have to get through. To ride out. Especially when the black dog comes sniffing around. I think about our little party last night. I think about my relationship with Lisa, which I thought I'd lost, about Uncle Jimmy's tale of misfortune on the staircase, about Ed's story of self-preservation, and I get it. In the space of twelve hours or so I've had four moments. Moments that were worth sticking around for. Moments I wouldn't have had if I'd followed it through. Had I not paused.

TEN DAYS AFTER

I pass Sharon's group as I race down the corridor, running late because of my shower. They're on the way back from art class. I look at Sharon and smile. Her eyes glisten with what I could only call pride.

'Where are you off to in such a hurry?' asks one of the women, whose name is Hannah and who can't quite grasp the concept that her name is a palindrome.

'I'm meeting someone downstairs in the cafe.'

'What's her name?' one of them shouts after me, which is followed by raucous and approving laughter.

They don't know that Lisa and I are back

together. I've kept that to myself in group. She's my delicious little secret. Our emails have become more and more intense, more and more charged.

I pass Ed as I near the lifts. He doesn't say anything. He doesn't need to. Ed uses an economy of words, though what he does say is worth listening to and, more importantly, he knows when *not* to talk. It's a rare commodity. Instead, he gives me a high five as I pass, which speaks volumes.

My mobile rings as I enter the cafe, which is tucked into a corner of the lobby. It's quite crowded — half-civilian, half-PJ-clad patients — but Chris and Maaaate have squeezed into a corner table. Chris is on his phone. I pull out mine and see that he's calling me. I don't actually own any PJs, so I'm in jeans and a T-shirt. I look normal. And thanks to Ed, the group, some drugs and, yes, me, I'm starting to feel normal.

'Sorry, guys,' I say, sliding into the booth next to Chris. Chris looks at his phone and hangs up. 'Time doesn't really mean much in here.'

'No worries,' says Maaaate.

'Good to see you, bro,' says Chris.

Maaaate gives me one of his complicated boys-from-the-hood handshakes. Chris is next to me so he gives me that one-armed, back-patting hug. Although he can't tell me, it's his way of saying 'stick around'.

Chris is on his second coffee while Maaaate's onto his third milkshake and what appears to be about his tenth donut. There's more of Maaaate since I saw him last.

'So, er,' begins Chris, awkwardly, 'how's things?'

One thing that group has taught me is that you can't sweep things under the rug. If you try to repress stuff it'll grow like a cancer until it consumes you.

'Okay, guys,' I say. 'I had a mental breakdown. I went nuts. It happens. It happened to me. It can happen to anyone.' I've learnt from Ed and the group that depression and anxiety do not discriminate.

Chris and Maaaate shift uncomfortably in their seats.

'I didn't see it coming and it almost killed me,' I continue. 'But it's over now – I hope. I'm getting better. Any questions? Good.'

Chris and Maaaate laugh at this because I'm channelling our science teacher, Mr Williams, who always finishes his lesson preambles with, 'Any questions? Good.'

'Was it just what happened with Lisa?' says Maaaate.

'Yeah,' I say. 'That was a big part of it. But there's other stuff, too. Stuff I thought I'd let go. I'm handling it better now.'

'So you're getting out soon?' says Chris, who obviously doesn't want to talk or hear about my other stuff.

'Released into the wild?' offers Maaaate.

Chris glares at Maaaate.

'What?' says Maaaate.

'It's okay, guys. I'm not hiding from anything. No more bottling shit up. Lisa's kraken of a mother practically kidnapped her and it fucked me up completely because I didn't know how to talk about it. Release the pressure valve.'

'Do they teach you to swear in here?' asks Maaaate.

Another glare from Chris.

'No,' I say. 'But they teach you to be honest.'

'So when *are* you getting out?' asks Chris.

'In a couple of days, maybe. There's no rush. What's everyone been saying at school?'

Chris and Maaaate look at each other.

Maaaate sucks down some more milkshake. 'Rumour has it you threw yourself on the tracks but went under the train and it missed you.'

'The Christians at school reckon it's a miracle,' says Chris. 'They're all praying for you.'

This time it's Maaaate who glares at Chris.

'It wasn't quite like that,' I concede. 'I paused.'

'God?' says Maaaate.

I shrug. 'Maybe Mum. Maybe Lisa. Maybe Kate. Maybe Dad. Don't know, really. Something just stopped me.'

'Could have been God,' says Maaaate. I often forget that Maaaate's as big a Christian as Lisa. 'It's possible.'

'Sure,' I concede. 'It's possible.'

'Then why didn't he stop those whack jobs on September 11?' says Chris. 'Or help that little girl out your way whose mum and step-dad beat her to a pulp and then burned her body?'

Maaaate just looks at Chris and shakes his head. It's not an easy position to defend and he knows it. At least he didn't say God moves in mysterious ways or God has a plan.

'Tell everyone I appreciate their prayers,' I say, because I do.

'What's it like in here?' says Chris.

'It's really nice. I've got my own room, friends, a bunch of people looking out for me, a really cool psychologist, and the food is almost edible.'

'If any of us were going to be in here,' says Chris, 'I wouldn't have thought it'd be you. I thought it'd be me. Or *him*.' Chris gestures across to Maaaate.

'Hey,' says Maaaate. 'What's wrong with *me*?'

'Where do I even begin?' says Chris.

I look at Chris. The most together member of our group. 'Why would you be in here?'

Chris looks down into his coffee. He picks up his spoon and stirs it. 'You've never figured it out, have you?'

Maaaate and I look at each other, unsure where this might be heading.

'Your old man?' I suggest.

'Never knew him,' says Chris, shaking his head. 'Don't want to.'

'I give up,' says Maaaate.

'If you say a word about this to anyone, I'll kill you.' Chris looks at us, one after the other, to show that he's serious.

'You'll kill us?' says Maaaate, who never knows when to shut up. 'That's a bit heavy, isn't it?'

'Okay,' concedes Chris. 'I might not kill you but I'll be severely pissed.'

I look at Chris and try to use my experience in group to see inside him, but soon admit defeat. He's a wall. What could it possibly be? He's a wonderful son – his mum regularly tells me. In fact, she tells us *every* time she sees us. And he's my best mate. He's academic and sporty. He's so good looking it should be illegal, but he doesn't exploit his good looks by using girls even though they drool over him. I mean, I've never even heard him talk about a girl let alone seen him with –

Chris sees the realisation wash over me and nods.

'You're gay?'

'Shut up,' says Maaaate about as subtly as a fox tearing into a chook pen.

Chris looks at Maaaate but doesn't contradict him.

'Holy crap!' Maaaate's eyes widen. You can almost hear the hamster running the maze inside what passes as his brain.

'Any questions?' says Chris, himself lapsing into Mr Williams' mode. 'Good.'

'I've got one,' says Maaaate.

I roll my eyes at Chris.

'Go on,' says Chris.

'So if you're really gay, does that mean when you have a shower after sport, it would be like me and Declan showering with a netball team?'

I look at Maaaate and shake my head. 'Seriously? *That's* your question?'

Maaaate shrugs and seems to drift off momentarily.

'Stop it!' I glare at Maaaate.

'What?' says Maaaate.

'You're imagining the whole netball-team-shower thing right now, aren't you?'

'Yeah, so?'

'Well, you can keep that thing away from me.' I look about the cafe. 'There're little kids around, and you're sitting there with a netball-induced throbbing trombone.'

Chris laughs, happy to have the moment lightened.

'How long have you known?' I ask.

'About the netball team?' says Maaaate.

'Shut up, Maaaate.'

'As long as I can remember,' says Chris. 'Even in kindergarten I was never attracted to girls.'

'We used to hate them,' I say to Chris. 'Girls, I mean. They were like aliens.'

'Yeah,' admits Chris. 'But you used to hate them in that not-really-hating them, chasing-them-around-the-playground sort of way. For me it was different.'

'Do you . . .' starts Maaaate.

Chris and I look over at Maaaate. You can almost hear the stupid question formulating in his mind.

'What?' says Chris.

'You might think this is a dumb thing to ask but I really want to know.'

Chris groans. 'Go ahead.'

'Do you . . . er . . . like, dress up in your mum's clothes when she goes out?'

'You dumb fuck!' snarls Chris. 'I'm gay, not a cross-dresser.'

'Okay. Sorry,' says Maaaate. 'Thought it was more or less the same thing.'

Chris glares at Maaaate. 'You're such an idiot!'

'All right! Keep your shirt on. Or your mum's dress.' Maaaate bursts out laughing. Alone. 'I'm only asking.'

Chris and I look at each other and then at the cup full of sugar packets on the table. We nod, then pick them up and start throwing them at Maaaate.

'So what's it like?' says Maaaate after we've made him pick up all the sugar packets. Watching him squeeze himself beneath the table to get the ones on the ground is like watching a sumo wrestler trying to wedge himself into a SmartCar.

'What?' says Chris. 'Being gay? It's bloody hard.' Chris quickly checks himself. 'And don't even think about saying anything about me being hard.'

'No,' says Maaaate. 'What's it like being, you know, with another guy?'

As insensitive as it is, this is the most sensible question or comment that Maaaate has brought to the table so far.

'I don't know,' says Chris. 'I haven't . . . I haven't been there. Yet.'

'So how do you know?' asks Maaaate. 'That you are . . . you know?'

'You know. When you are you know,' says Chris, lapsing into Maaaate speak. 'It's just something you know. I can't explain it but I know, you know?'

'But *how* do you know?'

Chris glares at Maaaate. They came to visit me together in Chris's mum's car, but I suspect Maaaate will be taking the bus and train home. 'How do *you* know you're fat?'

'Oh, duh!' says Maaaate. 'I look in the mirror.'

'Same with me,' says Chris. He turns to me but looks downcast. 'The worst part will be having to tell Mum that I won't be having kids, that she's not going to be a grandmother.'

'Why can't you have kids?' asks Maaaate, and for once I'm with him. 'Man, did you even watch those *Modern Family* eps I lent you?'

'Yeah,' says Chris. 'But it's just the whole normal thing.'

'Mate,' I say. 'If there's one thing that being in here has taught me, it's that there is no such thing as normal. They admitted a guy last night. He'd totally flipped. They found him naked on the beach about to swim to New Zealand because his dog told him to.' Okay, I made up the bit about the dog for effect. 'Know what he does for a living?'

'Dog trainer?' asks Maaaate and I can't help but laugh.

'He's a psychiatrist. He's an expert in this stuff and yet there he was about to head off to New Zealand without a passport.'

'Or anywhere to put it,' suggests Maaaate and even Chris laughs at this.

When we've calmed down, Chris looks at both of us and then stares off into the distance. 'There's a storm coming,' he sighs.

Maaaate looks out the cafe window. 'There isn't a cloud in the sky, you moron.'

I look at Maaaate and raise my eyebrows. 'I think he means metaphorically.'

'Then why didn't he just say that?' says Maaaate.

'Does it change anything?' says Chris. 'Between us, I mean?'

'No!' I say. 'Don't be ridiculous, mate. You're still the man.' I'm referring to Chris's position as the head of our group.

Chris and I look over at Maaaate, who is clearly about to say something breathtakingly stupid and insensitive.

Maaaate looks at Chris. 'Nah. Doesn't change a fucking thing.'

Chris nods and I wink at Maaaate. When it mattered, he came through.

'Though if you guys are crashing at my place,' says Maaaate, 'you're in the spare room.'

We bombard Maaaate with more sugar packets as he pleads with us that it was a joke.

NON-SPACE

Being dead is supposed to clear up the ultimate mystery. The final riddle. Is there an afterlife? Does God exist? Yet here I am, deader than a mouse that's been run over by a steamroller and I'm still none the wiser.

But if you think about it, and I mean *really* think about it, the universe is a staggering place. Its beauty is brain freezing. The mind-blowing swirl of the seemingly infinite galaxies, the warmth and life-giving qualities of the stars, even the crunch of black holes and glow of supernovae, the mystique of nebulae, and the concept that despite it having a beginning, it has no end. Yet if the universe had no life, had nothing to witness its stunning beauty, then surely it would have no point. Without us to awe and marvel at it, the universe is kind of redundant.

I was raised a Christian because of Dad, but a questioning one thanks to Mum. It was the nutjobs who turned me agnostic. The righteous, the zealots, the egocentrics, the narcissists, the extremists – they destroy it for the rest of us.

The arrogance of people who believe that God has an individual tailored plan mapped out for them is the very height of narcissism, I reckon. Do they ever stop to think about that photo of that little girl in Ethiopia? The one where she is squatting down in exhaustion on the way to a UN food station when an enormous vulture lands next to her? Was it God's plan for the vulture to eat that little girl?

I heard a story about a man who emerged from a bus crash in Egypt, where the bus had rolled down a mountain, killing everyone but him. He claimed in an interview that Allah was looking out for him. Does that mean Allah was ignoring the rest of the passengers? Was Allah displeased with them? Were they unworthy, or was the guy just lucky?

It's when people enter into a private dialogue with God and gain strength from such conversations that the true beauty of faith emerges. But unlike Maaaate, I don't think for one second that God is going to stop me from jumping into the path of an oncoming train. He's not going to stop Lisa's skin being whacked raw by The Kraken. He's not going to pluck one guy out of a bus crash in Egypt to prove that he exists, just as he's not going to make your football team win, your Lotto numbers come up, or help you with your parallel parking. For that is the price we pay for free will. And if God does in fact exist, then apart from life itself, that is the greatest gift he could give us.

ONE MONTH AFTER

I insist we get to the *yum cha* restaurant early. It's Saturday morning, the day after I've been released into the wild, and from what I remember from my last visit here with Lisa, it can get quite crowded. Too much longer and all the tables will be taken and we'll have to wait around for about an hour or maybe more.

Kate nudges me in the ribs as we walk in. 'Look, douche,' she says excitedly. 'Is that for real? Is it allowed?'

I turn around to Mum. 'Have you cut back her Ritalin again?'

'Declan,' says Mum. 'You know she doesn't take it anymore.'

'Seriously!' says Kate, practically leaping out of her skin as she points at the sign above the door. 'Fuck me.'

'Kate!' snaps Mum.

But Kate's wound up like a caffeine-affected chihuahua. 'It's called "Fuck Me", Mum.'

'"Fuck Me, Mum"?' I say.

'No,' says Kate still looking at the sign. 'Not "Fuck Me, Mum". That'd be silly. Just "Fuck Me".'

'Kate!' snarls Mum. 'Stop it, before we're escorted away by security.'

I sigh and look at Kate. She has absolutely no filter. She doesn't care who hears her or who she offends. In fact, I don't even think it would occur to her that she might be offending anyone. Meanwhile, I'm attempting to display the sophisticated air of someone who has been to *yum cha* more times than he can remember. Well, okay, six: three times with Lisa, twice with Chris and Maaaate, and once with Mum.

'It's "Fook Mei",' I say, though my Cantonese seems destined to remain at kindergarten level. I try to make the 'Fook' rhyme with 'puke', which is probably not great now that I think about it.

But Kate's so hypo by this point I don't think she can hear me, so I decide to toy with her for a bit. 'That's actually its shortened name.'

'Declan, don't,' says Mum from behind as the balding man in beige leads his clan towards the 'Wait to be Seated' sign.

'The full name,' I continue, 'is "Fook Mei Sideways".'

I can hear Mum's intake of breath as if she's about to tell me off, but she snorts with supressed laughter instead.

'"Fook Me Sideways"?' says Kate.

'Yeah,' I continue, because playing with Kate's gullibility is a bit of a hobby of mine. 'Before the renovations you could only access the restaurant through the alley, which was so narrow that you had to turn sideways to get down it, so they named the place . . .'

'"Fook Me Sideways",' says Kate again and Mum is snorting so much now she sounds like an asthmatic warthog.

'Stop it, Declan,' she says, but it's hard for her to speak and for me to take her seriously when she's biting her lip. 'Don't listen to him, Kate. He's having you on.'

'It makes sense though,' says Kate. 'I mean, if you could only get in sideways.'

If I look at Mum at this point I know we'll both end up rolling about on the floor kicking and screaming.

Captain Embarrassment decides to draw attention to himself, as if his beige pants and battery-operated Hawaiian shirt weren't bad enough. '*Lei ho ma-rrrr*,' says Dad, ratcheting up the cringe factor which, on wardrobe choice alone, is already running pretty close to DEFCON 1.

'Morning,' says the bored waiter, who is about as Chinese as me.

'We'd like a table for four, please,' says Dad.

Not one to waste words, the waiter hands Dad a ticket and gestures towards the stairs.

'You're not allowed to ask for a knife and fork,' I say to Dad as he leads us up the stairs.

'Oh,' he sulks. 'You know I'm next to useless with chopsticks.'

'Too bad,' I say. 'Either use your hands, go hungry, or sharpen one of your chopsticks and use it as a spear.' I turn to Kate. 'Same for you.'

'You're not the boss of me,' says Kate, lapsing into tween cliché.

But I'm adamant. 'No knives and forks. Got it?'

'It looks like the floor will be eating well today,' says Mum.

A waitress greets us at the top of the stairs with a warm smile. She's wearing a blue, figure-hugging traditional Chinese cheongsam. 'Table for four?' she says.

Dad nods and hands her the ticket. We follow the waitress to our table, which is right at the back of the restaurant.

'Drinks?' asks the waitress when we're seated.

'*Mm goi bei cha ngoh?*' I say.

The waitress looks at me as if I've just asked to inspect her bra. '*Ha? Lei sik gong joong mun?*'

'*Ngoh jeng hai sik giu cha,*' I reply.

I can feel Mum, Dad and Kate all staring at me with their mouths hanging open.

The waitress gives me a stunning smile. '*Dung yut dung, ngoh lor bei lei.*'

I nod. '*Mm goi.*'

'Well,' says Dad after the waitress has taken everyone's drink orders and gone. 'As you know, it takes a lot to impress me, but son, you just impressed the shite out of me.' Dad, like a lot of Irish people, thinks saying shit with an 'e' tacked on the end makes it less offensive.

'What did you say to her?' asks Mum, equally taken aback by my bilingualism. If there is such a word as 'bilingualism'.

'For all I know, I just ordered a deep-fried hedgehog and two sautéed badger balls on a stick. But I *think* I asked her for some Chinese tea. Lisa taught me.'

Mum reaches across the table and pats the back of my hand. I don't pull away.

'Well, fook mei sideways,' says Kate and the four of us practically explode.

*

'Douche, look at that,' says Kate, pointing at the far wall. I look over at the lobster tank as the unfortunate invertebrate (or whatever they are) try to clamber over each other with their spindly legs to get at something that appeals to their pea-size brains. If I were a lobster and I saw the waiter heading my way with his scoop, I'd try to make myself look really thin (not easy, I suppose, with an exoskeleton) or else use my spidery legs to point at the big fat one skulking in the corner. Or maybe I'd teach myself how to tap-dance. No one is going to throw a tap-dancing lobster into a boiling pot, surely. It'd just be too cute.

'Do you reckon they're bred in captivity?' asks Kate, interrupting my thoughts on tap-dancing lobsters. 'Or are they wild?'

'No,' I say. 'These are free-range lobsters. It's the law now. They're bred on a farm outside Dubbo where they can come and go as they please and get into territorial disputes with the crabs on the neighbouring ranch.'

'Really?'

In deference to Dad's meat-and-potato palate, we opt mostly for *gweilo* food. I bite into the nuclear-hot spring roll, relishing the sound of the crispy deep-fried pastry shattering between my teeth, and the explosion of flavour of what's inside. My favourite dish is *siu mai* (pork dumplings). I'm a bit of a greenie at heart and rapidly heading towards vegetarianism, but I'm forced to suspend my principles when the waitress lifts the lid of the bamboo basket and reveals its mouth-watering contents. This is Lisa's favourite, too, so I insist on two servings and gobble Lisa's share as well, without telling anyone why I have momentarily turned into Homer Simpson.

A little while later, the waitress reveals her chicken feet to us (the chicken's — not hers), which is a Chinese delicacy. Kate is intrigued. She doesn't want to eat them, she wants to know what happened to the rest of the chicken, or if these chicken feet are in fact grown in a lab or something, kind of like mould or a pancreas.

Not being one to let an opportunity pass, I inform her that they only use free-range chickens, which are bred on a farm near the lobsters, and when they have removed the chickens' legs for market, the chickens are given little off-road wheelchairs in which they can manoeuvre about the farm and team up with the lobsters to drive off the warmongering crabs.

Kate looks at me and then over to Mum, who is biting her lip so much that she's practically drawing blood. 'You're such an idiot!' Free-range lobsters she buys, but wheelchair-bound chickens is apparently a step too far. Still, I suppose it's what you might expect from someone who names her pet guinea pig Pooey McFartpants.

'Okay,' says Dad when he's devoured several spring rolls and a couple of *char sil bau*. 'Down to business.'

I look at Dad, wondering if he's about to announce that he and mum are splitting up, which I reckon has been coming for a while — they've been arguing more and more recently and, rather than making up afterwards, the tension seems to linger. So maybe they *are* getting a divorce. Or worse, maybe they've taken up linedancing.

'We're going on holidays after Christmas,' says Dad.

'We *always* go on holidays after Christmas,' says Kate.

'Ah,' says Mum, 'but this year's different. Your father and I have —'

'You mean *you* have,' interjects Dad.

'— have *decided*,' continues Mum, 'that we all get an equal vote about where we go this time.'

I look at Mum and smile. I know what she's getting at. In an effort to stave off his boredom and introduce it to us, Dad generally drags us off to some godforsaken corner of the globe to look at some fossilised dinosaur crap. We actually spent last summer on a four-day trek through northern India, wading through waist-deep mud and being eaten alive by mosquitoes the size of helicopters, just to see a hut that some supposed guru or other had once stopped to take a dump in. And as if to add a certain poetic symmetry to things, poor Mum ended up in hospital with a severe bout of dysentery when all she'd wanted to do was sit by a pool with a good book and a glass that contained a tiny umbrella and copious amounts of pina colada. So this year, when Dad announced that he was keen for us to venture into the Amazon Basin to see for himself if there was any evidence of a certain breed of fish that was thought to have been extinct for thousands of years, Mum told him where he could stick his fish and cancelled our subscription to *National Geographic*. Obviously the vote thing was a sort of compromise.

'So,' says Mum, 'where do we want to go?' Mum looks at me and nods. She's obviously counting on my vote and I won't let her down. Well, I won't be voting for the extinct fish thing anyway.

Ever the accountant, Dad takes out a pen and paper ready to take notes and tally up the count. 'Okay, Katie Bear,' he says, 'you're up.'

Kate thinks for a moment. Then her eyes go manic. 'I want to go to Disneyland.'

I look at her and shake my head. 'You go nuts staring at a lobster tank and a painting of some fish on a psycho hospital wall. How could you possibly cope with all the stimulation offered up by enormous mice, waistcoat-wearing bears and talking ducks? You'll be having nightmares for years.'

'I wanna go to Disneyland, I wanna go to Disneyland,' says Kate in her cutesy singsong voice that makes me want to throttle her with her *Frozen* scarf.

'So that's one gorgeous girl for Disneyland,' says Dad.

'Thank you, Daddy,' says Kate, and I think even Mum has to hold back a puke.

'Declan?' says Dad.

'Ladies first,' I say.

'Nope,' says Dad. 'Youngest to oldest.' Dad gives me a look that lets me know that he's well aware of what I'm up to. Mum could say she wanted to spend the holidays having her bikini line waxed on a herbal-tea plantation just outside Kandahar and I would go with that too, just to avoid the Amazon fish thing or the agonising possibility of having to search for a tree in some remote corner of Asia that Buddha or Gandhi had once taken a leak behind.

I try to second-guess Mum. Where would she want to go? She likes shopping and art and sitting by the pool. Mmm, tricky. 'Okay. I vote Paris.'

Dad writes Paris on his list. 'Not what I would have expected, but good choice.' Meanwhile, Mum gives me a weird look. She's gritting her teeth and making her eyes bulge. Not having a clue what she's on about, I shrug.

Kate obviously sees Mum's facial gymnastics. 'Hey. That's not fair. They're cheating.'

'How can we cheat?' I say.

'Gabriella?' says Dad.

'Well, as you all know I love shopping and five-star hotels, so I'm going for somewhere in Asia.'

'Oh, not the guru poohouse again,' says Kate, and Mum and I burst out laughing. Kate looks over at Dad. 'Sorry, Daddy.'

'"Sorry, Daddy",' I mock.

'That's okay, darling,' says Dad.

'Thank you, Daddy.'

'Anywhere in particular?' says Dad before the vomit starts to fly.

'I was thinking Hong Kong.' Mum gives me her best exasperated look and I pretty much want to beat myself over the head with a rice-bucket stand. What an idiot. Kate's right. I'm a complete douchebag.

'But you go there all the time with work, Mummy,' says Kate.

'That's right, darling. Work. But I never get to see it properly. It's just hotels and boardrooms.

I thought it would be nice to go as a tourist.' Luckily neither Dad nor Kate has made the Lisa connection. 'There's a Disneyland there too, Katie,' continues Mum.

'Really?' says Kate.

'It's not as good as the real one,' interjects Dad, trying to take Kate's mind off changing her vote to Mum's. 'Mickey Mouse looks more like a rat.'

I try to find my Zen centre through breathing, which isn't easy when my Zen centre wants to pour my Chinese tea over Dad's balding head.

'Which leaves me,' continues Dad. 'And this year I'm opting for the stromatolites.'

'Oh, God,' sighs Mum. 'Please tell me that's not some type of petrified dog turd in the middle of the Simpson Desert.'

Kate bursts out laughing. 'Mummy said "turd".'

I cast Kate a look that only a sibling can.

'No,' says Dad. 'The stromatolites are *not* petrified dog turds in the middle of the Simpson Desert.'

'The Mojave Desert?' I offer.

'They're in Western Australia,' says Dad.

'So they *are* dog turds?' I say.

Dad ignores me. 'Shark Bay to be accurate. About nine hours' drive north of Perth.'

'And just what,' says Mum with a world-weary sigh, 'are stromatolites supposed to be?'

'Well, they're kind of like living rocks that sort of sit in the water,' says Dad, warming to the subject and perhaps hoping, in his own deluded way, that he'll be able to convince us to change our vote because we'll be positively aching to see a bunch of rocks with him.

'Rocks?' says Mum. 'You want us to fly across the country and then drive nine hours to look at some rocks?'

'Ah, but they're not just rocks,' continues Dad. 'They're three thousand years old, the first known ecosystems, and they're similar to life forms that are about three-and-a-half *billion* years old! It is thought the original ones started the oxygenation of the atmosphere and so they're kind of responsible for all life on earth. They're sort of like our earliest ancestors.'

'It's always difficult when you drop in on relatives you haven't seen for three billion years,' says Mum. 'I mean, you never know what to bring. Somehow, a bottle of wine and a tin of shortbread doesn't seem enough.'

Hawaiian shirt and beige pants aside, I want to respect Dad as much as I can. But, unfortunately, when Mum does sarcasm I can't stop myself from laughing.

'Well, if you're going to mock,' says Dad.

'No,' says Mum. 'Let's hear the rest of it. So do these rocks actually do anything?'

'Yes, well, occasionally they'll walk up the beach and play volleyball against each other.'

'Really?' says Kate.

'Oh, come on, Katie Bear,' says Dad. 'Even you must have seen that I was pulling your leg with that one.'

'Okay,' says Mum. 'Back to these . . . rocks of yours.'

Dad scratches his head. Surely he must realise that Mum and I would rather drive a sharpened chopstick into our ears while watching the shopping channel than visit a bunch of rocks with him, living or dead. 'If you watch the water closely, you might get to see some oxygen they've released bubbling to the surface.'

'Seriously?' I say to Dad. 'Nine hours in the back of a car with Hypo Girl so we can see some burping rocks? Are you friggin' kidding me?'

'They're responsible for all life on earth. You should be grateful.'

'I'll send them a thankyou card and some chocolate brownies,' I reply and Mum totally loses it.

'Okay,' says Mum, trying to contain herself. 'That's one for Disneyland, one for Paris, one for Hong Kong, and one for the burping rocks.'

Dad begins to lose what little cool he has, which isn't much. 'They are *not* burping rocks!'

Mum and I can't control ourselves.

'I get no respect around here.'

'Diddums,' says Mum, and I crack up again.

'You shouldn't be laughing at Daddy,' says you-know-who.

'We're not laughing at him,' I say to Kate. 'We're laughing at his farting stones.'

'They're not . . .' Dad bails out — but it's too late. Mum and I are snorting so loudly that people at other tables are looking over at us.

'I change my vote,' says Kate. 'I want to see the burping rocks, too.'

'Thank you, Katie Bear,' says Dad, and he's so pleased that his comrade is on board he doesn't correct her about the burping rocks.

'Okay,' I say. 'Well, in that case, I vote for Hong Kong.'

Mum looks at me and winks.

'Two all,' says Dad. 'And as I get the deciding vote, it looks like we're off to see the stromatolites. Pack light, people. It gets hot over there in January.'

I glare at Dad as he and Kate give each other a high five. 'Why the hell do you get the deciding vote?'

Mum piles on. 'And if you even think about saying it's because you're the man of the house, then you'll be sleeping on a park bench for the rest of eternity.'

'It's because I'm the oldest,' says Dad, case closed.

'You're certainly the baldest,' I offer.

'No casting vote,' insists Mum.

'So how do we settle it?' says Dad.

Mum looks at me and smiles. It's clear that we're going to Hong Kong no matter what Dad says. 'Easy. You and Kate go off and see your regurgitating rocks, while Dec and I go to Hong Kong.'

'Fine!' says Dad. 'If that's your idea of a family holiday.'

'Don't get all narky, Shaun,' says Mum in barrister mode. 'You're obviously not going to give in and neither are we, so it's the perfect solution.'

'Okay, Katie Bear,' says Dad. 'Looks like you and me are off to do some exploring.'

'Yay,' says Kate, but she doesn't sound too convincing.

'C'mon, Shaun,' says Mum when she sees Kate's reaction. 'Are you seriously going to drag her across the country to see a bunch of flatulent boulders? You'll have DoCS after you.'

Dad looks at Kate and realises Mum's right. 'You know what, Katie Bear? I've changed my mind, too. I'd love to go to Disneyland.'

'Really?' screeches Kate, practically peeing her pants.

'The original one,' says Dad. 'In America.'

'Then it's settled,' says Mum.

Kate looks like she's ready to explode with excitement.

Dad stares at the mess he's made in his bowl. He signals a waiter over.

'Yeah?' says the waiter.

'Yes,' says Dad. He gives me a look. 'Could you get me a knife and fork, *dor je-eee-h*.'

I look at Dad and roll my eyes. Disneyland's welcome to him.

'Two please,' says Kate. Her, too.

'And a beer,' says Dad.

Mum and I clink glass and cup. Dad and Kate go over to investigate the free-range lobsters.

TWO MONTHS AFTER

It's the last school day of the year. My final day of year eleven. We have a six-week break before the HSC work really begins, though the rest of my year group has been into it since the start of term four. I'm still playing catch-up, though my teachers at the school have been incredible. They know – and in their own subtle way they have told me – that compared to what I've been through, the HSC is practically irrelevant. I do want to get into uni and study history and politics – I wouldn't want to miss out on that – but there are many ways to skin that particular cat. What I have to do is take care of myself and let others take care of me when I need it.

I stare out at the sea of faces — students, parents, grandparents — and find Mum sitting with Dad. She sees me looking at her and jokingly gives me the finger by pretending she's got something in her eye. I smile and rub my nose with *my* middle finger. It's always been our little joke: to try to make each other laugh in inappropriate situations. And if there's ever been a more inappropriate situation than this then I can't think of it — and that includes Aunt Mary's funeral, when Mum wanted to tap dance on her grave.

I notice Ed Chiu coming in through a side door and taking a seat along the wall. It was nice of him to come. Although there's a squadron of butterflies in my stomach, I feel better for seeing Mum, Dad and Ed.

I've come a long way since hospital, when I shuffled along the corridor with my food tray like a hundred-year-old sloth, and sat in my first group session and cried in Sharon's arms. I think about Sharon, about her posse, and I feel a twinge of regret. I never got to see her again once I was told that I was going home. I never got to thank her. I never got to say goodbye. I wonder what happened to her. Did she go back to her home, back to her life, back to her husband? Or did she throw herself off a cliff or under a train, or chase down a bottle of pills with some vodka?

I think about that moment on the station when I paused. Had it not been for that pause, the end-of-year assembly would still be going ahead. The only difference would be that it would be going ahead without me. Everyone's life would have carried on. I'd barely be missed now. And although what I'm about to do absolutely terrifies me, had it not been for that pause, what was left of my body when the train had finished with it would now be rotting in the ground somewhere, or else my ashes would be fertilising a shrub or a rosebush. So as scary as this is, it's so much better than being dead.

Surveys have shown that when it comes to humanity's greatest fears, people would rather die than speak publicly. Clearly those who tick the 'Death' box have never been at the cross-roads. Have never had that pause. Now that the miasma of depression and anxiety has started to clear and the rest of my life with all its possibilities and wonder and moments stretches out before me, I know which I prefer.

Mrs Morelli sits down next to me. 'You okay, Declan?' Mrs Morelli is the deputy principal but also our year adviser. She came to see me in hospital – several teachers did. When she walked into my room, she never said a word. She just marched over to my bed, plonked herself down next to me, and hugged me.

'I'm fine, Mrs M.' But who am I kidding? This was her idea and I only agreed because she helped me. Helped me like so many others did. And I guess it's time to give a little something back. When she asked if I would speak to the school to remove the elephant in the room, I didn't think she'd approve of what I wrote. She took one look at it and said, 'Go for it.' But now that I'm about to deliver it, I'm having serious doubts and would rather be anywhere else, with the possible exception of linedancing.

'Actually,' I say, 'that's a complete lie. I'm packing it.'

'The secret to public speaking,' says Mrs Morelli as she squeezes my hand, 'is to imagine that every single member of the audience is sitting on the toilet trying to pass a house brick.'

I actually snort when she says this. You just don't expect it from your deputy principal.

'No one is superior to you if they're sitting on the loo. No one.'

The assembly starts and we all stand and sing the national anthem. We embarrass the principal and the local MP by staying silent during the line of the second verse that goes, 'For those who've come across the seas, we've boundless plains to share.' At least it's not as controversial as the student council's original plan, which was to replace the line with, 'For those who've come across the seas, we'll lock you and your kids behind razor wire.'

When everyone is seated and the uncomfortable silence falls across the auditorium, Mrs Morelli walks over to the lectern. No matter how gently she introduces me, there's no getting past the butterflies squirming around in my stomach that are now in some sort of mating frenzy.

My friends have been amazing since I returned to school, but everyone else has given me a wide berth. It's just too much to deal with. I'm kind of like a social leper. Most guys (both students and teachers) go the long way round just to avoid me, and if they spot me walking along the corridor towards them they make it look like they've forgotten something in the other direction, turn around and race off. And I get it. Blokes don't do this stuff very well, but to compare, teenage boys are so clenched up we make our fathers look like Oprah.

'. . . Ladies and gentlemen and students,' continues Mrs Morelli. 'It's my absolute privilege and honour to introduce Declan O'Malley.'

When Mrs Morelli has finished her introduction, I walk across the stage to the lectern. Mrs M smiles and winks at me as we pass.

'Remember,' she whispers, 'they're all on the bog.'

I smile at her and my tension is eased, but only momentarily. The audience doesn't seem to know if they should applaud or not, so they opt for silence.

I take a deep breath and unfold my note on the lectern. I look over at Chris and Maaaate, who are sitting in our usual spot. Chris gives me the thumbs up, but Maaaate doesn't see me. He's too busy ferreting around in his pocket for the remnants of a Mars Bar or Krispy Kreme or KFC to cram in his hole. He's got an entire end-of-year assembly to get through and badly needs a sugar hit to help. You've got to love Maaaate. Before, I thought he was hiding behind his food, withdrawing. But now I can see he's happy as he is. He just enjoys food and doesn't give a crap what anyone thinks about it.

I lean into the microphone and try to think of the toilet thing. It doesn't work.

'I never left a suicide note,' I begin, 'because I didn't plan on dying that day; it was a spontaneous act of insanity. Of stupidity. Of course people will miss you when you're gone, but you won't know because you no longer exist. You're not proving any point, you're not spiting anyone, you're just slipping into oblivion and there is no return. I never left a suicide note, but if I had it would have gone something like this:

'I'm sorry. Sorry for the pain I've left behind. Sorry for the unanswered questions. The absence. The hole in the air where I once was. I'm sorry to my friends, particularly Chris and Maaaate, who didn't see it coming and wouldn't have known what to do even if they had. I'm sorry to you, my teachers, who might have blamed yourselves and wondered why you hadn't spotted the signs — signs that simply weren't there, signs that only became apparent to me after it was too late, after I was gone. Signs that I'd learnt to hide from everyone — myself included. I'm sorry to you, my fellow students, for putting the idea in your heads that suicide is an option, when all it does is consign those you leave behind to a lifetime of hell. Of emptiness. Of sheer agony. I'm sorry to my family, but mostly to my parents, who gave me the greatest gift of all — life. A life that I tossed away on a whim, so carelessly, so needlessly, so pointlessly. To all of you, I'm sorry. I'm sorry. I'm sorry.'

I fold up my note and am about to walk away when there's a slight trickle of applause from the student council, who are on the stage with the teachers. Students sitting down the front join in and soon the applause builds and spreads throughout the auditorium until everyone is on their feet clapping and cheering and whistling. I look over at Mum who is bawling her eyes out. Dad's got his arm around her. I gulp down my tears as if I've learnt nothing from this whole experience.

But I *have* learnt from it, so I end up letting them out. The tears fall freely and I don't try to hide them. Mrs Morelli hurries across the stage and hugs me, tears streaming down *her* face. And now I'm starting to feel that I can let everything go — the pain, the darkness, the emptiness, Aunt Mary.

The principal gets up and comes towards the lectern to quieten things down — the local MP is with us after all — but I decide to go for it anyway. I tap the microphone with my hand, and sound booms around the auditorium. Silence quickly returns. Mrs Morelli stands beside me.

'I want you to do something for me,' I say into the microphone. 'Actually it's not for me. It's for you.' I have them. They're in the palm of my hand. Everyone is looking at me. Even the principal has stopped mid-stage, which sort of makes him look like a bit of a jerk. Which is fine, because he is.

'I want you to turn to the guy next to you, whether you know him or not, shake his hand and say this: "Stick around. You're worth it." And then when you've said that to him, turn around and say it to the guy on your other side, and the one behind you, and the guy in front. Say it to everyone around you. Got it? Okay. Go.'

Everyone is cautious at first — we're not used to expressing stuff like this, but I guess this is the point of what I'm trying to show them, what I've learnt since it happened – but a couple of groups start it. They're laughing and being self-conscious about it at first but they're doing it anyway. And then they're all at it. Bedlam overtakes the auditorium. It's borderline anarchy, kids standing on chairs and seeking out their mates, their brothers, but they're doing it. They're all doing it. And they're doing it because they're worth it. Because the guy next to them is worth it. Because we're all worth it.

'Declan,' hisses the principal, joining me by the lectern. 'You were only asked to speak to the student body, not start this, this, this . . .' Having failed to find an appropriate noun, he gestures to the audience and the general this-ness that's going on in front of his – and the local member's – very nose.

I turn to him and smile. I offer him my hand. He looks awkwardly back at the local member but realises he has no option but to take it. 'Stick around, sir,' I say to him. 'You're worth it.'

THREE MONTHS AFTER

Kate and Dad left for Disneyland yesterday. We saw them off and did the photo thing before they went through customs. Dad tried to put on a brave face for Kate's sake but he had a bit of a hangdog expression when he and Mum hugged. They're not going to last. I could see it in their eyes and their hug. They grew up and grew apart. While we were little, I guess Kate and I were the glue that bound them. But now I'm bound to Mum as Kate is to Dad and there's nothing but history keeping our little unit together.

Like me, Mum's a bit of a greenie, so although we all took a taxi to the airport, we caught the train home. It was the first time I'd been on a train since . . .

(When I started back at school, Mum took some time off work and insisted on driving me to and from school.) And now, having emerged from the darkness, I know which side of the wheels I'd rather be on. Mum held me around the waist as we got off at our station — at *the* station. She didn't say anything. She didn't need to. I reached over and kissed the top of her head as we made our way up the escalator.

Mum wanted to take me to try this new restaurant which generally has lunch queues milling outside. At night it's a bit quieter. Luckily we managed to get a table fairly quickly, which I was grateful for given that, by the time the waiter showed us to our table, I was so hungry I could have eaten the quack out of a low-flying duck.

We studied the menus but it wasn't an exhausting task. This was one of those restaurants where the chef has only a very tenuous grasp on reality or else thinks he's just too cute to kiss and offers up dishes like pureed bat's testicles served on a bed of natural henna that has been curing under the armpits of an old Ukrainian woman for seventeen years. The food is generally served on white plates the size of tractor tyres with the portions so small you need a microscope or homing beacon to find them. The menus were made of compressed plywood and the options written with candle wax. Mum and I looked at each other and tried not to snort at the pretentiousness of the place. Mum grew up in the Western Suburbs and is a bit of a class warrior.

'Do you have any specials?' asked Mum.

The waiter leered at Mum. 'This is a fine-dining establishment, ma'am. We cater for certain . . . tastes.'

After giving us a few minutes to consider our choices, the waiter reappeared and loomed over us like a sentinel, with an air of practised superiority.

He looked at Mum, contempt etched across his face for no discernible reason. 'And what has ma'am decided on?'

Mum looked up at the snooty git. 'Ma'am has decided to go next door for a pizza, because ma'am has a growing teenage son who needs feeding and will get precious little nourishment from' – she looked back at the menu – 'quail and alfalfa chowder. Especially not for twenty-eight dollars.' Mum handed the waiter his wooden menus and we stood up to leave.

'As you wish,' said the waiter, a leer creeping across his face.

'And take the silver spoon out of your arse: you're a bloody waiter, not the Duke of Kent.'

We practically stumbled into Angelo's Pizzeria giggling like a couple of nuns who have inadvertently wandered into a male strip show. I watched on proudly as Mum spoke to Angelo in fluent Italian and ordered us a family-size seafood pizza with extra prawns, which we took home and scarfed down in front of the TV. Barrister or not, she's a working-class hero. She's *my* hero.

I gaze out the window and notice with increasing alarm that the wing wobbles as we taxi towards the runway. I didn't know they did that. I don't know much about engineering and aeronautics but I thought wings would be rigid. When I think about it, though, I suppose they need to be unstable in order to function properly. I'm not sure I get that, but I kind of like it.

As the plane waits for take-off clearance, I try to distract myself from the wobbling wings and imagine Kate being let loose in Disneyland. If Dad buys her a soft drink and some candyfloss, a switch in her brain will flick and she'll end up tearing around like the Tasmanian devil in those old Looney Tunes cartoons. Little kids might even mistake her for a ride and try to leap on her as she goes spinning past. Poor Dad. Poor Disneyland.

The pilots gun the engines and I'm pushed back into my oversized seat. I've never been keen on air travel. If people were meant to fly we would have been born with boarding passes in our hands. I grip the armrest while Mum holds the back of my hand. My heart is pounding so fast that there's no discernible gap between the beats. 'When closing gate to secure dog in yard,' says Mum, trying to interest me in what she's just written on her iPad, 'it is essential that dog not already on other side of gate.'

I appreciate Mum's efforts to take my mind away from the take-off. It's one of our favourite family games. We recount all the stupid things Dad's done down the years but make it sound like a self-help book. Dad plays too, and sometimes I'm pretty sure he does some of the spectacularly dumb things he does just so that we'll laugh at him because surely no one in their right mind would attempt to trim their nostril hairs with barbecue tongs, especially not while they are actually barbecuing and their wife is looking on from the upstairs window holding a bowl of water.

The plane banks over Botany Bay while my fingers leave an indentation in the armrest.

Mum hands me her iPad. 'Your turn.'

The plane dips suddenly and my heart pretty much flatlines. Is she serious? I can't let the armrest go to take her stupid iPad. It's my clenching the armrest that's keeping us in the air.

'C'mon, Dec,' she encourages. 'If you come up with one, I'll get you a beer when the trolley comes around.'

I look over at Mum. 'Seriously?'

She nods.

Mmm. Motivation. 'Okay.' Thinking back to the time when the sink in their ensuite was blocked and the tong/hedge trimmer thing, I release the armrest (miraculously the plane stays airborne), take the iPad, and opt for a Newtonian approach. 'When bowl of water is tipped out of upstairs window, water will continue in downward motion until encountering object, usually husband, who will then generally gush, with equal and opposite force, "Jesus Christ, Gabriella!"'

Mum snorts like a wombat in a pepperbush when she reads it. The elderly woman across the aisle glares over at Mum with a look of superiority. Obviously snorting is unbecoming for business-class passengers. If her nose reached any higher it would start to haemorrhage.

'Lighten up, vinegar tits,' says Mum, just loud enough for the woman to hear but soft enough for her to pretend to ignore it if she chooses not to get into it with Mum. The woman turns to her husband, who looks over at us, but that's as far as it goes.

'Did you just call her "vinegar tits"?' I whisper to Mum, who gives me an innocent, butter-wouldn't-melt-in-her-mouth doe-eyed look.

Mum is such a frequent flyer that she is auto-matically upgraded whenever she checks in. She also had enough frequent flyer points to upgrade me, as well as Dad and Kate. I'm positive Qantas business class would never have encountered the likes of Kate before, and I'm certain that Dad's latest Hawaiian shirt would have required the cabin crew to hand out complimentary sunglasses.

'I've got one,' says Mum. She takes back her iPad and types it in. 'When catching train home from work, it is best not to wait until one is halfway home before remembering that one drove in that day.'

Me. 'When sawing branch off tree, it is vital not to be sitting on branch.'

Mum. 'In order to establish one's position of alpha male, it is essential not to scream like a seven-year-old girl when encountering a daddy-long-legs.'

Me. 'When checking under car bonnet, it is imperative to put up that arm thingy or bonnet will collide with head when released.'

Mum. 'Never floss teeth with razor blade, no matter what is stuck between them.'

Me. 'Socks with thongs is never okay.'

Mum. 'When returning from the dog park, one should first ensure that the dog one took is the same dog that one brings home.'

I decide to opt for Mum's use of the formal British 'one' – I think it's really effective. 'When one has the coordination of a baby giraffe and has consumed four pints of Guinness, one should not attempt to dance anywhere near the wedding cake.'

Mum. 'When one is trying to locate work colleague's home in Sydney, greater success will be achieved when not using Melbourne street directory.'

By the time the drinks trolley is open for business, Mum and I are practically in hysterics. When she is able to speak, she asks for a red wine and gets me that promised beer. I'll be eighteen in four months so it's no biggie.

'To the future,' says Mum as we clink glasses. 'Whatever it may bring.'

I'm about to wash down my peanuts with Stella Artois (I am flying business class, after all) when Mum stops me. 'And, to sticking around,' she says, 'because you're worth it.'

I smile and squeeze the back of her hand.

It's not the first time I've had a drink but my memories of my first session are not fond ones. Chris, Maaaate and I got completely trashed on Maaaate's old man's putrid home-brew when we crashed there in year eight, and I hurled so much that I practically turned myself inside out. And before that, Aunt Mary forced some whiskey down my throat the night she went over the cliff. She did it to numb the pain (hers not mine), but I hoicked it up quicker than she could pour it down so she beat four shades of shit out of me, threw me in the back seat of her car and took us on a one-way trip to the coast.

But now that I'm an adult (well, four months away from being one), I am going to drink maturely and sensibly and so I sip my beer and enjoy every mouthful. Before I've finished half, Mum's onto her third glass of red.

After dinner, we both recline our seats to the comatose setting so we can watch a movie. I opt for an action/adventure/thriller that involves lots of car chases, buildings being blown up for no adequately explained reason and bathrobes cascading provocatively to the floor. Mum settles for a period piece that seems to involve the male protagonist spending an inordinate amount of time staring out of windows at lush green fields and rolling hills, either contemplating the nature of existence or whether or not he really ought to be getting on with something other than spending so much time staring out of windows.

Mum's movie kind of reminds me of Lisa. I spent a good bit of time staring out of windows (at home and in psychiatric hospitals and class-rooms) thinking about her. Missing her. Craving her. I can't believe I'm actually going to see her. I can't believe I almost . . . died. I would have missed this moment and thousands of others like it.

On approach to the airport on Lantau Island, Mum tells me about the old one in Kai Tak, which was so close to the city that you could be in your hotel room fifteen minutes after touch-down. Apparently the planes flew between the buildings as the pilots aimed at an enormous checkerboard on a hill before banking sharply to the right and plonking the plane down hard either onto the runway or, as was sometimes the case, into Victoria Harbour. The new airport is fast and efficient but, as far as Mum is concerned, dead boring. She used to enjoy the thrill of landing at Kai Tak, waving at people eating dinner in their high rise as you flew past their window.

When we get through customs, Lisa isn't there to greet me, which is how I planned it. Although I've teased certain information out of her such as her school, timetable, address and so on, I have been very subtle about it and haven't mentioned our coming here because I want it to be a surprise. I'm dying to see her reaction. To see if she's missed me half as much as I've missed her.

We take the Airport Express into the city and then the regular MTR to our hotel on Nathan Road. Had I been by myself, I could imagine that finding my way around Hong Kong would be about as easy as eating Maltesers with chopsticks, but Mum guides us through the complexities of the rail network like a professional tour guide and doesn't need to call on my Cantonese — which wouldn't get us very far anyway, as there are very few opportunities to order tea as we navigate our way through the labyrinth of the Hong Kong underground.

By the time we get to our hotel room, I feel like something the cat's dragged in and then dragged out again. Mum decides to take a shower but I just flop onto my bed and sleep like the dead. The dead that is happy to be alive.

THREE MONTHS AND ONE DAY AFTER MORNING

Mum looks at me through the steam of her second double espresso. The three glasses of wine before dinner on the plane were one thing, it's the couple she had with dinner I think she's now seriously regretting. She might have also given the minibar in our room the once-over before the room began turning about her.

I'm having the full English buffet breakfast in our hotel's restaurant, while Mum has opted for coffee and Nurofen with a Berocca chaser. Despite her vastly decreased brain functionality, she's playing with her iPad, which is practically surgically attached to her hand.

'Mum. Your eyes look awful.'

She takes another sip of coffee. 'You should try them from this side.'

Poor Mum has clearly woken up with a hangover of biblical proportions. She looks like Death is skulking over her shoulder, scythe unsheathed.

'What do you want to do today?' asks Mum, through eyes so bloodshot the world must look maroon.

'Seriously?' I say. 'I want you to go back to bed.'

She shakes her head and then groans. Bad idea. 'Sorry,' she says. 'Pushed the boat out a bit last night. Not a very good example. Celebration went a little too far.'

'They say you shouldn't really drink alcohol on long flights,' I offer, as if this will actually help. 'Dehydration doubles the impact of jet lag, apparently.'

'Thank you, Mr Temperance.'

'What were you celebrating?'

She looks guilty. 'Oh, you know.'

'Oh, I don't.'

'Just getting away from . . . things.'

'You mean Dad?'

'Sorry,' she says. 'Probably not what you wanted to hear.'

'Are you guys okay?'

She sighs deep and loud. 'I don't know. Things are a little complicated right now.'

'You mean because of what I . . .' I look down at the table in shame. '. . . What I went through?'

'A little.' She reaches across the table and holds the back of my hand. 'But don't worry about me. I'll be fine.'

'You and Dad had nothing to do with it. You have to do what's right for you, Mum. You deserve it. You're worth it.'

Her face breaks into a warm smile, but there are tears welling in her eyes.

'Right,' she says, changing the subject. 'School gets out around three, I imagine.' She flashes me a watery wink. 'So let's do some tourist stuff before you pay your social call.'

I nod and try to hide a smile.

'Now there are two aspects to Hong Kong. Do you want to see the real one? Or would you prefer the bling version? Where does Lisa live?'

I open my phone and bring up Lisa's contact details. 'Um. North Point.'

Mum nods. 'Nice. Hong Kong Island. She's more bling. Relatives must be doing okay. So how about we go gritty first. We can traipse out to the markets, and then swing back to Hong Kong Island later?'

'Sounds good to me.'

After heading back to our room to change and load Mum up on some more Nurofen, we step out from the hermetically sealed safety of our hotel and after a short walk during which I am bombarded with offers to buy suits and copy watches, we disappear down the escalators into the Tsim Sha Tsui station and the rabbit warren of the Hong Kong MTR. Even though we have left daylight far behind, Mum's eyes are protected from the world (and it from them) behind the duty-free sunglasses she bought at the airport.

In Sydney you can wait ten, sometimes twenty minutes for a train. Here, they seem to come every minute. No sooner have we started milling on the station than a train arrives. Once the passengers have poured off, we bustle onboard with everyone else. Mum makes for a pole with me in tow. She doesn't even bother to go for a seat and I'm left to strap-hang next to her, because although it's mid-morning, the train is packed. The young women all look so classy. They've clearly spent ages getting ready but try to make it look like they've just thrown something on. Most of the guys are so busy trying to be hipsters and checking each other out that they fail to notice the young women. It's kind of pathetic, really.

A couple of teenage school girls with white socks pulled up to their knees are nudging each other, giggling and staring at me. I try to catch them out by glancing back at them but each time I do they look away and giggle even more.

I look up at the MTR map. The stations reveal a curious mixture of old Hong Kong and its former colonial masters: Tsim Sha Tsui, Jordan, Yau Ma Tei, Mong Kok, Prince Edward, Sham Shui Po.

We alight at Mong Kok and head up the escalators, the aromas from outside becoming more intoxicating the higher we go. I can't place the smell, though I suppose it's kind of a hybrid of sizzling woks, McDonald's, car exhausts, toil and industry all rolled into one.

'You were quite a hit on the train,' says Mum.

'You saw that?' I ask, embarrassed at being sprung. 'I thought your eyes had ceased functioning.'

'I'm a barrister,' she says. 'And your mum. I see all.'

We finally emerge, blinking into the daylight like the Eloi out of the Morlock's subterranean abattoir. Mong Kok is mostly locals. Foreigners are few and far between. Several men stare at Mum as we walk by and are so unsubtle about it that their heads swivel around like those circus clowns whose mouths you stuff balls into to win a prize. After one guy's head practically does a three-sixty, I feel like shoving a couple of balls in his mouth myself. Tennis balls, that is. Even hung-over, Mum's Italian looks are enough to draw a crowd.

We continue through the tight crowded streets until we turn into the markets.

'The thing about shopping in Hong Kong,' says Mum, 'is to shop where the locals shop. If there are more foreigners about than locals, you're being ripped off. Also, don't forget to haggle.'

'Haggle?' I ask.

'Yes,' she says. 'Haggle. Negotiate a price. Barter. Bargain.'

'But what if I don't want to haggle?'

'You have to haggle,' continues Mum, 'otherwise the stallholder will pass it down the line that a thick-as-a-brick teenager, ripe for the picking, is heading their way and they'll bump up the price when they see you coming.'

Mum looks at me and smiles. I know what that smile means. We are out and about in Hong Kong — our first of possibly many holidays together. It's a gorgeous, sunny day. The warmth is spreading through me as if I were a lizard on a riverbank, and, to use an old Australianism, "You wouldn't be dead for quids". And yet I came within a whisker of throwing it all away. The memory of that moment, of that pause, causes my heart rate to quicken and my throat to constrict.

'Okay,' says Mum. 'See that cafe across the street?' She points out a French patisserie not surprisingly called Le something or other. 'How about we meet there in a couple of hours?'

A couple of hours? I try to hide my shock.

I don't want to split up. I don't want to be on my own. 'Er, okay. You don't want me to carry your bags or something?'

'I wouldn't do that to you.'

'So why are you ditching me?' I try not to sound completely pathetic and fail.

'I'm not ditching you, Dec. You can come with me if you want. But remember: unfortunately I adhere to every shopping cliché surrounding my gender. Guilty as charged. And you're a man. Well, a close approximation of one.'

I scratch my nose with my middle finger.

Mum laughs and continues. 'So you'll be done in about half an hour, tops.' She opens up her purse and hands me some Hong Kong dollars to add to what she gave me this morning. 'Get yourself a coffee and a bun or profiterole or something and sit in the cafe and read or maybe write Lisa some poetry.' I cringe when Mum says this, thinking back to my earlier haikus which, if I remember correctly, are still in my bedside drawer. To think that I came within a whisker of committing suicide, having failed to destroy any and all evidence of my poetry. Oh, the horror.

A seasoned consumer, Mum's eyes are bulging like those of a startled puffer fish at the thought of the shopping and browsing that awaits. She pulls me down and kisses the top of my head, tells me to call me if I need her, and is soon swallowed up by the crowd, leaving me a bit lost and vulnerable, which scares me a little. I don't like being left alone since it happened. My thoughts and what they almost did frighten me. They're kind of like voices in my head, and I want to keep that voice that appeared when I was on the platform buried deep. I hate that voice for what it tried to make me do. For almost destroying me. For almost destroying my family. My life, my love, my world, my soul. Me.

I take a deep breath and absorb some vitamin D through my eyelids before beginning a slow stroll through the markets where the stallholders want to give a special price just to me.

The markets themselves have everything you could possibly desire, providing everything you could possibly desire includes copy watches, handbags, towels, toys, costume jewellery, mobile-phone covers, jeans, dresses, scarves, Hello Kitty accessories, or Lionel Messi, Cristiano Ronaldo and Robin van Persie replica shirts – otherwise you're kind of stuffed. I find myself in little need of any of these things. In fact, I don't really need or want anything. I'm just happy to be out and about. Just happy to be alive. Thrilled at the possibility of seeing Lisa this afternoon. Happy that the voice is silent.

Apparently the thing that surprises a lot of Americans when they travel overseas for the first time is encountering people who are completely ambivalent about America. They simply can't imagine anyone not wanting to at the very least visit. They seem to think that the rest of the world is queuing outside their international embassies desperate to migrate to the land of the brave and the home of the free. And so when they meet people who have no concept of the Super Bowl and don't know or care what the New York Yankees and Chicago Cubs get up to, or, for that matter, give a rat's what Paris Hilton or Kim Kardashian had for lunch that day (a lettuce leaf and spring water — fizzy, not still), it comes as a shock.

I feel a little that way myself as I meander along through the stalls. These people are Hong Kongese and, unless they have relatives Down Under, simply have no concept of Australia. Or if they do, it's the heavily clichéd one of the kangaroo in a corked hat surfing down the Opera House while eating a jar of Vegemite, which, as far as I know, has never happened.

After about half an hour, I abandon my quest for anything worth buying and settle on a Hello Kitty pencil case for Lisa as a sort of a joke, which I hope she gets. The stallholder wants to give me a special price if I buy two or more. Seriously?

What the hell would I do with multiple Hello Kitty pencil cases? She kind of growls at me like a rabid dog when I insist on just the one but then I change my mind and get one for Kate as well and so when I hand her the money she smiles.

Having survived the experience with the stall-holder, I take Mum's advice and escape from the maddening throng to the sanctuary of Le Café (groan). I order a coffee and a blueberry friand and take a seat in the corner. While I am waiting for my coffee, I open up Lisa's Hello Kitty pencil case. There's a little card inside on which I write 'Hello Kitty says Hello, Kitty'. And yes, before you ask, I call Lisa 'Kitty', or 'my Kitty Cat' or (and please don't let this get out) 'Snuggle Bunny'. Fortunately Chris and Maaaate are back in Sydney, coming to terms with either their sexuality or the fact that they regularly scarf down the contents of the pantry, otherwise I would have to write something more blokey on my Kitty Cat's Hello Kitty card. God! Kitty Cat? Snuggle Bunny? What's happened to me? I've turned into a complete sap. Still, it's a damn sight better than being turned into mulch on train tracks.

As I'm waiting for Mum, I take out my writing pad and try to think about what I'll do with my life now that I have one. I was thinking of doing an arts degree majoring in English and history as well as a bit of politics and then joining the army with a view to getting into the SAS. Though if I'm going to be honest, that career plan was largely to impress the chicks. A guy who could quote Tennyson while taking out a Taliban stronghold? You really couldn't go wrong. But, I suppose, in order to take out a Taliban stronghold, you generally have to shoot a couple of people, and that goes against my pacifist principles. And I'd imagine that the SAS would have a way of weeding out any pacifists in their midst, so I'm kind of forced to rule that option out. And besides, I've got a girlfriend, so I don't need to impress anyone with my Tennyson-quoting manliness.

I jot down a list of possible careers:

Doctor

Investigative journalist

Paramedic

Psychiatrist

Psychologist

Youth worker

Spy

Writer

Historian

Liberal Party politician

High-school English teacher

Human-rights lawyer

Aid worker

Giggolo

I figure that it's okay to have one joke career option on my list. As if I'd join the Liberal Party! Ha ha ha.

Several coffees and a couple of pastries later, Mum bustles into the cafe doing a fairly decent impression of a bag lady. She plonks herself down in the seat next to me and lets the multitude of bags fall where they may.

'What the hell did you buy?'

Mum looks at her bags. 'Pretty much one of everything.'

'Looks more like two.'

'Get me a coffee, please, Dec. I'm dying.'

'Of what? Alcohol withdrawal?'

It's only when I return with Mum's latte and croissant that I realise I've left my writing pad open and, showing strict adherence to the mother stereotype, she's snooping through it.

'Thanks, darl,' she says, as I put the coffee in front of her.

'Mum! That's private.'

'Nonsense,' she says, mainlining what must be her fifth coffee of the day. If I sliced her now – and it's tempting given that she's reading my private thoughts – she'd bleed caffeine. Though having practically sculled down a bucket of coffee myself, I can't really talk. 'We *should* talk about prospective careers.'

She runs her eyes down my list and they widen slightly when she reaches the bottom. 'If you're going to be a gigolo, I don't really want you bringing your work home with you. We could clear out the garage, I suppose, and you could take your clients there.'

'Cut it out, Mum! It was a joke.'

'Maybe you should think about it. You're handsome and you have a good physique and you can quote Tennyson.'

I groan. KMN. 'The Tennyson, SAS stuff was a joke, too.'

'There's only one "g" in gigolo, by the way.'

'And how would you know?'

'I read, Declan.'

'What, *Fifty Shades of Beige*?'

'Don't talk about your father like that,' she says, and we both laugh at poor Captain Beige who's probably being driven around the bend right now by a sugar-infused Katie Bear.

I think about Dad and Kate in Disneyland, about Kate's general weirdness and Dad's overall annoyance and hopelessness, and I have to admit that I miss them. I miss my dad and my sister. I miss my family. A family I came within a whisker of giving up. A family that I genuinely believed would be better off without me.

We leave the cafe and head for the MTR. I'm still feeling a little raw when we emerge blinking into the daylight from the Tsim Sha Tsui MTR station. I'm feeling raw not because again I'm being bombarded with offers to buy copy watches and suits, though that's certainly a contributing factor. It's more that I'm feeling bad about the way I (well, we – Mum isn't innocent in this) treat Kate and Dad. It's kind of us and them rather than just us, which is how it should be. I wind up Kate (and she does me) because we're siblings and that's the law. But Kate has issues that I should be more understanding and sensitive about; instead I treat her with disdain. She finds it hard to make friends because she's so exact and not very good at social stuff, so she can be made fun of at school. She used to want to blow out the candles on whoever's cake it was. We would be at a restaurant and some random spawn of Satan would be having a birthday party and Kate would run over and blow out the candles. By the time she was in year two she wasn't getting invited to parties anymore. Mum had to put on special birthday parties for her stuffed toys just so that Kate could blow out the candles. In primary school she used to hide in the library at lunch time. Occasionally I would venture in myself and see her reading alone in the corner or nestled into a beanbag. I wouldn't even say hello. I completely ignored her. I didn't want to be associated with her for fear of being recognised as her brother and being tarred with the same brush. I feel disgusted that I treated her like that and I promise myself that I will make it up to her. Somehow. Because she's a total brainbox – well, her mind's brilliant at storing facts and figures; she got into Reeve Road High, which is the top-ranked school in Sydney. But she chose Grosvenor Girls' instead because she claimed that she had a friend who was also going there, a friend whose birthday party she'd obviously never attended. Because it's still a selective school, she's surrounded by other brainiacs, so I suppose things are easier for her now and, yes, she does have some friends – girls like her, I guess. Girls who, just like any other tween girls, love boy bands but, when all is said and done, would prefer to come up with a mathematical model predicting their decline from both the charts and teenage girls' consciousness. So Kate's doing okay, with or without me, though I still feel bad about how I treat her. And I will be better with her from now on. I *will*. That's a promise.

Then I think about Dad and I feel even worse. I'm going to make more of an effort to laugh at his jokes and to not tease him, but sometimes I just can't help myself and Mum makes it worse by piling on. The problem is that he gives us so much material. I could pay out on him for a year about his Hawaiian shirts alone. And then there are his shorts. Since when is it okay to wear shorts with zipper cut-offs or those little triangular cut-outs on the side. What the hell are the triangles for? Do they make it easier to maintain the optimum sprinting stride as you tear away from a ravenous pack of lions as you streak across the Serengeti plains? See what I mean? I just can't help myself. It's one of those things that I know I'm going to think about when he's on his deathbed. We won't be talking about that time we went fishing (well, I guess we haven't been yet) or bushwalking or mountain-bike riding or that time we went to see a concert and we ended up bouncing off each other and slam dancing in the mosh pit. Though who the hell would appeal to the both of us is anyone's guess: AC/DC plays Enya maybe. No, I'll be thinking about his stupid Hawaiian shirts and triangular cut-out, zip-up shorts, and I'll be all choked up and when he dies I'll ask Mum if I can keep them – his shorts and Hawaiian shirts, I mean – and I'll end up wearing them as a sort of tribute to him and my son will pay *me* out because I'll be wearing Hawaiian shirts and embarrassing triangular cut-out shorts. But he won't understand that I'm doing it ironically and then when I die he'll feel sad because he paid me out and on and on it goes . . . Maybe it's one of those circle-of-life things.

I feel sad about the way I treat Dad. Really sad. But that's okay. I should feel sad. It's normal. It's part of what makes us human. And I'm going to feel sad at other times in my life but the thing is, I will recover. I'll recover from sadness, from grief, from bereavement, because they're all parts of life. And I know now that life will improve. That I won't throw myself in front of a train because my girlfriend or wife dumps me. That I won't throw myself in front of a train because I feel bad about how I treat my sister or my dad and his Hawaiian shirts and triangular cut-out shorts. And if that voice in my head starts up again, I will stamp on it or take medication to shut it up. Because feeling anything – even if it is pure agony – is better than feeling nothing.

'You right, Dec?' says Mum as we walk towards the Ocean Terminal shopping centre through the artificial wind tunnels created by all the buildings.

'I was just thinking we should buy Dad a present. Maybe a Hawaiian shirt.'

Mum smiles at this suggestion. 'What about Kate?'

'I bought her something at the markets.'

'I'd like to get them something, too. From me. From both of us.'

I nod.

Mum reaches over and holds my hand.

THREE MONTHS AND ONE DAY AFTER AFTERNOON

It's a quarter to three and I'm lurking across the road outside Lisa's school trying to appear inconspicuous. Though I suppose trying to appear inconspicuous while you're lurking around outside a school kind of makes you conspicuous. If I get any closer to the front gate, the school will probably go into lockdown.

After lunch at a noodle bar, Mum and I shopped in the upmarket Ocean Terminal for a while. We bought Kate a GoPro and a heart necklace, which kind of makes my Hello Kitty pencil case look a bit sad. However, rather than buy Dad a Hawaiian shirt, we decided on a complete makeover. It's the sort of silver fox/David Jones' catalogue look that will enable him to stroll along the beach at sunset thinking his poetic and poignant thoughts as a storm rolls in and a designer labradoodle frolics about beside him with a stick. The thing is, even in these brand labels he'll still somehow manage to look like a farmer at a wedding. I mean, the mannequin in the shop looked more stylish than Dad, and it only had half a head.

After Mum had *finally* had enough of the shops, we caught the Star Ferry across the bustling and choppy Victoria Harbour to Hong Kong Island, the salt spray churned up by the wash both cooling and invigorating. We took a tram up to the Peak for that panoramic postcard view that you see in every travel agent's window.

We had a quick drink in one of the bars then, around two, Mum said that she was meeting up with a friend for high tea in the Peninsula Hotel. I had been wondering why she'd only bought me a one-way ticket. Before catching the tram back down she put me in a red taxi and together we were able to give the driver directions to Lisa's school. As we were heading off, I told the driver that I was a student at the school, hoping that he wouldn't take me on a costly and time-consuming detour around the New Territories.

Around three, a bell goes off somewhere in the school and soon enough a couple of students trickle out. It eventually builds to a steady flow. Ten minutes later, there is a torrent. Being an international school, the student body is a cross-section of race and cultures, the way the planet is supposed to be.

And there, in the midst of the multitude, is Lisa, weighed down by an oversized backpack and what I assume is a violin case and just life in general.

If this were a movie I would raise my hand to attract her attention but then we would cut to a close-up of my face as it freezes with the sudden realisation that she's with someone – a guy. An extremely good-looking, confident guy. They would be laughing and carrying on, safe and happy in their clichéd couple bubble. After they disappear into the afternoon, a storm would hit and I would just stand there staring, the torrential rain only marginally masking the tears that would be cascading down my cheeks. I would montage my way back to the hotel, walking in a slow-motion trance as everyone else runs for cover from what turns out to be a once-in-twenty-years typhoon. Later that evening, after looking out my hotel room's window at the lights far below, I would phone Lisa and terminate our relationship. I would protect her from my breaking heart by citing the tyranny of distance, how I've only ever wanted her happiness and will always love her, and if she ever needs a friend then I will be here for her, blah, blah, blah . . . (well, not here as such, but back home in Sydney because she would be blissfully unaware that I am actually in Hong Kong). And I would assume her silence was the masked joy of being let off the hook and that she was now free to pursue her burgeoning relationship with a guy who would have designer glasses and a hairstyle that would be just shy of an Elvis duck arse and yet he would still somehow be able to pull off. But then later, just as I'm about to leave for the airport, Lisa would call one more time, and it would slowly be revealed that the guy she was with wasn't her boyfriend, just a friend who happens to be both good looking (haircuts aside) and has zero interest in Lisa (apart from as a study buddy). With the confusion cleared up, but our airport taxi inbound, a noise in the background (possibly someone ordering tea in Cantonese – perhaps even me) would reveal that I'm actually in Hong Kong. With our wires finally uncrossed, Lisa and I would race towards each other down Nathan Road, dodging shoppers, commuters and those annoying a-holes peddling suits and copy watches, before leaping into each other's arms hugging and kissing in the rain while the camera circles around us, credits rolling.

Fortunately this isn't a movie and there is no Elvis-hairstyle impersonator to muddy the waters. Instead, Lisa is struggling with her violin case and backpack, which must weigh more than her.

I quickly cross over and sidle up beside her as she begins her trek down the street towards a set of shops. I can see that she is aware of my presence, but she hasn't looked over at me yet, possibly in case I'm a fat old guy with a balding ponytail who lurks around parks with a video camera . . .

'Can I give you a hand, miss?'

Other than a gulp there's no response.

'Your backpack looks heavy.'

Lisa keeps her eyes locked to the pavement. 'Piss off or I'll scream.'

'Lisa.'

She stops and turns towards me, a look of realisation and relief slowly washing over her. 'Oh my God!' she screeches like a banshee. 'Declaaaaaaaaan.' She shrugs off her backpack, drops her violin case and, as per the end scene of my movie, she leaps into my arms, her legs wrapped around my waist. And even though she's wearing her school uniform and is still in sight of the school grounds and is in danger of losing her, her family and her school a tremendous amount of face, she showers *my* face with kisses. The feeling of being needed, of being wanted, is so mind blowing, so overwhelming, that I can hardly breathe.

When she unhitches herself from me, I hitch on her backpack and pick up her violin case, which seems bigger and heavier than a violin case ought to be.

'When did you take up the violin?'

'Saxophone. Not all Asian kids play the piano and violin, Declan. Only about ninety-seven per cent.'

'You're such a rebel.' It's tough: she probably wouldn't have wanted to continue with the piano, even if she was good at it. Too many bad memories, I guess.

We walk down the street, fingers interlocked, hearts racing.

'I've got about a million questions but firstly, what are you doing here?'

'I came to see you.'

'Seriously?'

'Seriously.'

Lisa is quiet for a moment. I look over and realise that she's crying.

'Is everything . . .?'

'No one has ever done anything like that for me before. Not even close.'

I don't know what to say to this, so I unhook our fingers and put my arm around her. 'I'm with you, Lisa. I'm always with you.'

We walk in silence for a while.

'How do you get home? Bus?'

'My . . . my aunt picks me up. If she's not working.'

'What? Where?'

'Just down the road here.'

'Is that where we're going? Shit. Oughtn't I get out of here?'

Despite the danger, Lisa laughs. '"Oughtn't". That's not a word.'

'Yes it is. It's a contraction of "ought" and "not". As in, "Ought not I get out of here?"'

'Who would say that?'

'Why are you so calm? There's a fire-breathing dragon just down the road who toasts penis-wielding teen *gweilo*s for breakfast, and you're arguing about grammar.'

'Relax, Declan.'

'Relax? That's easy for you to say. She doesn't want to barbecue *your* testicles and serve them with fried rice.'

'Boiled rice, Declan. Testicles don't work with fried rice.'

'Ha ha.'

Lisa stops and turns to look at me. 'Declan. Susanne's nothing like my *mother*. Nothing. I've told her a couple of our stories and she thinks it's hilarious. She wants to meet you. In fact, she was going to look you up and take you out for coffee when she was in Sydney next time.'

By the time we enter the cafe, I'm not hyperventilating quite as much. I do a quick scout around, trying to spot Lisa's aunt and any possible exit points in case Lisa is wrong about the whole aunt-not-being-psycho thing. There're a few kids from Lisa's school buying coffees and smoothies, but no one who strikes me as Lisa's aunt. Certainly no Kraken look-alikes. There's a flight attendant talking on her mobile in Cantonese.

'There she is,' says Lisa, gesturing towards the flight attendant, who waves us over.

No way did she emerge from the same womb that spat out The Kraken.

Lisa's aunt hangs up as we are squeezing our way through the tables towards her. She gives Lisa a hug and then looks over at me. She runs her eyes up and down me.

'Susanne,' says Lisa, 'this is my friend Declan.' Lisa's aunt's handshake is as warm as The Kraken's wasn't.

'Have a seat,' says Susanne, with a look that lets me know that *she* knows we're a little more than friends. 'So. This is the guy who's been getting old Joy's knickers in a twist.' Susanne's face lights up. 'It is an absolute pleasure to meet you, Declan.'

I look over at Lisa as the penny finally drops. 'Your mum's called "Joy"?'

Lisa's raised eyebrows tell me everything I need to know. No one need mention the word 'irony', though if the people at Webster or Collins were looking for a definition, they could do a lot worse.

'Mum?' says Susanne. 'Some mother she turned out to be.'

Lisa and Susanne share a look. Lisa shakes her head. Something passes between them and although I'm pretty good at subtext, I have no idea what it is.

We order coffees and engage in small talk for a while. Susanne speaks four languages (Cantonese, Mandarin, Japanese and English) and is currently learning a fifth (French). She makes me feel like an illiterate baboon. I ask her about her work and she says that although she loves the travel, the work itself is pretty boring and repetitive and also the next bloated businessman who pats her bottom is going to get a jug of nuclear-hot coffee poured onto his lap. Even though the work itself is pretty monotonous, Susanne has made enough money to buy a little apartment in Paris to go with the one her father left her in Hong Kong – out of guilt, she reckons. Lisa and Susanne share another look. I discover that Susanne is taking Lisa to Paris during the next school holidays, which makes me feel a bit upset that she didn't think to arrange it so that Lisa could visit me in Sydney instead, and also a little green: I wanted to be with her when we first saw Paris, at the start of our motor-cycling holiday through Europe. Still, I'm happy for her and it's better she's here rather than being smacked by The Kraken's cane on a regular basis or having her knuckles whacked for hitting the wrong note on the piano.

Susanne asks me what I want to do with myself after school and I give her a few things from my list, omitting both the Tennyson-quoting commando and the gigolo bits.

'But if you could do anything,' says Susanne, 'what would you choose?'

'Seriously,' I reply, 'I just want to be with Lisa.'

Lisa turns her head slightly to the side and gives me a look that liquefies my heart.

'That's so sweet,' says Susanne. 'A little nause-ating, but sweet.'

With the treacle and cheese flowing, Lisa reaches over and grabs my hand. I feel I should pull away but Susanne just smiles and tells us to get a room. It's clear that Lisa will be okay now that she's with Susanne.

'I'm sorry about what's happened to the two of you,' says Susanne, reaching across the table and holding Lisa's free hand but looking at me, 'but I've got her now. And I'm not letting her go again.'

Again?

Lisa and Susanne share a smile.

'But what if "Joy"' — I'm forced to put air quote marks around her name because I can't say it out loud and still expect to be taken seriously — 'decides she wants Lisa to come back?'

'Well then "Joy"' — Susanne matches my air quotes — 'can kiss my arse.'

'But how can you stop her?' I don't know much about the law or what sort of extradition rules exist between Australia and Hong Kong, but if The Kraken insists on Lisa's coming home, short of going into hiding, surely there isn't much that Susanne and Lisa can do about it. I feel as though I'm missing something crucial.

'I'll let Lisa explain the details,' says Susanne. 'But she *is* staying with me. At least until she's finished uni. Then she can make up her own mind. It's her life, after all, but the next bit is going to be with me.'

I suddenly realise what Susanne is saying. Lisa is a year behind me at school so she has a full two years to go of high school, then at least three at university. I always assumed that Lisa would eventually come back. After year twelve, maybe. Stay with that aunt of hers on her father's side.

The one she mentioned. The one who loathes The Kraken. Though listening to Susanne it seems as though The Kraken is not exactly short on people who loathe her. But Susanne is saying that's not going to happen. Lisa is staying in Hong Kong for at least five more years. Whether she realises it or not, Susanne has just ended our relationship and Lisa is smiling at her. I've come so effing far, and now this. It's tearing my heart out. But as much as this sucks — and boy does it suck — I know I'll get through it this time. I know I'll be able to ride it out.

Susanne gives Lisa some money to pay for the coffees. When Lisa heads off to the counter, Susanne leans towards me.

'I want to thank you for what you've done for Lisa,' she says.

I shrug. 'I didn't do anything really. I just liked her. Loved her. Still do.' I glance over at Lisa, who's waiting at the counter. She smiles back at me. It's the sort of smile that makes my pulse quicken. The sort of smile that would have stopped da Vinci from arsing around with half-baked helicopters and break out the paints again.

'We've spoken, Declan. *Boy* have we spoken. You showed her another life. You showed her how to have fun. To be a bit rebellious. She needed that. To stand up to Joy.'

What? Lisa stood up to The Kraken? I don't remember that.

Susanne continues. 'I tried to stay in touch. Be an influence on her life. But you know Joy. She isn't exactly the most communicative person in the world. Quite frankly, she's nuts.'

I'm only really half-listening to what Susanne is saying as I'm too captivated by Lisa to take my eyes off her. But I suppose Susanne is right. I have had an influence on Lisa. Even if it was only small. And she's happy now. Happier than when she was with The Kraken, certainly, and I'm partly responsible for that. I may have just lost her, but I helped save her, and I suppose it was worth it.

'And so she goes back to live with that bitch over my dead body.'

I sigh and Susanne gets it. She understands where I'm coming from.

'Declan. This is the age of technology. You have Skype and FaceTime. Relationships aren't what they were. Don't give her up.'

'Isn't it inevitable?'

'That's up to you. I had a long-distance relationship for five years. She lived in New York.'

I'm looking over at Lisa again, who's paying our bill . . . did Susanne just say 'she'?

'She was a flight attendant with British Airways. But she was based in New York.'

I'm trying hard to be mature, to be her niece's bookish, intellectual boyfriend, to not imagine Susanne with another woman, but she's not making it easy. If only 'Joy' knew of Susanne's 'lifestyle', she'd be turning in her grave at the thought of sending Lisa back here to live under her influence. Okay, 'Joy' isn't dead, worse luck – I haven't managed to set those pit bulls or bees on her yet – but still.

'It didn't last, though?' is the best I can manage.

'She went all hetero on me,' says Susanne. 'Went and got married, had kids, white picket fence and everything. Barf! Still, we run into each other occasionally and, you know.' Susanne smiles enigmatically. 'Just live for the moment,' she says quietly. 'Enjoy the now, because tomorrow might not come.'

Lisa has to leave for her saxophone lesson because, according to Susanne, having music lessons after school in Hong Kong is the law, apparently. Susanne suggests that the four of us catch up for dinner tonight. I think she's just being polite but she insists on writing down Mum's mobile number so that she can arrange it with her.

A couple of hugs later and they're gone.

I should feel miserable because I suppose Lisa and I have sort of just broken up. Because no matter how much Bill Gates and Steve Jobs have enabled couples to stay in touch across the planet, there's just no substitute for being in the same city, the same room. But I don't feel miserable. I feel content that Lisa is happy. Besides, breakups, sadness, grief, despair are all a part of life. Unless you know agony, you'll never truly know joy — and that's joy with a lowercase 'j'. And I know that I will never throw myself under the wheels of a train for Lisa. For anyone. Because no matter how low I get (and I will get low again, that's a given), happiness will always be just beyond the horizon. Just around the corner. Also — and I can't stress this enough — the thought of Captain Beige discovering my haikus would haunt me across all eternity.

THREE MONTHS AND ONE DAY AFTER NIGHT

There's no doubt about it, having dinner with three stunningly beautiful women is good for the ego. I'm drawing jealous looks from the men in the restaurant and I feel about ten feet tall. Okay, it would probably be better if one of the women wasn't my mum, another one wasn't gay and I hadn't recently broken up (sort of) with the other, but still . . .

Susanne and Mum chat like old friends, which means that, although we've kind of broken up, for the first time since we've been together in Hong Kong, Lisa and I can disappear into our couple bubble. I have never seen Lisa looking more relaxed. More gorgeous. Hong Kong obviously agrees with her. Or maybe it's just being 4583 miles/7375.63 kilometres/3982.52 nautical miles from The Kraken that's agreeing with her. It's certainly doing wonders for me.

I'm half-listening to Susanne and Mum's conversation but Lisa keeps putting her hand on my leg, which doesn't make it easy to concentrate. From what I can gather, Susanne was a bit of a wild child. Apparently she was born after her mother had died (though I can't quite get my head around that), but after she died, Joy took her mother's place at the head of the family while the amah (?) took her mother's place in bed, and the resulting shame that was brought down on the family was enough for Joy and her husband and their two young sprogs to eventually flee to Australia, and good riddance. Susanne was okay at primary school but when she got to high school she fell in with the wrong crowd, or maybe Susanne *was* the wrong crowd and others fell in with her, and when *it* happened – whatever *it* was – Susanne was packed off to live with relatives and attend school in England, while Joy returned briefly to Hong Kong to take care of things and try to keep a lid on the shame. In England, Susanne managed to get her act together and did well enough at school to get into university to study languages. It's clear that Susanne absolutely despises Joy (and from what I can gather, the feeling is mutual), and yet despite there being four other sisters spread across the globe, Susanne was the one Joy turned to when she wanted to get Lisa off her hands and away from me. It doesn't make a whole lot of sense. Then again, I once saw The Kraken at the supermarket at ten o'clock in the morning wearing canary-yellow PJs and her slippers, so I suppose sense doesn't really enter into it.

I turn to Lisa and make it look like I'm kissing her while I whisper in her ear, 'Did Susanne say she was born *after* her mother died?'

'Yep.'

'How does that work? Was her mother in a coma or something?'

'Oh, Declan,' says Lisa, giving me one of those looks that I would happily die for. 'You really are quite naive at times. "Mother" wasn't Susanne's actual mother.' Lisa continues because I obviously look like a goldfish that's trying to solve a Rubik's Cube using telekinesis. '"Mother" was the matriarch. Susanne refers to her as "Mother" because everyone else in the family does. Though Susanne never met her.'

'So who's Susanne's mother?'

'The amah.'

I lapse back into looking like a goldfish again. 'The armour?'

'No. Her mother wasn't some sort of medieval knight's attire, you doofus. "Amah" means "maid", or "servant".'

'So Susanne's mum was . . .'

'A Filipina servant girl, yes.'

'Seriously?'

'Quite the scandal,' says Lisa. 'After Susanne was born, Joy wanted to ship her and the amah off on a one-way flight back to Manila — or at least she *did* want to, until the amah, Grace, leapt off a thirty-storey building, which shamed Father into taking Susanne in. Grace killed herself to protect her daughter: she knew that had she gone back to Manila with her daughter, the chances of someone employing a single mum were next to nothing, and the chances of Susanne ending up as a street kid or a prostitute were way too high. Now look at her. And all because of what Grace did. Now that's real love.'

As the skeletons in Lisa and Susanne's family closet come out to play, I am practically speechless. After what happened to Susanne's mother, I feel kind of guilty. Okay, I'm not supposed to minimise or trivialise what I went through — anxiety and depression are silent killers and do not discriminate — but what I was going through seems like nothing compared to what happened to Susanne's mum.

After dinner, Mum has a coffee (big shock there) while Susanne ducks out for about ten minutes. When she comes back she hands something to Lisa in a paper bag and then Susanne and Mum announce that they're going out clubbing and, since we're having dinner on the Kowloon side of Hong Kong, just down the road from our hotel, they want us to wait in the room until they get back. They'll be gone about four hours, or so they reckon. Mum also tells me that we're not allowed to touch the spirits in the minibar but we can help ourselves to the champagne, wine and beer. Lisa and I try to avoid eye contact during what has to be the most awkward conversation of our lives.

I wrap myself around Lisa as we stroll down Nathan Road towards our hotel. In the lift I pluck up the courage to kiss her and she kisses me right back. It's the most wonderful feeling in the world. Certainly one worth sticking around for.

We exit the lift and walk along the corridor, fingers interlocked, my stomach in knots thinking about where this might lead.

'Well, that wasn't weird,' I say to break the tension, thinking back to Susanne and Mum bailing on us.

'Tell me about it,' says Lisa. 'Do you know what Susanne gave me in the restaurant?' She blushes slightly as she says this.

I shake my head as Lisa opens her bag to reveal a twelve-pack of condoms.

Now it's me who's turning red. 'We could always blow one of them up and play volleyball.'

Although I'm holding Lisa's hand, it's all become a little awkward and I can feel my hand sweating. Our parents/guardians are out clubbing and pretty much insisting that we have sex and get drunk. It's like we're the parents and they're the irresponsible teenagers. Or maybe this is some sort of high-end reverse psychology. By telling us that it's okay to have a drink and mess around, they're hoping we won't do either. Whatever it is, it's strange.

I fumble nervously with the keycard and insert it in the slot. The light flashes green and I push open the door.

'Wait,' I say to Lisa as she is about to walk in. I scoop her up in my arms and carry her into the room and lower her gently onto the bed. She weighs almost nothing.

'Oh, Declan.' She swoons like a fifties movie star. 'Y'all is just so romantic.'

'Stop speaking like that,' I laugh. 'You're putting me off.'

'Whatever you say, daaaaahling,' she replies. 'You're the maaaaan.'

I latch the door and slip off my T-shirt. I return

to the bed and puff out my chest, tense my stomach and flex my arms.

'Oh my,' says Lisa as she runs her eyes over my bulging pecs and rippling six-pack. (Hey. This is *my* road not travelled. I can have all the bulging pecs and rippling six-packs I want.)

Lisa licks her lips. 'Come give me some of that sugar, sugar.'

I crawl onto the bed and advance on Lisa who moves and squirms like a cat. We kiss deeply and passionately and then I make my way down to her sexy, succulent neck, which I love devouring. Her back arches as I pretty much turn into a vampire. I help Lisa remove her top but as I toss it aside I look deep into her eyes and stop. Despite the Southern belle routine, she looks frightened. I smile at her, lay back on the bed and pull her into me so that her head is lying on my chest.

'Sorry,' she says.

'It's okay,' I reply.

'It's just . . .'

'I get it.' Lisa is right. The timing is wrong. The moment contrived. Contrived by Mum and Susanne who, in their own progressive yet clumsy way, are encouraging us to do something that we're not ready for. No means no and that's the end of it. And despite her alluring talk and her passionate kisses, the look in Lisa's eyes just now said 'no'. I know if we carry on we'll both regret this moment and when Lisa looks back on our time together, no matter how long, or short, or how imagined it is, I want it to be a beautiful memory. I only want to bring her joy (lower case) because she's been through enough.

'Thanks for understanding,' she says.

'I love you, Lisa. Always have. Always will.'

Lisa props herself up on her elbow and looks at me. 'We should do something though,' she says with a mischievous grin. 'We've got the room to ourselves for hours yet.'

'Room service? Banana split or something disgustingly chocolaty and sweet?' I suggest.

'If I eat any more I'll explode,' says Lisa.

'What then?'

Lisa grins at me again. 'Spa bath?'

'Seriously?' Now it's *my* eyebrows that are raised.

'Seriously. And champagne.' She gets up from the bed and sashays towards the bathroom. 'Give me five to get it ready.' Even though she's wearing her jeans and a bra, she still covers her breasts with her arms as she disappears into the bathroom.

While Lisa organises the bath, I delve into the minibar and take out the champagne. When five minutes are up I carry two wine glasses and the champagne through to the bathroom. I try not to swallow my Adam's apple when I see that Lisa is already in the bath. Naked and – gulp – all wet and slippery. Double gulp. Well, I have to imagine that she's naked, wet and slippery because she's covered with an avalanche of suds. I can only see her head. She looks like an otter poking its head out of a snowdrift.

'Where did you get the bubble bath?'

Lisa looks about her as if she hasn't even noticed the mountain of foam. 'It came out of the tap that way.'

'Seriously?'

'No, Declan.'

Duh!

'I used your mum's shampoo and some bath gel. I was surprised how much it frothed up.'

Stupid Mum's shampoo and bath gel.

I pop open the champagne like a seasoned champagne popper and pour us both a full glass.

Lisa sips hers. 'Mmm. More bubbles. Delicious. So,' she says after she's placed her glass on the side of the bath. 'You coming in?'

Uh oh. Big problem. 'Er.'

'Don't be embarrassed.'

'That's easy for you to say. You're already in there and what's more, you don't have a part of your anatomy that has a mind of its own.'

'What?' she says, then immediately snorts in laughter. 'We could always use an extra towel rack.'

'Close your eyes,' I insist.

'No,' she says, taking another sip of champagne.

'Please.'

Lisa is loving my predicament. 'Absolutely not.'

'Right. Then stand up and wash all that foam off you.' That hot, slippery, wet foam. Gulp.

'Okay then.'

Double gulp.

She closes her eyes. Blast.

I quickly remove my clothes and clamber into the bath about as elegantly as a rollerskating giraffe on a slip 'n' slide.

The water is hot. Seriously hot. Almost – but not quite – hot enough for me to leap into the air like a frog that's accidentally landed on a barbecue. I man up and take the heat.

When I'm used to the temperature, Lisa moves over and lies back against my chest. It's a little awkward at first but Lisa is eventually able to wiggle into a position that is comfortable for both of us.

I decide to wash Lisa's hair, massaging the shampoo into her scalp slowly and firmly with my fingertips. Her sighs tell me that she's enjoying it. That I'm doing it right.

Lisa goes quiet and suddenly I feel the elephant entering the room. 'Declan. We haven't talked about it yet, and I think we need to.'

I knew this was coming.

'What happened to you when I left? On the station. Was it a su– . . . an attempt?' She can't say the 's' word. No one can say the 's' word. It's too big.

'I paused.'

'What do you mean, paused?'

'What happened with your mum?' I ask.

'Declan . . .'

'I'll tell you but please tell me what happened with you and your mum first. Susanne said that you stood up to her. To Joy, I mean. Is it true?'

'Yep.'

'So if you stood up to her, why are you still living here?'

She turns and looks up at me. 'You haven't worked it out yet, have you?'

'Worked what out?'

'It was the night we came back late from Bombay Bicycle Club – you remember. The last time we saw each other.'

It's not something I'll ever forget.

'Reverend Tong had phoned Joy and told her that it had been weeks since he'd seen me at youth group and the few times I had been, he'd seen me with a boy. And what's more, there wasn't any Christian youth concert that night. I was obviously lying. As soon as I kissed you goodnight and walked inside the house, she was waiting there with her cane.'

'When did she start hitting you?'

'As soon as I walked in the door she just went berserk.'

'No. I mean, how old were you when it started?'

'Oh. She'd always hit me. For as long as I can remember. It wasn't just the physical stuff, it was emotional abuse, too. Name calling. Mind games.'

'Such as?'

'Like taking family photos but deliberately leaving me out.'

'What about your sister and brother. Did she . . .?'

'Nope. Just me. For a long time I wasn't sure why. I spoke to my school counsellor about it. She said sometimes it's one child who cops the lot.'

I feel her relax even more against me. I enjoy the moment, the silence, and use my empty champagne flute to rinse the shampoo out of her hair.

'I started fantasising that I was adopted. I suppose all kids do, at some point. You know that one where you pray you're the long-lost Princess of Manchuria sent to live with commoners but now emissaries are on their way to restore you to your rightful place on the throne . . .'

'Can't say I've had that fantasy.'

'Well, if you'd had my life, you would have.

I fantasised about it every night. It became my safe place. Somewhere to escape to, every night as I cried myself to sleep. I was alone, Declan. All alone with no one to turn to. I hated my life so much, I just wanted to die. And then a handsome prince showed up on a train quoting some guff about *To Kill a Mockingbird*.'

I feel myself choking up. I practically did nothing for her and she thinks I'm a prince.

Lisa looks up at me and sees the doubt in my eyes.

'You showed me another life. You showed me that it was okay to be a bit rebellious. You made me feel worth it. No one, not even my family, *especially* not my family, made me feel like I was worth anything. You showed me that I was. You made me feel special.'

'You *are* special, Lisa.'

Lisa turns around and kisses me. 'And it turns out that I was.'

'You were what? Special?'

Lisa eases herself up from my chest, still covered in foam (when will these bloody bubbles burst?) and moves back to her side of the bath. She takes a sip of champagne and looks at me. 'Adopted.'

My chin practically goes under water. 'So you're like, what, a Chinese princess?'

'Not quite a princess.'

'I'll be the judge of that.' I scoop up some bath-water with my empty glass and toss it over her chest, clearing away the suds so that I can finally see her in all her glory. 'I anoint you Princess Lisa of Hong Kong.'

Lisa looks down at her breasts but doesn't attempt to cover them.

'Now arise and take a bow.'

'Nice try, Declan.'

'Seriously, though. You're adopted?'

'Yep. Well, sort of.'

'When did you find out?'

'That night we arrived home from the concert. The night I stood up to her.'

'So what happened?'

'She'd been hitting me more than usual since — I have to say it, sorry — since I started seeing you.'

I reach over and hold her hand. I pull her towards me so that we can hug. I love her warm skin against mine, the feeling that I'm protecting her as she is me. I soap and massage her back as we hug. Anyone can have sex. I'll choose love, I'll choose closeness, I'll choose friendship every time.

'Well, you remember how I told you about how when I got home she went crazy? She was screaming at me that I was a worthless, black-hearted whore. I knew I was going to get caned, and I could tell that this was going to be the worst one yet. And it was, but I guess even worse than the beating was what she was saying. She kept telling me it was *my* fault, that this is what happened to deceitful, disgusting, ungrateful, selfish hearts. And all the time I knew what she was doing was wrong. So wrong. None of my friends' mothers treated them this way. She never laid a finger on my sister or brother. Just me. Susanne's right. She's crazy.'

I could kill Joy right now. What an effing sadist.

'Well, she was so mad she started stomping on the floor. It was only then that I realised that she was left-footed. She probably didn't even know herself because, seriously, how many middle-aged women get the opportunity to play football? And I was kind of laughing at the idea of her trying out for the local Aussie Rules team when her slipper went flying off. And this made it worse — I was hoping that the slipper would decapitate one of those stupid figurines she decorates the house with, and I couldn't stop laughing. And then when she went to retrieve the slipper she said it, the . . .' She trails off.

'Said what?'

Lisa holds up her fingers, one after the other, as if she's counting. 'Hang on a sec.' She mouths as she counts. 'Okay, got it. She said the eleven words that changed my life.'

'Eleven?'

'I know. Ten would have been better – rounder – but it was eleven.'

'So what were they?'

'"You are nothing but a cheap whore, just like your mother."'

Although she'd prepared me for it, it still takes a moment for this to sink in.

'It was like the world just stopped for a second and then we exchanged this look. I actually smiled at her because we both knew that she'd just lost her leverage and she was in a very awkward position.'

'Awkward position for what?'

'Well, after she got her slipper, she came back and she was leaning over me but she was off balance, so I used my judo skills and threw her off me.'

'You know judo?' I know this isn't the point, but it hits me that there's still so much I have to learn about Lisa.

'I don't. But I went for a lesson with my cousin when I was ten and I remembered this one throw. It's about using your opponent's weight against them.'

'Lisa. You are my hero.'

'She kind of flew off me. I saw it all in slow motion. She was actually airborne for a moment, and she squeaked when she hit the floor. She literally squeaked! Then she was rolling around on the ground as if *she* was the victim. I got up and ran to my room and slammed the door, daring her to come in.'

'Where was your dad?'

'He usually went into hiding when she went ballistic. Probably scurried away to the pub.'

'What a guy.'

'A couple of hours later, the phone calls started. She was screaming down the phone to Hong Kong, and it didn't take me too long to figure out who my mother was.'

'Susanne?'

'Susanne.'

'How old was she when she had you?'

'Fifteen. She bought us the condoms tonight because she doesn't want us making the same mistake.'

'So who's your father?'

'He was some guy from school she was seeing at the time. Works in New York now. Financier or something mind-numbingly boring. Never wanted to know anything about me. Has his own family now.'

'His loss.'

'Okay, that's me. Not exactly Anastasia or Anne Frank but there it is.'

'Why didn't you tell me about what happened when we spoke the next morning?' I ask her.

'I was still processing it myself. And it wasn't definite that Susanne was my mother. She only confirmed it when we went out to dinner the first night I arrived back. Now, what about you?'

The water's getting cold and we're out of champagne. We scissors, paper, rock to see who goes for a beer. I can't believe my luck when my paper covers Lisa's rock. I promise to close my eyes (yeah, right) as she climbs out of the bath and glides across the bathroom without bothering to cover up with a towel or robe.

I top up the hot water while Lisa slides gracefully back into the bath, more swanlike than my earlier rollerskating giraffe. I twist the top off the beer and pour us both half a glass.

'What happened to you at the station?' She hesitates. 'Please tell me that it wasn't me. I don't think I could take it . . .' She trails off.

But I'm not going to sugar-coat it. If we're going to stay friends, a couple, or whatever this is, then we have to be truthful. 'Your leaving kind of tipped me over the edge.'

Lisa slumps. I reach forward and pull her to me again.

'It wasn't you, though, Lisa. I promise. It wasn't you that put me on that platform. There was something that happened that I kind of tried not to think about. It was *our* dirty family secret and it was chewing me up inside even though I didn't know it. Everyone thought I was pretty normal, but until I met you all I ever did was go to school, do a bit of weight training in the garage, then hide in my room reading and watching movies.'

'Same as me.'

'So we were good for each other. We kind of saved each other.'

'But you almost died.'

'Almost.'

'Tell me, Declan. Tell me what happened.'

I tell her and she cries for two hours.

ELEVEN YEARS BEFORE

I sit at the breakfast bar listlessly stirring the dregs of my Coco Pops and feeling like something that the cat pooed out.

'He'll just have to go to school,' says Dad. 'That's all there is to it. He can't have the day off for every little sniffle.'

'Look at him,' replies Mum. 'He's not well.'

'His temperature's fine. He's just putting it on.'

'I'm not!'

'Don't talk back to me, Declan.'

'He's got a cold coming on, Shaun,' says Mum. 'For God's sake, show a little compassion.'

'When I was his age . . .'

'Stop!' snaps Mum. 'Spare us the "When I was

a lad we used to walk barefoot to school across broken bottles and arctic icefloes to get to class" routine. You went to a bloody private school.'

'Gabriella! Language.'

'Can you take the day off work?' says Mum.

'You know it's the end of financial year.'

'And the world will stop turning if those accounts don't get reconciled.'

'Well, can *you*?'

'I'm in court today.'

'What about your mum?' says Dad. 'Surely she's the obvious solution.'

'You know she can't handle the two of them at once. Even Kate's too much for her at times.'

Right on cue from the playroom, Kate attempts to beat a Lego policeman into compliance with a lump hammer.

'Could you ask Mary?' suggests Mum. 'I'm assuming she's still on the wagon.'

'Mary's fine,' says Dad. 'She hasn't had a drink in years.'

'I don't want to stay with her,' I say.

Dad crosses his arms. 'And why not?'

'She smells.'

Despite the domestic bind that they're in, Mum has to snort back a laugh.

'Aunt Mary does *not* smell,' says Dad.

'Does too.'

Before Dad has the chance to issue his 'Does not' rebuttal, Mum chimes in.

'Actually she does. Kind of like mothballs and gin.'

'This is my mother's sister you're talking about, Gabriella.'

'Okay,' says Mum. 'Your mother's sister smells like mothballs and gin.'

*

After dropping Kate at Grandma's, we pull up outside Aunt Mary's house in the Western Suburbs. The house resembles Aunt Mary. It's neat enough on the outside, but inside it's falling apart.

This is a big detour for Dad and he isn't happy about it. He's been grumbling like a wino's dog since we left home. He's going to be late for work and late home tonight. Despite this, I stand my ground. 'I don't want to stay with her,' I say. 'She's mean.'

'So what is it, Declan? She's mean or she smells?'

'Both. And she's ugly.'

'She took me in through the goodness of her heart when I first came to this country,' says Dad. 'I know she's got a bit of a temper but she's a good person. She hasn't had an easy life.'

'She's still ugly.'

'That's enough!' snaps Dad. 'You used to like staying with her when you were little.'

'She's mean and she hits me.'

'She does not! Don't lie, Declan. You know I can't stand liars.'

'Can I come to work with you?'

'There are no crèche facilities at the office.'

I don't have a clue what crèche facilities are, but I suppose it means that I can't go to work with him.

'Okay, I'll go to school then,' I plead.

'You don't have your uniform.' Dad's got me with this one.

'I can tell Miss Stevely it's in the wash,' I suggest.

'You should have thought about that this morning before you decided to skive off.'

Dad carries my toys and library bag up the path. I trudge along behind him, staring at the creepy-looking gnomes that are scattered about the garden.

'And put a smile on your face when you see her. Don't you embarrass me in front of her, you hear? She's doing us a favour.'

The door creeps open before we even knock.

'Hello, Aunt Mary. You well?'

'Grand, Shaun. Yourself?'

'If I was any fitter I'd be dangerous.'

Aunt Mary's disturbing screech-like laugh is the type you would normally associate with the sort of person who owns a squadron of flying monkeys. I wish I had a pair of red shoes that I could tap together and fly away to Kansas in.

'And here's the wee fella,' she says. 'Are you feeling poorly, my love?'

'He's fine,' says Dad. 'Got a bit of a sniffle, that's all. Nothing fatal.'

Aunt Mary takes my stuff and Dad ruffles my hair. 'Behave yourself,' he says. He then winks at the Wicked Witch of the Western Suburbs. 'Both of you.'

'Ah, Shaun, get away with you, you big tease.'

When Dad leaves, Aunt Mary tells me that we're going to have a grand time. We're going to have lots of 'crack' (which is Irish for 'fun' — I hope). She's going to be doing some baking and if I'm a good boy she'll let me stir the mixture and if I'm a *really* good boy she'll let me lick the bowl afterwards. She's in a happy mood, for now. I just hope it stays that way. It's when she goes for that bottle under the sink that she turns into the Witch. I swear if there were an instruction manual for Aunt Mary, it would say, 'Instant psycho — just add alcohol'.

She sets me up at the kitchen table so that I can draw and read while she gets the cake and scone mixture ready. She leans over me as I try to keep myself busy and off her radar. 'What are you drawing there?' She examines my picture a little closer. 'What's that big fella with all them legs doing on that boat?'

'They're not legs, they're tentacles. It's a giant octopus. And he's taking over the ship.'

'There's no such thing as giant octopuses.' Even though it's only around nine in the morning, I can tell from her fumes that she's been under the sink already.

And like an idiot I decide to go all David Attenborough on her. 'There might be. In the really deep parts of the ocean. Where no one has ventured yet.' I actually use the word 'ventured'.

Big mistake. I look at Aunt Mary. She sees the fear in my eyes as I see the fire in hers.

'So you think you know more than me, you little smart alec?'

'No, Aunt Mary. I'm sorry.'

'You know I used to be a school teacher. Back in Ireland.'

'Yes.'

'You think you know more than a qualified school teacher, do you?'

'No, Aunt Mary.'

'That's your mother coming out in you, so it is,' she hisses. 'Thinks she's such a big shot, that one, in her fancy black robes and ridiculous wig. Correct me again, young man, and I'll wash your filthy mouth out with soap.' She grabs the back of my hair. 'You got that?'

'Yes, Aunt Mary. I won't do it again.' And right now I hate my stupid father. Him and his psycho aunt. Why doesn't anyone believe me?

After that, we retreat to our corners for a while. She busies herself baking while I carry on drawing – though I reduce the size of the attacking octopus significantly. It's no longer a serious threat to the sailors; it's more something to have a bit of a laugh at and poke with a stick. Despite my concession, there's to be no mixing or bowl licking for me. Not now that I've had the audacity to suggest that there might be larger than usual molluscs lurking in the depths of the ocean somewhere.

Aunt Mary is still coming to terms with the latter part of the twentieth century so she doesn't have a DVD player. It's lucky she even has electricity. Deciding to give me a reprieve from her death stares, she relocates me to the 'sitting room' and puts on an old *Wallace & Gromit* video, which, apart from a few episodes of *Pingu* and *Spot the Dog*, are all she has for when Kate and I visit.

When Wallace forgets the crackers to take up to the cheese moon, I try to stifle my laughter with a pillow in case I'm laughing the wrong way.

I'm mid-snort when Aunt Mary summons me into the kitchen.

'Declan! I called you.'

I leap up and hit stop on the video player, which is so old it has a wood-grain finish. I race into the kitchen just as she's putting the bottle back beneath the sink.

'Yes, Aunt Mary.'

'Ah. There you are. Good boy.' She ties up a plastic bag and hands it to me. 'Be a love and bring this out to the bin for me.'

I take the rubbish bag from her and walk out through the laundry towards the backyard and realise that I'm in serious trouble. Aunt Mary owns three dogs: an Irish wolfhound, a Jack Russell and something that looks like a cross between a goat and a weasel. And like the dogs themselves, Aunt Mary isn't exactly the cleanest person in the world. It's not so much that her backyard has a bit of dog poo in it, more that her dog poo has a bit of backyard in it.

I open the laundry door and try to plan a route through the teetering, festering and steaming piles of dog crap, all of which are in various stages of decay and stench. This tiptoeing might have worked had it not been for the half-starved demented hounds leaping up at me and the rubbish bag like dolphins after a fish at Sea World, which wasn't something that I'd factored into my trip across the yard.

When I arrive at the bin, one of the dogs, the wolfhound I think, knocks me off balance and I stumble awkwardly. I only just manage to retain my footing by steadying myself on the wheelie bin, blissfully unaware that I've stepped backwards into a dog turd of such dimensions and freshness that every fly within a ten-kilometre radius is currently inbound to worship its very wonder.

Aunt Mary notices, though. Boy does she notice.

Task complete, I wander back into the kitchen, determined to stay in Aunt Mary's good books by asking if there are any other jobs that need doing. I am completely oblivious to the faeces trail that I'm leaving in my wake, like some sort of urban Hansel and Gretel.

Aunt Mary turns to look at me. She sees my turd track and practically spontaneously combusts.

A rational person would have said something like, 'Declan. Don't move. You've accidentally walked some dog poo through the house. Stay there while I help take your shoes off and then we'll get it all cleaned up.'

The thing is, if she'd said that she would probably still be alive. It's funny how these things work. Your life changes with the toss of a coin, the smear of some dog shit. But Aunt Mary wasn't a rational person. She was a raving lunatic into whose care I should never have been trusted.

'Will you look at the feckin mess you're leaving, you useless little gobshite?'

I'll tell you another thing that a rational person doesn't do. When your psycho aunt comes running at you clutching a rolling pin, a rational person doesn't just stand there and see what the psycho aunt might do with the rolling pin. A rational person goes into flight-or-fight mode. And when your attacker is a half-pissed, completely insane psycho with a hair-trigger temper who's armed with a heavy wooden rolling pin that she's waving about like a marauding Viking wielding an axe, then fight doesn't come into it either. You take flight. Even if the route of your flight takes you across said half-pissed, completely insane psycho's brand-new recently laid cream-coloured carpet.

By the time she finishes chasing me and my poo-coated shoes through the house and has cornered me in the bathroom, her new carpet looks more like the pattern was taken from a zebra.

She grabs me by the hair and holds me down, raising the rolling pin above her head as I close my eyes. She only hits me once. That's all she needs. We both hear the bone snap.

She covers my screams with her hand and carries me from the bathroom and lays me gently on the sofa. She doesn't seem to care about the crap on the carpet anymore, or that I'm now getting it on the sofa with the hand-knitted white (though not-so-white-anymore) doilies.

'You just rest there, love,' she says. 'I'll get you some ice and a couple of aspirin. You'll be right as rain.'

I curl up in a ball as she disappears into the kitchen and returns with the pills and a glass of water.

'Right so. Sit up and take these.' I do as I'm told, swigging the pills down with the water. 'Now let's put a little ice on this arm of yours.' As soon as she touches my arm, the jolt of pain is so excruciating that I immediately vomit the pills back up.

'Stop that, you disgusting boy.' She clips me over the back of my head and then hugs me by way of an apology, but this hurts my arm even more and I scream out in agony.

She covers me with a blanket and I spend the rest of the day drifting in and out of conscious-ness. At one point I stir in my delirium where I see narwhals in the hallway and hear Aunt Mary talking on the kitchen phone. I think she's speaking to Mum.

'Ah, we're having a grand old time. Making scones and cakes. He's a great little helper, so he is.'

'Mum!' I call out from the sitting room. But

I'm too weak from the pain and vomiting. She can't hear me. 'Mummy.'

Aunt Mary hears me and closes the kitchen door.

When I wake up it's after six o'clock and dark. Mum and Dad both work late so it's not surprising no one's picked me up yet. Aunt Mary is wandering around the house muttering and mumbling incoherently. She's also drinking something from a bottle. Not the one under the sink with the clear liquid. This stuff is brown.

'My arm hurts, Aunt Mary.'

'"My arm hurts, Aunt Mary,"' she mocks. She squeezes my cheeks which forces my mouth open. 'Here. See if this deadens the pain. It certainly does wonders for me.' She pours some of the brown liquid down my throat but it's so disgusting that I immediately start choking and hoick it straight back up.

'You dirty little fecker. That's a bottle of Jameson's you're throwing up. Do you know how much that costs?' She lays into me again but by this point I'm beyond caring. 'This is all your fault. If you'd watched where you were stepping, none of this would have happened.'.

'Please, Aunt Mary. I'm sorry.'

'No one will believe you fell over. No one will believe me. Just like back in Dublin. They didn't believe me then, and they won't now. You've ruined everything. I didn't ask to look after you today, and now look where it's got us.' She sways for a moment, the drink throwing her off balance.

'There's only one thing for it, God forgive me.'

She scoops me up off the sofa and half-carries, half-drags me out to her car. She opens the door and more or less throws me in the back, covering me with a dirty old blanket. She climbs in the front and turns on the engine, which splutters to life.

'Where are we going, Aunt Mary?' I ask. 'To the hospital?'

Her rosary beads clack through her fingers as her old Volkswagen coughs along the road. 'We're taking a little trip to the seaside, my darling. The air'll do us good. Give us a chance to think.' The *click clack* of her rosary beads continues all the way to the coast.

*

I don't remember how we got over the fence. Maybe I fell asleep or passed out from the pain and Aunt Mary lifted me over. I hear the crash of the waves onto the rocks far below and smell the salt spray being whipped up by the thermals. A lone seagull cries overhead.

We're standing on the edge but I feel safe

because Aunt Mary is holding my hand firmly. My other arm — the broken one — hangs limply beside me like an empty shirtsleeve. It's dark so I can't see how far it is down to the ocean. To the rocks. A watery moon drifts in and out of the clouds.

'Hail Mary, full of grace. The Lord is with thee. Blessed art thou amongst women, and blessed is the fruit of thy womb Jesus. Holy Mary, mother of God, pray for us sinners, now and at the hour of our death . . .'

'Can I help you in some way?'

'Stay back!' snaps Aunt Mary at the kind-looking man who seems to have snapped her out of her trance. 'Don't come any closer.'

'Would you like to come back to my house for a cup of tea? I just live over the road there.'

'No one will believe me,' says Aunt Mary. 'They never do.'

'I know it gets hard,' says the man, 'but there's always hope.'

Aunt Mary grips my hand tighter and sways against the breeze. She'd emptied the rest of the bottle of brown stuff down her throat on the drive. 'His mother's a barrister. Know-it-all. She'll have them throw the book at me.'

'What's his name?'

'What's it matter? He's coming with me. He has to. I have to explain it to St Peter otherwise he'll never let me in.'

'You don't need the young fella with you. God's compassion is infinite.' The man stops when he senses Aunt Mary hesitate. 'C'mon, love. Give the young fella a chance. He's hardly lived. Come and have that cup of tea. My wife's made scones. Fresh out of the oven.'

'I was making scones myself,' says Aunt Mary.

'And you will again, love. Everything will sort itself out.'

'Not this time,' she says. 'Not this time.'

She squeezes my hand tighter and steps forward.

'No!' yells the man.

I look over at the man and then back down at my hand. Although I can still feel Aunt Mary's fingers interlocked in mine, she's no longer there.

'Don't move, young fella,' says the man as he clambers over the fence. 'Stay right where you are.'

The man edges cautiously towards me. I look down into the gloom, wondering where Aunt Mary has got to but there's nothing but darkness and the distant crash of wave on rock.

'Name's Bill,' says the man. 'I'm very happy to meet you.' He scoops me up in his strong arms and I bury my face in the nape of his neck, never wanting to leave.

NON-SPACE

It seems that now is an opportune moment to remind us all that I'm actually dead. Aunt Mary didn't drag me over the cliff and into oblivion with her that night. At the last second, her basic decency shone through. But maybe she was supposed to. Maybe I'd been on borrowed time since. I'm not a fatalist, but I suppose that when your time's up, your time's up. And my time finally ran out that day on the station when my depression and anxiety became too much. The weight too heavy.

That beautiful, healing evening with Lisa, and countless others just like it, would only have happened had I paused. But I didn't pause. I carried it through and my timeline came to an abrupt stop.

Everything else is just conjecture. A fragment. A taste of what might have been. That night with Lisa in Hong Kong, when we both shared our pain like two broken souls coming together and healing, would have been a memory burner, a near-perfect moment to talk about for the rest of our lives.

And there would have been others. In Hong Kong alone, Mum and Susanne would have become besties, leaving Lisa and I free to spend more time together. We would have caught the train out to Disneyland and another day we would have gone out to Ocean Park, riding the triple-loop dragon, which darts exhilaratingly out over Repulse Bay. We would have ridden the cable car back down and then jumped a bus to Stanley Markets and walked along the beach at sunset with our fingers interlocked, feeling the sand between our toes, and we would have danced cheek to cheek as a storm rolled in, using one earpiece each from Lisa's iPod, and I would have promised to spend the rest of my life with her, or else searching for her if we ever became separated again, even though we both would undoubtedly know that our time together was drawing to a close.

Golden moments. Priceless moments. Death-bed moments. Moments to let you know that life is worth living and that you need to embrace all its joy, all its wonder, all its pain.

But in order to have those moments you have

to work through the pain, find a way out of the darkness. You have to pause. You have to live.

It's only now that I *am* dead that I truly understand it. Lisa wasn't worth dying for. She was worth living for.

TWO YEARS AFTER

The intercom buzzes but I haven't got a clue how to operate the thing.

'Mum!' I knock on the bathroom door. 'Are you in the shower?'

'I can't hear you properly,' she calls back. 'I'm in the shower.'

'Someone's here but I don't know how to let them in.'

'Well, who is it?'

'I don't know.'

'Look at the screen,' she yells back through the steam.

'Oh, right.'

The intercom buzzes again and I do as Mum

instructs but reel back slightly. I don't know what the hell is out there but it kind of looks like a whale rolling and sliming over a bunch of headstones. Headstones that are connected by wires . . .

'Kate, you idiot. Don't put your stupid mouth up to the camera.'

Kate laughs down the intercom. 'Let us in, douche.'

'Us?'

'Dad's coming up.'

I press the big silver button and downstairs the door buzzes open.

A couple of minutes later, Kate bustles in with her bags. Dad kind of hovers around behind her.

'How was your weekend?' I ask.

'Cool,' she says. 'Went to the zoo.'

'And they let you out again?'

'Don't, Declan,' says Dad. 'She had a nice time.'

'Hello, Father,' I reply, annoying him with my formality.

I look at Dad's hair and try not to let him see me smirking. In all honesty it actually looks quite good. I just wonder if the horse misses it.

Mum emerges from the bathroom in her robe and with a towel wrapped around her head.

'Hey, baby doll,' says Mum, giving Kate a hug. 'Shaun.'

'Gabriella.'

269

It's like a friggin roll call.

'You're back early,' says Mum. 'I thought you were dropping her this evening. That was the arrangement.'

'Yeah, sorry,' says Dad. 'Slight change of plan. I have to fly to New York this evening.'

'So you're going?' says Mum.

'We're going to look at apartments.'

'"We're"?' says Mum, inviting the elephant into the room so that it can plonk itself on Dad's face.

'Yes,' replies Dad, defiantly. '*We*.'

Here are three sure-fire signs that your father is having a midlife crisis:

1. He dumps his wife for a younger, blonder, dafter version, whose only qualification is an advanced degree in lip-gloss application.

2. He buys a red (seriously – *red*) convertible that actually complements the younger, blonder, dafter version's lip-gloss.

3. He invests a small fortune in the sort of hair transplant that only talk-show hosts and international cricketers can carry off and even then, only just.

There's a part of me that understands he's starting to feel the sand that remains in his hourglass running out at an alarming rate and he wants to recapture what's left of his rapidly declining youth. So I kind of get it. But seriously, his midlife crisis is so clichéd he should be arrested for showing such a cavalier regard for stereotype. Still, at least he's ditched the beige pants and Hawaiian shirts for the sort of smouldering black-turtleneck look that was generally the domain of Jean-Paul Sartre and Albert Camus as they strolled along the banks of the Seine at dusk discussing existentialism, long cigars and Sartre's belief that he was being followed by crayfish.

Since their marriage went down the gurgler, I'm happy to spend time with Dad (even if we still haven't been fishing), but I steadfastly refuse to waste one more second in the company of Cindy (Mindy, Bindy, or whatever the stupid-y she claims to be) – someone who, when she heard that Mum was a barrister, thought she worked in a cafe.

'So your mind's made up?' asks Mum.

'It's too good an opportunity to pass up,' replies Dad.

'What about the kids?'

'Well, Katie's already looking forward to spending the holidays with us.'

'You have a son, too.'

'Really, Gabriella?' replies Dad, applying the sarcasm with a high pressure hose. 'I wasn't aware of that.' Dad turns to me. 'You're welcome to come, too. You know that, Dec.'

I nod.

'Do you want to stay for lunch?' says Mum, changing the subject and saving me because, seriously, I do not want to spend my uni holidays having Mindy play step-mum, especially when she's closer to my age than she is to Dad's.

'I can't,' says Dad. 'I have to go home and pack. And besides, Mindy's waiting.'

'You left her in the car?' says Mum. 'I hope you wound one of the windows down, or she'll overheat and run around the back seat.'

'Ha ha,' says Dad with possibly the worst comeback in history. 'It's a convertible.' Like that's the important bit.

'Seriously. Bring her up.' Mum turns on the coffee machine. 'We could always use a laugh.'

'Okay, I'm leaving now,' says Dad, 'if you're going to be mean.'

'Mean?' snorts Mum. 'How old are you, five?'

'It's really unbecoming, Gabriella. You know Mindy has an economics degree, and yet just because she's blonde . . . If you can't say anything nice, don't say anything.'

'Well, that's me struck mute. No, seriously,' continues Mum, whose muteness lasts about two seconds. 'Bring her up. Kate probably has some old books. She could always do some colouring in while she waits for your hair to set.'

I try not to snort but fail.

'If you went bald,' says Dad, 'what would you do?'

'Well, I'll tell you what I wouldn't do,' says Mum. 'I wouldn't stick a dead porcupine on my head and expect to be taken seriously.'

'Bye, Katie Bear.' Dad gives Kate a hug and marches off in a huff.

Mum looks at me and nods towards the door suggesting that I should go after him.

When I get outside, Dad is waiting by the elevator.

'Have a good trip, Dad. I hope things work out.'

'You seriously mean that?'

I nod. 'Yeah. With work, anyway.'

'But not with . . .'

'Cindy Doll?'

'Mindy.'

'Dad, it's embarrassing. She's young enough to be your daughter.'

'She's twenty-nine.'

'Is that her age or IQ?'

'I'm forty-six, Declan. You do the maths.'

'Dad. She'll want to go clubbing. And you dance like a praying mantis caught in a spider web.'

We look at each other not quite knowing what to say. We've never quite known what to say.

I have to admit, I've been grossly unfair on Dad with his midlife crisis list. Firstly, it was Mum who ended their marriage, not him, and not only does Mindy have an economics degree, she also has an MBA. Second, while they do have a red convertible, it's actually Mindy's not Dad's. He still drives around in his clapped-out Triumph that belongs in a museum not a garage. And third, while he *did* get a Ken-doll hair transplant, it was a birthday gift from Mindy so he didn't really have a whole lot of choice.

'I know you blame me,' says Dad, completely out of left field. 'With Aunt Mary and everything. I didn't know how damaged she was.'

I hesitate. We've never had this conversation. The closest we've been to intimacy throughout the whole ordeal with Aunt Mary was his writing 'Get well soon, son' on my cast. 'I tried to tell you. Both of you.'

'She left you in the car while she leapt off the cliff. I can't even begin to imagine what that was like. How terrifying it was. The not knowing what was going on.'

'That's not exactly what happened.'

'What do you mean?'

I take a deep breath. It's time he knew. 'She tried to take me with her. That was her plan.'

'How could you possibly know her plan? You were six years old.'

'I was there, Dad. I stood on the edge of the cliff with her. She dragged me over the fence and she was squeezing my hand while she was summoning up the courage to jump.'

Dad is practically speechless. 'But why would she want to . . .'

'To cover up what happened. With my arm.'

'You tripped over, taking out the rubbish. That's what your mother . . .'

I shake my head. 'She clubbed me with a rolling pin.'

Dad is gobsmacked but it's right he knows. Finally.

'This guy – he just came out of nowhere. He intervened. Talked her round. Got her to let me go.' I can still feel her squeezing my hand sometimes, late at night when I can't sleep.

Dad looks stunned, as if he's rethinking his whole life. 'Why have you been lying to me all these years? Mum said you were in the car.'

'That's what she wanted you to believe. She . . .'

'Protected me.'

I nod.

'I didn't even understand it myself at the time. That night was just a blur. It was all jumbled up.' I do remember the police taking me to the station, letting me turn on the siren. And I remember Mum and Dad picking me up from there – I must have known our home number.

'It was only when I thought about it later, when I started having nightmares, that I remembered everything. I woke up screaming one night. Mum came in and rubbed my back and asked me what I'd been dreaming about. When I told her … she said to me she thought it might be best if you didn't know.'

'Why?'

'She didn't want you blaming yourself. Said that if you didn't have any fond memories of Aunt Mary, then no one would. It wasn't a conspiracy, Dad. It's just how it was.'

'But it's just led to a lifetime of resentment. From you. From your mum.'

'It's not your fault Mary was out of her friggin' mind.'

'But you used to tell us that she hit you.'

I start to choke up because I can see that Dad's eyes are watering. I swallow the pain that Dad is feeling. I see now that it was wrong of Mum to keep this from him. Although I think she did it with the best intentions, it created a sense of us versus him and he never knew how to fix it, because he never knew why it had come about. I feel for Dad right now, I truly do. None of this is his fault. Mum instigated the marriage breakup, my suicide attempt was due to his aunt, not him. All he's trying to do is stitch *his* life back together and I haven't exactly been there for him.

'That's right. I used to tell you. *Both* of you. And I don't resent Mum.'

'Just me.'

'I don't resent you, Dad. Never have.'

'But you're always laughing at me. Poking fun.'

'That's because you used to do — and still *do* do — some pretty dumb stuff, and that's how families work. We take the piss out of each other.'

'I'm sorry I let you down, Declan.' A single tear runs down Dad's cheek. He doesn't try to hide it.

'You didn't let me down, Dad. I just work better with Mum, like you do with Kate. It's just one of those things. It's no one's fault.'

We stare at each other, not quite knowing what to say or where to go from here. Dad's good with accounts, not words.

I break the silence. 'I reckon we're going to work better as adults.'

Dad wipes his eyes and holds out his hand. 'Deal.'

I look at his proffered hand. I don't want to leave him hanging, but still. 'What is this?' I say. 'The nineteen-forties? Come here.'

I pull Dad to me and hug him. Really hug him. It's the first time we've hugged in as long as I remember. His body wracks with sobs. I leave my tears on his shoulder. But even though we're father and son and there's so much left to say, we still can't quite carry off the hug and after a moment it descends into one of those back-patting deals.

We pull apart and look at each other.

'If you come to New York, I'll buy you a beer.'

'*When* I come to New York, you'll buy me a slab. And you'll tell me how you managed to get a hot chick like Bindy.'

'Mindy.'

'Whatever.'

The lift door dings open and Dad steps in.

'See you, Dec.'

'Later, Dad.'

The doors start to close.

'And don't forget,' I shout after him, 'you still owe me that fishing trip.'

'It's a deal,' he yells through the door.

'And shave your head,' I call back.

From the depths of the elevator shaft comes a distant, 'Bite me.'

*

We celebrate our first full night in our new home with Thai takeaway and a bottle of Moët. Even Kate is allowed a small glass, which she pronounces disgusting and, despite Mum's yelp, tips down the sink and replaces with some lime cordial. Philistine.

We've swapped the burbs for the inner city so it's closer to Mum's work and to Sydney Uni for me. Kate has a forty-five-minute train ride to school and back each day but she's okay with it and she and Mum are talking about her spending six months here and then six months at school in New York, which Kate finds as exciting as Mindy (Cindy, Bindy, Windy) won't.

'So tell us about Kim,' says Mum out of the blue.

'How do you know about that?'

'She called your mobile a couple of times while you were lugging boxes up from the garage; I thought I should get it for you. She sounds nice. And she's certainly keen. You meet at uni?'

'Yeah. She's studying commerce/law. Though she wants to be a humanitarian lawyer.'

'Good for her. So you and Lisa . . .?'

'We email sometimes. But . . .'

'But . . .?'

'We're in different hemispheres, Mum. How's that supposed to work? Besides. She's seeing someone. They met through her church. He's a bit older than her. Works in finance. Probably a total douche.'

Lisa and I were good together. We'd both been abused – she more so than me – and we helped each other heal. But things pass. We learn. We grow. We move on. We just have to avoid killing ourselves over pain that will pass. Though I do miss her. I miss her smile. I miss her subtle sense of humour, too. I miss her.

'She'll be right with Susanne looking out for her.'

I'm not being entirely truthful with Mum about Lisa. Yes, she is seeing someone, as I am. But we still email and text each other about eight or nine times a day. With Maaaate enrolled at some private college in Perth studying business, and Chris backpacking around Europe with his 'friend', and despite my growing relationship with Kim, Lisa has long since become my best friend. I miss my best friend. And I miss what might have been.

EIGHT YEARS
AFTER SYDNEY

A phone call at four in the morning never brings good news. When that phone call occurs at four o'clock on the morning of your wedding day, it's only ever going to bring disaster. And I'm not about to be disappointed. Actually, I am going to be more than disappointed with both the news it brings and the subsequent ramifications.

Kim stirs in her sleep but my ringtone is soft enough not to wake her. I'm happy to let this call go through to the keeper. It'll probably just be Chris or Maaaate still whining about the fact that I didn't want to kick on with their bucks party/ pub crawl last night, preferring instead to bail around midnight for home and bed with Kim.

'It's bad luck to sleep with the bride the night before the wedding,' said Chris as he saw me into a taxi at the end of the night.

'It used to be bad luck just to *see* the bride the night before her wedding,' offered Maaaate, as he stood on the side of the road, tucking into an ill-advised service-station kebab. 'What's next? Bad luck to sleep with the bride *and* the bridesmaids the night before her wedding?'

I wound down the window. 'Maaaate. That's my fiancée and her friends you're talking about.'

Maaaate buried his face into his road-kill kebab and then came up for air. 'No it's not. I'm not referring to Kimberly; I'm just talking hyper . . . hoperthetical-l-ly . . . hi-i-iperthotical-l–'

'Pathetically?' suggested Chris.

'I'm out of here,' I said. 'Come round early tomorrow for breakfast. I'll make eggs benedict with smoked salmon and industrial-strength coffee, then we're going to go for a morning surf and do blokey stuff.'

'Like what?' said Chris. 'Play darts and dress up as lumberjacks?'

'If that works for you,' I replied.

And so I ditched them on the side of the road with Chris, my best man, looking forlorn, and Maaaate staring into his kebab, perhaps wondering if its contents were in fact fit for human consumption.

Now it's the morning of my wedding. My phone rings again, but this time Kim *does* stir. 'Declan. Your phone keeps ringing.'

'Sorry, babe. I've been trying to ignore it.'

'You'd better answer it,' she says. 'It might be important.'

'Maaaate's probably eaten an entire Krispy Kreme franchise and is now in the emergency liposuction ward.'

Kim doesn't laugh at my joke. Kim thinks Maaaate (or 'Simon', as she insists on calling him, even though he has asked her not to) is deeply sad, which is why he eats so much. When in actual fact Maaaate's one of the happiest people you could ever meet and he eats so much not because he's deeply sad but because he's deeply fat and absolutely loves food just about as much as he loathes exercise, which is why he opted out of the corporate world and is now a trainee chef.

I pick up my mobile but I don't have my glasses on so I can't make out who it is. 'Just a sec.' I take the phone out to the kitchen and sit at the breakfast bar, not wanting to disturb Kim.

'Hello.'

I was right. When your phone rings at four in the morning, it brings nothing but bad news. The worst kind, in fact.

After I hang up, I walk back into the bedroom

and stare at Kim's silhouette, knowing that our lives are about to change. Mine already has. I want to let her sleep a while longer, to put it off, but I can see that she's aware of my presence.

'Who was it?'

'There's been an accident.'

Kim sits up in bed. 'Oh, my God. Who?'

'Lisa.'

'What happened?'

I sit down on the bed. Kim crawls over and hugs me.

'Susanne, her mum, was pretty vague. She was hit by a car.'

'Is she . . .?'

I shake my head. 'She's in a coma. It doesn't look good, though.'

Kim pulls away and stares at me. 'You're going, aren't you?'

Guilty as charged. 'I have to. I need to. Sorry.'

Kim nods. 'You should. She is your best friend, after all.'

I don't think Kim means it as a criticism, but I still feel a slight stab to the heart. I take my travel bag out of the wardrobe and start throwing in a few things.

'Thanks for being so understanding. Not everyone would.' Who am I kidding? 'No one would.'

'We can get married any day,' she says. 'I mean, let's face it, we've been living together for two years already. Today is – was – just the official ceremony.' Luckily we opted for a small, civil service in a park with only a few guests and a small party at a restaurant afterwards. Still, I feel guilty that Kim will have to do all the ringing around to reorganise things.

I take my passport from the bedside drawer.

'Can I ask you a question?' says Kim.

'Of course.'

'How many people would you drop everything – including your wedding – for, to fly halfway across the world to be with?'

'Only one,' I reply, without even thinking. 'Just Lisa.' As soon as it's out there I realise that I can't take it back. I could seriously kick myself. 'And *you*, of course.' But no matter how nonchalantly I put it, the ship has sailed. I realise now that the 'of course' made it worse. Kim doesn't look shocked or even surprised. In fact, she looks like she's known this for some time.

'Declan. I need to be with someone who would drop everything to be with me. I can't be anyone's "and".'

I sit down next to Kim and rub her back. 'It was just a slip of the tongue.'

'No, it wasn't. It's when we don't plan what we're going to say that we're at our most honest and our most vulnerable.'

I try to pull her to me but she tenses up. 'Why are you so suspicious, anyway? She's married.'

'I can't be your consolation prize, Declan. I'd be your wife but Lisa would still be your best friend. I need to be both.'

'You are. You will be,' I say, but I don't sound too convincing. I change tune, Susanne's words hitting me again. 'Let's not do this now,' I whisper. 'Lisa's dying.'

I give her a hug and pick up my bag. She doesn't say anything. 'Thanks for understanding.'

I walk towards the door.

'Declan.'

I turn back to face Kim when I'd rather be anywhere else. I know what's coming. We both do.

'I know you need to be with her. I get that. I truly do. And you are an amazing person because of it. But I need someone who'll fly across the world to be with *me*. So if you *do* go — and I believe you should because she *is* your best friend — then the wedding isn't postponed. It's off.'

It already is.

*

The problem with leaving your fiancée at your North Sydney apartment at four-thirty in the morning to fly to your stricken best friend's bedside is that by the time you get down to the street and google flights to Hong Kong on your phone and realise that there isn't one for another four-and-a-half hours, you can't then go skulking back up to your apartment and slip back into bed for a couple of hours. You can't even slink back up and sit at the breakfast bar and have a coffee. Having made such a grand gesture and dramatic departure, I have no choice now other than to follow it through or I'll look and feel like a complete idiot.

Fortunately it's only a short walk to the train station. Unfortunately I have about a thirty-minute wait until the trains start running. It gives me time to think about the decision I've made, and what shocks me is that my decision doesn't come as a surprise. Have I always known, deep down, that Lisa is more than a friend?

By the time I get to the Cathay Pacific sales desk at the airport, some residual memory – as well as the lanterns and dragons they have decorating the desk – reminds me that it's only a couple of days until Chinese New Year, meaning that quite possibly the only way I'll be going to Hong Kong today is by renting a canoe.

'*Kung hei fat choy*,' I say to the sales clerk.

'Good morning, sir. How may I help you?'

'I need to get on the next available flight to Hong Kong.'

She pulls the sort of face that makes me wonder if I should start work on that canoe. Still, she goes through the pretence of checking seat availability.

'I'm sorry, sir. We're fully booked today. Chinese New Year.'

'When's the next available —'

'I could waitlist you.' She checks her screen again. 'But there are already twenty people ahead of you.'

I try the sympathy card, knowing that it's next to useless. 'My friend's in hospital, you see, and it doesn't look good. And I know it's no one's fault, certainly not Cathay's, but is there anything you can do?'

She taps her computer again, perhaps looking to see if there's anything under the Cathay Pacific 'Friend's had an accident and probably won't make it' special reserved-seating clause.

'There are a few seats still available in business class if you have the means.'

This lights me up. 'Oh, that's brilliant. Yes, please. Get me on this flight. Whatever it takes. First class if I have to.'

'Don't you want to know how much it costs?'

I shake my head. 'She's my best friend. I don't care how much.'

The sales clerk takes my credit card and smiles at me. 'So she really *is* in hospital?'

'Yeah. Of course. I wish she wasn't, but I wouldn't lie about something like that.'

'You'd be amazed what people will say and do to get on a flight.'

She processes my credit card and hands me the receipt. I look down at the charge, preparing for a serious cringe and knowing full well that my English teacher's salary is about to take a massive hit. 'Er, I think there must be some mistake. This is the economy rate, surely.' I point to the charge.

'Oops,' says the sales clerk with mock shock. 'Have a pleasant flight, Mr O'Malley.'

I look at her and am practically speechless. Because of the doom and gloom thrown up by the nightly news, you sometimes forget how wonderful people actually are. 'May flights of angels sing you to your rest,' I say, then remember that that's the sort of thing you say to someone when they are dying, or at least when they were dying in the Elizabethan period. 'And I mean that in the strictest non-celestial sense.'

*

No matter how comfortable Cathay Pacific business class actually is (and it is pretty bloody comfortable) at thirty-five thousand feet, you are kind of isolated from the world. I don't know if Lisa is still in a coma, if she's alive or dead. Unlike Lisa, I'm not religious, but I do find myself praying that she will hang in there. That she finds the strength to fight. To live. And if God needs to take someone early to balance the books or whatever, then let it be me. She doesn't deserve this. There was that time years ago when I nearly called it quits on the train platform anyway, when I almost gave up my life willingly, so carelessly, so recklessly, so cheaply, so pointlessly. But I paused. And I've had a wonderful – what is it – eight plus years, since that day. Bonus years. Amazing years that I wouldn't have traded for the world. Years I would now happily trade for Lisa's life.

Being on a long-haul flight, especially a morning one where you can't get hammered at least until it's midday somewhere, you're kind of left alone with your thoughts. And after offering my life for Lisa's, my mind turns to those people that I would die for.

Kim. Although she didn't believe me, if there's one word to sum up Kim it would be 'perfection'. So drop-dead gorgeous that she paid her way through uni modelling. She is a truly wonderful and intelligent person and I am (was) lucky to have her in my life. But I pretty much left her at the altar to be with my married friend who may already be dead. Now that I think about it, there was something missing from our relationship. And I'm not sure if that something wasn't me.

Mum. Since the divorce, she has wanted for neither attention nor company but seems to be at her happiest when she's on her own. She travels a lot for both business and pleasure. She and Kate still live together, while Kate finishes uni, and she's still my hero. The best mum anyone could ever have. Ever. She's not just my mum, she's my friend, and I am so happy I was able to spare her the lifetime of agony that my suicide would have rained down on her. She deserves better and because of my pause she has it.

Kate. She recently finished her honours degree in biology (big shock there) and is now studying for her PhD in neuroscience so she can finally understand or dissect her own brain, I imagine. When it comes to academics, she kind of makes me look like a sea monkey – and I'm currently doing my master's in English literature. As far as I'm aware, she's only had one serious-ish relationship, and that was with a guy ('Donga', if you can credit it) who worked on a fishing trawler. Watching them together (and they *are* still together as far as I'm aware) is kind of like watching Madame Curie dating Fred Flintstone. Donga had a thing for neck tattoos, the Southern Cross – his ute was covered in stickers of them – and a strong belief that the only degree worth having was awarded by the university of life. Seriously, holding a conversation with Donga on anything other than fishing, engines, football (rugby league) and refugees (he held some pretty strong views there until Mum shut him up one Sunday lunch) is like trying to communicate with toast.

Dad. He moved to New York and actually married Mindy (Bindy, Cindy, ~~Windy~~) who is now – hold onto your stomach – pregnant. I started spending time with them because part of Dad's package to relocate to New York was six-monthly visitation trips for his children. (Though before I became engaged to Kim, I would insist on his paying for the triangle – Sydney, New York, Hong Kong, Sydney – so that I could catch up with Lisa.) Dad eventually bowed to societal pressure (well, me and Mum) and either shaved off or melted his hair and now sports the shorn-down look. Just as I thought, we *do* work better as adults, and though we *still* haven't been fishing, I really do like spending time with him.

Lisa. We lost touch for a little while in our early twenties when we started seeing other people but reconnected after she got married, when she started emailing me again. She started studying languages like Susanne had but added on nursing when she realised she could combine the two. Lisa's husband, Gary, works in finance. Just why she married him is a complete mystery to me. They met through their church and my guess is that he represented safety for her. Boring to the point at which you would seriously consider throttling him rather than hear him utter one more word on the subject of derivatives or the share price index (whatever the hell derivatives and the share price index are), Lisa's husband has the emotional intelligence and warmth of a lump of wood. Spending time with him is about as interesting as watching a four-hour instructional DVD on basket weaving. God knows what Lisa was thinking. On one of my trips, shortly after they were married, they took me out to dinner. Gary had recently been on one of those corporate personal development courses and so he spent the evening regaling us on how he could cure misery and depression. The secret, he maintained (and the alarming thing was that he was deadly serious), was to draw a smiley face on one of your fingers and if people started to get you down, you simply hold up your smiley-face finger and everyone would fall about laughing at the sheer side-splitting hilarity of it all. When the evening was finally over, I wanted to hold up my finger to Gary, only it didn't have a smiley face on it. I was disappointed with Lisa for settling when she could have had anyone.

When we said goodnight outside the restaurant and Lisa gave me a kiss and a hug, Gary said, 'Steady on there, Declan. She's *my* wife.' I then had to endure the agony of watching them stroll off with Gary's arm wrapped around Lisa's shoulder.

And that thought, that image, plagues me for the remainder of the flight. The best thing I ever did in my life was pausing on the station that day. The worst thing I ever did was letting Lisa go.

EIGHT YEARS AFTER HONG KONG

Susanne is just emerging from Lisa's room when I arrive. She's shocked to see me, which is not surprising, I suppose, given that in our hasty exchange on the phone this morning I neglected to tell her that I was coming.

Susanne leads me towards a small waiting room that is just along the corridor.

'What's the latest?'

Susanne asks me if I want a coffee. When I decline she makes one for herself.

'The good news is that she's out of danger.' Susanne's voice cracks. I can see that there's more to come. I help her into a seat and finish making her coffee.

'And the bad news?'

'She'll never walk again.'

Now *I* need to sit down. I want to scream at the injustice of it all but there's no one to whom or nowhere I can direct my anger so I just have to choke it down for Lisa's sake. For Susanne's.

'She also lost the baby.'

'She was pregnant?' I reply, stating the bloody obvious.

Susanne nods. 'It was only a few weeks. I guess I'm not going to be a grandmother after all.'

I gently rub Susanne's back.

'Is Gary in there with her?' I gesture towards Lisa's room.

'He's at work.'

'What the . . .?'

'Reckons he had a meeting that he couldn't get out of. Said it was pointless him being here while she was unconscious. Wants me to call him if there's any change.'

'Oh, so he *can* get out of this meeting.'

'I know, Declan,' says Susanne. She takes a sip of coffee. 'He's a jerk. But he's her jerk.'

'And has there been any change?'

'She came round just a minute ago. I was coming out to phone Gary when I ran into you.'

'Does she know? About not being able to walk?'

Susanne nods. 'How on earth is she going to cope, Declan? She loves her work. Lives for it.

How can she reach the beds and look after her patients in a wheelchair? Before she fell pregnant, she was even thinking of going back to uni and studying to become a doctor.'

Susanne is thinking too far ahead. 'Let's get her through this first. Then we'll see what she can do. One step at a time.' I cringe at my clumsy wording but fortunately Susanne is too caught up in her thoughts to have processed it.

'Would you like to see her?'

'Is she up to visitors?'

'She's resting, but I know seeing you will do her a world of good.'

Susanne and I walk back along the corridor to Lisa's room. 'She's always talking about you.' She stops and looks at me. 'You want my opinion?'

I don't think I have much choice.

'I don't believe in destiny, but if ever two people were supposed to be together, it was the two of you. God knows why you let it go. Now look at her.' Susanne has tears cascading down her face, anger in her eyes. 'I blame you, Declan.'

What?

'You'd both been through hell and were drawn to each other because of it. You saved each other, but you stuffed it up. You both did. You let it go and now it's *all* gone to hell.'

We arrive at Lisa's room. Susanne stops,

composes herself as best she can and wipes her face. 'Sorry,' she says quietly, and gives me a hug. 'Just needed to vent.'

I hate that she's right.

'Hey, baby doll,' says Susanne quietly. 'Look who I found lurking around the corridor.'

Lisa opens her eyes and looks at me. Despite what's happened to her she smiles. My heart quickens at seeing her lying there immobile. I want to crawl in beside her, spoon her, and never let her go.

'Declan. What are you doing here?'

'Oh, you know. Just passing. Saw your light on.'

I walk over to her bed. Given her condition, I don't know what I can and can't do. I kiss her cheek and taste the salty tang of grief. I sit down on the chair next to her bed and hold her hand, interlocking our fingers like old times before . . . before it all went to hell.

Susanne holds up her mobile. 'I'll just go and call . . .'

'No!' snaps Lisa. 'I don't want him here.'

'Lisa.'

'Please, Mum.'

'Darling. He has a right to know about . . . things.' It's too big to say.

When Susanne goes, Lisa turns away from me to hide her fresh tears. 'What are you doing here? You're supposed to be getting married today.'

I shake my head.

She turns back to face me when I don't say anything. 'Oh, Declan. I ruined your wedding day. I've ruined everything.'

'It wasn't you. It wasn't working. We saw it just in time. Dodged a bullet, really.'

There's a long silence.

'I'm going to be stuck in a wheelchair for the rest of my life. My baby's gone . . . I don't want to live, Declan.'

I squeeze her hand. 'It's awful at the moment but the pain will pass.'

'How do you know?'

'I've been down this path, remember? When I thought I'd lost you all those years ago. I didn't want to live then, but I made myself push on. And look at the times we've had – the times I've had – since. You have to give it time. You have to pause. The sun will smile on you again, babe. The good moments are just over the horizon. That's a promise.'

'Declan,' says Lisa.

'Yeah?'

'You just called me "babe".'

'Sorry,' I reply. 'Slip of the tongue.' I've been doing that quite a bit today.

Lisa squeezes my hand. 'No. I liked it. Reminds me of how things used to be.'

'Rest now, Lisa,' I say. 'You need to regain your strength.'

'For what?' she says.

'So you can get back to . . .' I trail off. I don't know her life. Not really.

'Back to my life?' she asks. 'What life? My life's over, Declan. All I am now is a burden.'

'You ever heard of Erik Weihenmayer?' I don't even wait for her to reply. 'Completely blind but he climbed Everest.'

'Good for him.'

'Anne Frank. Holed up in a wall with her family, hiding from the Nazis. Wrote one of the biggest-selling books of the twentieth century. Jean-Dominique Bauby. Locked-in syndrome. Could only move his left eyelid. Managed to blink a book – *The Diving Bell and the Butterfly*. And it strikes me that Stephen Hawking has done pretty well for himself. Even appeared on *The Simpsons* and *The Big Bang Theory*.'

'I know you're making a point but I –'

'Your life's not over, Lisa. It's just taken a different direction.' I've just decided that tonight, when visiting hours are over, I'm going to go out and buy *The Diary of Anne Frank*, *The Diving Bell and the Butterfly*, *A Brief History of Time*, and Erik Weihenmayer's autobiography if he has one, and I'm going to sit by her bed and read them to her. One after the other. And then, when she's ready, I'm going to take her shopping for a wheelchair . . .

I've overstepped. It's not my role to do any of that. I lost that right when she said 'I do' to Gary.

As if reading my thoughts, Lisa squeezes my hand again. 'When he comes, I want you here. Mum, too. I don't want to be left alone with him.'

'Why?'

'Please say you'll stay. Promise me.'

'I'm not going anywhere. I promise, babe.'

I stroke Lisa's forehead until she drifts off to sleep. I'm tired myself so I shuffle the chair a little closer to the bed and lean back and close my eyes as the minutes, the hours, the years just drift away.

*

'What do you think you're doing holding my wife's hand?'

I open my eyes not having a clue where I am. I'm obviously holding someone's wife's hand and her husband isn't at all happy about it. I kind of get it and so I release my grip.

I remember where I am. And although I've just let go of Lisa's hand, she refuses to let go of mine. She squeezes even tighter, so I squeeze right back.

Susanne comes in after Gary, obviously having heard his rant. 'Relax, Gary. It's only Declan.'

Gary turns on Susanne. 'If anything happens to him, I'll kill her.'

I don't understand why he's being protective of me, and then it dawns on me. He's talking about their baby. He doesn't know that Lisa has had a miscarriage. Lisa squeezes my hand even tighter.

Susanne glares at Gary. She has fire in her eyes. 'If anything happens to *her*, I'll kill *you*.'

I'm not fast enough to prevent Gary from pushing Susanne back and calling her all sorts of vile names, his face millimetres away from hers. But I am quick enough to prevent him for doing it for very long. Before I and, more importantly, *he*, realises what's happened, I have his arm behind his back and the rest of him shoved up against the wall.

'Let go of me!' he yells. He struggles against me but I have him pinned.

'You need to settle down. Then I'll let you go.'

'It's too late,' says Susanne. 'The baby's gone.'

'Everyone's a little on edge, and that's understandable,' I say, trying to be the voice of reason. 'But we all need to calm down a little for Lisa's sake.'

'For *her* sake?' yells Gary. 'That bitch killed my baby. She should be up for murder.'

'Get out!' screams Lisa. 'Get him out of here, Declan!'

I've been calm up until this point but now he's got my hackles up. 'She's not an incubator. She's a person. And she wants you out.'

I nod to Susanne, who opens the door. I shove Gary outside, letting him go in the process. He turns and glares at me.

'Get out of my way!' he yells. 'I'm going to see my wife. That's my right.' He starts towards me.

'You want to see her, you'll have to come through me. It'll end badly for one of us, and I don't think it'll be me.' He stops in his tracks and so I try reasoning with him again. 'I don't know what's gone on but I'll do whatever Lisa wants and right now she doesn't want to see you, so you're not coming in. I'll talk to her, and once everyone has calmed down . . .'

The noise we're making has attracted attention, and a nurse or matron is coming along the corridor with a security guard.

The conversation takes place in Cantonese but I get the gist of it from Gary's gesticulating. He wants to see his wife but *I* won't let him in.

The security guard turns to me. 'You need to stand aside, sir. This man has every right to see his own wife.'

I eyeball the security guard. 'Why don't you ask what she wants?'

Fortunately Susanne emerges from the room

and verifies what I'm saying. The nurse goes into the room while there is a stand-off in the corridor.

'Get out of my way or I'll . . .'

'Or you'll what? Sit on me? Quote the latest share price index to me? Bore me to death?'

The nurse returns and informs Gary that he's not allowed in. He looks at me, turns and leaves. I genuinely feel for him. I don't really understand what's going on, but part of Gary's life has been destroyed too and I feel awful that I've taken on a bouncer's role. If I were him I'd hate me, too.

Having returned to check on Lisa, the nurse comes back out and actually apologises to me.

Susanne also comes out and tells me that she's going to duck out and get us some lunch because despite everything that's happened to her, Lisa has a craving for a Quarter Pounder.

Lisa's eyes are all bloodshot when I resume my seat beside her.

I'm still playing catch-up. 'What just happened? Why won't you see Gary?'

Lisa looks at the wall for a moment. She takes a deep breath. 'It was our wedding anniversary yesterday and we were having dinner out. Everything should have been perfect. I was pregnant, I only just found out; Gary had just been made partner, and I was excited because I was thinking of going back to uni to study medicine.

But when I told him about studying he laughed at me. He said it was my place to raise the children now that I was pregnant. Nothing more. When I insisted that I could do both he actually thumped the table and said that I was being stupid. That I was selfish. That it was my job to support him and the children and that if I wanted to do something, then after the baby was born I should take up a hobby like yoga or tennis, but there was to be no more talk about further study.

'I realised right there and then what I had known for some time. I actually loathed him. We never discussed anything. Never talked. Not like you and I did, anyway. He didn't read novels. Thought they were a waste of time. He actually used to laugh at art. Said it was pointless. And if we ever went to the movies, I had to explain what was going on. We went to see an arty French movie once and I think he blew a circuit board in his brain. Anyway, I held my ground. Said that I was going to study and that was that. The argument continued on the way down in the elevator and out onto the street. Eventually he compromised and said that once the baby was born, if I still wanted to study medicine then we would talk about it.

'I felt this huge sense of relief: he'd heard me for the first time in our relationship, and maybe I didn't loathe him after all. Then he put his arms around me and hugged me and said that it was all just my hormones talking and that once I'd had the baby, I would dismiss all thoughts about becoming a doctor and be content to raise our babies. I just turned and looked at him and he gave me this daft grin. I knew that I had to get away from him. I had to escape. And so I ran. I ran out onto the road but a taxi . . .' She stops. Enough said.

I squeeze her hand. 'I'm so sorry, Lisa.'

'You know the first thing I thought about when they told me that I was paraplegic?'

I shake my head.

'I thought that you and I would never get to go motorcycling through Europe after all.'

For one of the few times since my breakdown, I'm stuck for words.

Lisa obviously sees that I'm struggling with this. 'I hope Mum hurries back with lunch,' she says, changing the subject. 'I'm starving.'

When Susanne arrives back, Lisa has two bites of her Quarter Pounder and announces that she's full. That she's had enough. I don't know if she's talking about lunch or life.

NINE YEARS AFTER

I stayed for two months. We talked, we read, we discussed rehabilitation and what she could still do. I took on the role that I was always supposed to. I became Lisa's best friend and anchor. Between us we bought her a kick-arse, all-terrain wheelchair. My school gave me leave without pay on compassionate grounds and although my accommodation in Hong Kong was free (technically I stayed in Lisa's old bedroom at Susanne's while Lisa was in hospital, though in reality I hardly left her side in case Gary turned up unannounced), I was still paying half the rent on the North Sydney apartment that Kim and I had taken out a long lease on and eventually things became tight. I had to return to Sydney and go back to work.

Although we stayed in touch by email and text, I had to give Lisa time to grieve her disability: to deny, to be angry, to bargain, to be depressed, to accept, and to divorce that a-hole she had mistakenly attached herself to. I was with her all the way. And while all that was going on in the background, I was busy finishing my master's thesis and writing my first book — about depression and creativity — so that no English department at any high school in the world would knock me back if they had a position vacant. Because for the first time in my life I had a plan.

Almost a year to the day since I visited Lisa in hospital, Susanne buzzes me up to their modified apartment in North Point.

Susanne hugs me at the door, having clearly forgiven me for messing things up.

I kick off my shoes in the vestibule. 'How is she?'

'She's in a good place. Got a high distinction on her last essay.' Lisa has followed her dreams and is studying to become a doctor.

'Lisa,' calls Susanne. 'You have a visitor.'

Eventually Lisa comes rolling into the lounge room. Her face lights up like a Christmas tree when she sees me, which sends my heart into bongo-drum mode. 'Declan. What are you doing here? You never said you were coming for a visit.'

I hug Lisa and kiss her forehead. 'That's because I'm not here for a visit. I live here now.'

Lisa's eyes widen to the size of frisbees. 'What?'

'Just down the road in Causeway Bay. You're looking at the new Head of English at Bayside International School.'

'You're kidding.'

'I start on Monday.'

'How did you manage . . . ?'

'Sent my résumé to every school in Hong Kong. I would have been happy just to teach. I would have been happy just to clean. Instead, I'm running the show.'

'Bayside International? That's my old school.'

'I know. Remember how I stalked you outside the gates all those years ago?'

Susanne looks at us and smiles. 'I'll just go and, er, put the kettle on for tea or something.' Susanne discreetly disappears leaving the two of us alone.

I opt not to beat around the bush. 'I know you've ditched the douche but . . . are you . . . are you seeing anyone?'

Lisa stares at me but she's definitely at the final stage of grief. She's accepted her lot. 'Seriously, Declan? Who would want to be lumbered with me? What have I got to offer anyone?'

'You're still the same you. Still the same girl I saw all those years ago on the station.' The first girl to make me crazy. And the last.

'It's not the years, Declan. It's the miles.'

I want to tell her that she's as beautiful as ever, but I have to play it cautiously. I've gone over this scenario countless times in my head. I've only got one shot at this. I have to get it right.

'Will you come out with me tonight? Dinner and a movie? We've never actually done that in all the time we've known each other. Bombay Bicycle Club aside, we've never really been on a proper date. We've just had a few stolen moments.'

She knows I'm not asking her out as a friend. She's knows I want more.

She shakes her head, which stabs me in the heart.

'Sorry, Declan. I can't.'

'Why not?'

'I can't. Okay? I just can't. Can we leave it at that?'

I'm about to get up and go. Admit defeat. But Lisa is worth fighting for. 'I moved to Hong Kong just to be close to you. I think I deserve to know why.'

Lisa takes a deep breath and composes herself. 'I can't be with someone who is only with me for pity. I can't be responsible for ruining your life.'

Lisa turns away from me and looks out the window. This isn't how I planned it.

'Ruining my life?' I say. 'Look at me, Lisa.'

She half-pivots her wheelchair so that she can face me. And despite the inappropriateness of the analogy, I suddenly feel my resolve forming in my back, sprouting vertebrae as it grows, generating a backbone in the very place where my spine ought to be.

'Now you listen to me, Lisa Leong. I'm going home. I am going to have a shower, get changed and make a few phone calls. And I will be back here at seven o'clock to pick you up, and we are going to the best restaurant in Hong Kong. That only gives you four hours to get ready. So you'd better get a move on.' Hey. I kind of like this spine thing. 'Because I'm not taking "no" for an answer.'

Lisa tries to be hard, to be stubborn, but she can't hide the sparkle in her eyes. 'Okay,' she whispers. 'But it'll only end in tears.'

'Only if you run over the maître d's foot.'

Lisa bursts out laughing. And I mean she seriously laughs. I suspect she hasn't laughed like this in years. Certainly not with that douche she was married to anyway.

'Tell me one thing,' she says when she's composed herself. 'Do you just want to be with me for the handicapped parking?'

That's my Lisa. I knew she was in there some-where. 'Well, that's certainly a contributing factor, I won't lie. Especially when we do this.'

'Do what?'

I quickly remove my iPad from my backpack and open the image I loaded before I left home.

'What is it?'

'It's called a trike motorbike.'

'You bought it?'

'Hired it. For the summer holidays. Six weeks travelling through Europe.' I tilt the screen so that she can see it better. 'Although your seat is behind me, see how it's actually a little higher? That's so you can bang on my helmet when I get us lost in Rome. And trust me, I *will* get us lost in Rome.'

'You really hired it?'

'We pick it up in Paris on day two of the school holidays.'

Lisa tries to keep her emotions in check but a single tear gives her away.

'I'm not here to be your knight in shining armour, Lisa. I'm here because you're the best thing that's ever happened to me. I let you go once and I'm not going to make the same mistake again.' I kiss her forehead.

I grab my shoes from the vestibule and leave. When I'm halfway down the elevator I hear Susanne's excited screaming erupt above me.

By the time I step out of the apartment complex into the chill February air, I'm the happiest I've been in my entire life. The world stretches out before me in all its wonder, all its possibilities. Nothing is written.

I draw my overcoat tightly about me and head off towards the MTR station.

NON-SPACE

Although it's fallen out of favour, there is a branch of philosophy called the Eternal Return that starts with the origins of the universe and is sort of linked to Newton's third law: for every action there is an equal and opposite reaction.

The universe started with the big bang (action) and will continue expanding until it runs out of energy after which it will start to collapse back in on itself with time running in reverse, finally ending with the big crunch (reaction) until we're back at the singularity. Then the big bang will occur again, as will the big crunch, over and over and over again ad infinitum, with time running in a circle. Some philosophers believe we will live (and have already lived) these exact same lives countless times over (which could well explain deja vu), while others maintain that there may be subtle variations. For instance, the next time around, Adolf Hitler might be born with a full complement of testicles so that he might not feel the need to overcompensate and therefore won't even bother with the whole formation of the Third Reich nonsense and instead he and his watercolours might just piss off back to Austria. Orville and Wilbur Wright might develop an interest in basket weaving as opposed to aviation and we might all end up boating and busing everywhere. The Second Amendment to the United States Constitution may be written so that someone's right to carry on existing supersedes someone else's right to bear arms. Gandhi might invest in a bulletproof vest. Lee Harvey Oswald might stop for a snack on the way to the Texas School Book Depository and end up with hiccups. The paparazzi might realise that they are a bunch of pointless pricks and not chase Princess Diana into that Parisian tunnel. Harold Holt might decide that swimming in an area that is well known for its rips, sharks and Chinese (or Russian) submarine activity is a breathtakingly bad idea. Kim Jong-un might look at himself in the mirror and come to the conclusion that he is a bit of a human turd who ought to start contemplating feeding his people rather than trying to blow stuff up. Someone in the Taliban might actually grow a functioning brainstem and conclude that access to education and power shouldn't be limited to penis possession. Every racist in the world might come to a sudden epiphany and realise that perceived superiority based on skin pigmentation or geographic location is pretty much the dumbest thing ever. And same for sexism. Next time around, female politicians might be allowed to get on with the business of running their countries and be praised or criticised based on their policies and intellect rather than on whether or not their pants suits make their posteriors look slightly larger than they actually are.

And, next time, I might pause.

Or maybe this whole thing has been a figment of my imagination. Maybe my mind, in an attempt to protect itself from self-annihilation, has not only played out a hypothetical, road-not-travelled future in which I paused, but also played out what might have happened if I hadn't.

Maybe there's still time.

SECONDS BEFORE

The train is almost here now. I have to make it quick. I can't hesitate. I stand up and run, but for a moment I do hesitate. Just for a moment. And it's enough. Because it's here I feel my life split in two. Part of me carried it through, but the part of me that wanted to live, the part that knew that at some point the agony would stop, was stronger. Just. And although I have to stop the pain, this is not the way. So I pause.

I slump to the ground and curl up in a ball. I feel that if I can make myself as small as possible, the pain won't be as intense. It won't find me. I'm wrong, of course, because my nerve endings are still rupturing, but at least now they're not being splattered beneath the train's wheels, though a strange sense of deja vu will not leave me.

Various arms scoop me up and half-drag, half-carry me over to a bench. Someone wants to give me water; someone else wants to give me air. No one seems to know what's wrong with me. They think I've had a seizure, that I've fainted, that I've OD'd, that I'm drunk. An ambulance has been called as have the police. A blanket appears from somewhere as if my problem is temperature related. A young woman in a business suit gently squeezes my shoulder while someone else strokes the back of my hand. A tradie in a bright orange shirt is kneeling down beside me as if asking for my hand in marriage. He might as well be because I can't hear or understand a word he's saying. He pats me gently on the head with a hand the size and texture of a baseball mitt. I look at the elderly lady who is stroking my hand. She smiles at me in that grandmotherly way that transcends generational, cultural and racial divides.

'Thank you,' I say to her. To all of them. I slowly get to my feet with the tradie lending a firm hand.

'I think you should wait for the ambulance,' says the tradie.

'You've had a close call,' says the young woman.

I've seen the future. The futures. And I know which I prefer.

'I'm okay,' I say to my guardian angels.

'You need help,' says the young woman.

'I know,' I say as the tradie hands me my backpack. 'I'll talk to my mum. She'll know what to do.'

My phone vibrates in my pocket. I take it out and see that I have a text. And although I don't know the number, deja vu tells me that it's Lisa's aunt's phone.

Hey D. Hope you're surviving.
Mum took my phone.
Email when I can. Love L XXX

The elderly lady stands up and takes my hand as I slip the phone in my pocket. 'You must live, young man. There are people who need you. People who love you.'

I look at her and smile. 'I'm okay,' I say. 'I had a bad moment but I'm going to be okay now.'

I hitch on my backpack and, a little lighter in my step, head off towards the stairs.

ACKNOWLEDGEMENTS

The Pause has been a long journey, both personally and professionally, creatively and mentally; a journey that I simply could not have taken alone. To that end I would like to say a special thanks to the following: Chantelle Larkin, Damian Larkin, Gabrielle Larkin, Louisa Chen, Natalie Chen, Daniel Chen, Jack Green, Alison Aprhys, Belinda Bolliger, Kerry Cumming, Ian Harrison, Richard Halliwell, Jacquie Harvey, Ian Harvey, Linsay Knight, Paul Macdonald, Russell McCool, Kathryn Morelli, Ted Quan, Irini Savvides, Bob Thomas, Stephan Wellink and Tara Wynne. Also to my wonderful friends and colleagues at Knox Grammar School — to name individuals would leave me in danger of inadvertently omitting someone which would be a terrible oversight, so a huge, heartfelt thanks to all of you. To the staff of The Hills Private Hospital's mental health unit and Hornsby Ku-ring-gai Hospital's Psychiatric Emergency Care Centre for their amazing and gentle care. To Don Ritchie, the real 'angel of The Gap'. To Ali Binazir, for his blog *Meanderings over heaven, earth and mind* (you can find his post 'What are the chances of your coming into being?' at http://blogs.law.harvard.edu/abinazir/2011/06/15/what-are-chances-you-would-be-born/). To Richard Baker and the legendary (in our own minds, at least) Pendle Hill O/45s football team. And last, but by no means least, to the incredible staff at Penguin Random House, especially Zoe Walton and Bronwyn O'Reilly. To all of you, because the sun has shone on me again, I owe you a debt that I can never repay.

NEED HELP?

If you're going through a tough situation that you don't feel comfortable talking about with friends or family, you *can* find help elsewhere. Reach out to a counsellor on a free anonymous hotline or website.

www.beyondblue.org.au or 1300 22 4636

www.kidshelp.com.au or 1800 55 1800

www.lifeline.org.au or 13 11 14

ABOUT THE AUTHOR

Sydney-based author John Larkin was born in England but grew up in the western suburbs of Sydney. He has, at various stages of his writing career, supported his habit by working as a supermarket trolley boy, shelf-stacker, factory hand, forklift driver, professional soccer player and computer programmer. He now writes and teaches writing full-time. John has a BA in English Literature and an MA in Creative Writing from Macquarie University. John's *The Shadow Girl* won the Victorian Premier's Literary Awards 2012 Prize for Writing for Young Adults.

READING GROUP QUESTIONS

1. Was Declan's breakdown preventable? What were the factors that contributed to it?

2. Declan's story contains examples of strategies you can use to help you recover from, and manage, mental illness. What strategies did Declan use? What else could he have done that might have helped?

3. *'I thought I would be stuck with this agony forever. But I just had the wrong mixture of chemicals whirring around in my brain. But how was I to know? . . . My mind was broken. And when your mind breaks you need help. External help. Because the thing you rely on most to get you through the*

screaming darkness is the very thing that's broken.' (p. 40) Declan's brain sends his body pain signals, so that he feels as though his nerves are rupturing, but in reality his pain is caused by a chemical imbalance that is contributing to his depression and anxiety. In what other ways can our brains deceive us?

4. How significant do you think Declan's family and friends are in his recovery? Or do you think that his recovery comes from within?

5. *'I'm sorry to you, my teachers, who might have blamed yourselves and wondered why you hadn't spotted the signs — signs that simply weren't there, signs that only became apparent to me after it was too late, after I was gone. Signs that I'd learnt to hide from everyone — myself included.'* (p. 185) Do you think there were any signs of Declan's mental illness? Do anxiety and depression manifest themselves differently in teenagers versus adults?

6. *'My friends have been amazing since I returned to school, but everyone else has given me a wide berth. It's just too much to deal with. I'm kind of like a social leper.'* (p. 183) Why do others find it difficult to talk to Declan after his break-down? Have you experienced this in your life? How can we create change in our society so that mental illness can be discussed openly

and honestly, and without discrimination or stigma?

7. *'Blokes don't do this stuff very well, but to compare, teenage boys are so clenched up we make our fathers look like Oprah.'* (p. 183) Do you agree with Declan that teenage boys are less likely to show their emotions and talk about their problems than others?

8. Declan's mother shielded her husband from the truth about what Great-Aunt Mary tried to do to Declan. Did she do the right thing? Would Declan's relationship with his father have been different if his father had known the truth? What other secrets in the book contribute to the suffering or emotional wellbeing of the characters?

9. *'Life is about enjoying the little moments . . . We're all going to fall on bad times and go through sadness, through breakups, through death, bereavement and depression. It happens. It's a part of life. But those moments will pass and you'll have good moments again. You'll have great moments. You'll have beautiful moments.'* (p. 145) Should we be happy all the time, or do we need to experience sadness and a range of emotions in order to appreciate the 'beautiful moments'?

10. Humour is an important part of Declan's story, and plays a role in his healing. How important is humour to you in your life?

11. Can humour also be destructive? (For instance, when Declan and his mother make fun of Declan's father?) What is the difference between healing humour and destructive humour?

12. Look up Don Ritchie, the real-life 'angel of The Gap', who saved many lives by offering a cup of tea and someone to talk to (as 'Bill' helps to save Declan, and tries to save Mary, in the story). Do you think Don saw himself as a hero, or was he just doing what anyone would do in his situation? What other strangers, as well as health professionals, help Declan in *The Pause*?